ALIEN MATE
COLLECTION

CONTAINS:
ALIEN MATE
ALIEN MATE 2
ALIEN MATE 3

NEW YORK TIMES BESTSELLING AUTHOR
EVE LANGLAIS

Copyright © 2011, Eve Langlais

Copyright © 2nd Edition 2016 Eve Langlais

Cover art © Dreams2Media 2019

Produced in Canada

Published by Eve Langlais

http://www.EveLanglais.com

PRINT ISBN: 978 177 384 122 9

E-ISBN: 978 177 384 121 2

ALIEN MATE

THE DAY DIANA MET HER FIRST ALIEN DAWNED LIKE any other—with a dry, cottony mouth and a bad case of bed head. She didn't even have any warning because, unlike *The X Files* and sci-fi movies, she didn't see any lights in the sky and her TV image didn't go all snowy. That kind of pissed her off because, had she known she would be having an up-close-and-personal encounter with life from another planet, she might have at least brushed her hair and worn something other than her ragged robe, plaid boxer shorts, and loose tank top. *This is definitely not my most attractive look.*

Anyway, there she stood, ironing her underwear —being single left her with way too much time on her hands—when, suddenly, *it* appeared in the middle of her living room. It wasn't a spectacular living room as living rooms went, outfitted with a second-hand, sagging couch and chair, a coffee table that wobbled, and some kind of Oriental print rug in bad need of a beating. A receptionist's salary didn't go far in the city.

Needless to say, when *it* appeared, it did so right on top of her flimsy coffee table, which under its weight collapsed, something her visitor absently noted when it looked down at its bare and fairly large feet.

Studying it in shock, Diana amended the 'it' part to 'Holy Hunk' because, if it hadn't been for the fact that his skin shone a startling sky blue, she would have mistaken him for some super-hot underwear model, one who magically appeared in her living room, only sans the underwear.

Good thing he's hung like a . . .

With flaming cheeks, Diana quickly averted her gaze, but his sizable endowment stayed with her, and flustered, she stammered, "Wh-Who are you?" *Other than the most gorgeous naked man I've ever seen.* She was so startled by her naked visitor that she accidentally left the iron lying on her underwear too long and a burning smell wafted up. Nose twitching, Diana quickly set the iron upright and looked down in dismay at the big burn mark on the ass of her favorite pair of undies. *Damn.*

So, of course, her blue alien chuckled. Yes, apparently creatures from space or alternate dimensions had senses of humor too.

"Greetings, earthling female," said a voice, smooth as hot, melted chocolate with just a hint of an accent. "I come in peace. I will be your leader."

Startled by her alien's horrible B-movie speech, Diana said the only thing that came to mind. "Um, isn't that supposed to be 'Take me to your leader'?"

Brilliant white teeth that shone opalescent like pearls between darker blue lips appeared when he smiled. "No, you heard me correctly, earthling. I've come to be your leader."

Diana laughed. She just couldn't help herself. Of all the things she expected him to say, that had to rank as one of the dumbest. His face remained quite serious, though, so, of course, she continued to howl, even when she saw a tinge of annoyance draw his handsome features tight.

"I fail to see the humor, earthling female. I will be your leader. You will respect me as is my due."

Diana cackled again, wiping the tears in her eyes with the back of her hand. "Oh, you are so funny. And just how is one naked alien going to convince the world that he's now their new leader?" Diana giggled anew at the thought of him aiming that weapon between his legs. Given its size, he'd definitely intimidate the male population and make the female one swoon.

A frown met her answer, followed by a wide Colgate smile, which made Diana wonder, *Do aliens brush their teeth?*

"I never said I intended to rule the world, earthling. I've come to be *your* leader. You have been chosen by the oracle and the spirits of my ancestors to be my mate," he stated with a self-satisfied grin.

That comment rendered Diana speechless. She could almost hear the thump as her jaw hit the floor. *His mate?* Diana knew, at this point, she had to be hallucinating. Super-hot aliens did not suddenly appear on a lazy Sunday morning to claim size-fourteen plumpers in their don't-answer-the-door-clothes as their mates. Maybe she'd eaten some bad potato chips.

Shame about the mental lapse, though, because Mr. Blue could probably be found under the definition of gorgeous. After all, what wasn't there to like on his six-foot-something frame with abs she could bounce quarters off? With short ebony hair that curled slightly at the tips, a tapered waist, muscled legs, bulging arms, and that club between his legs—which, shockingly enough, appeared bald—he also defined the word 'yummy'. While she contemplated his perfection, he assumed her acquiescence.

"Now that you understand," he said, gesturing to her impatiently, "disrobe that we may perform the bonding ceremony and be on our way."

Make that the definition of arrogance. Just who does he think he is? "Excuse me? Did you say you wanted me to undress?"

"Yes, this is part of the ritual. Fear not. Your

clothing will be replaced with something more appropriate for space travel. Besides," Mr. Blue said, looking at her outfit disdainfully, "you cannot mean to tell me that you are attached to such unattractive garments."

Diana drew her ratty robe more tightly around her and tilted her head regally. "Ugly clothes or not, they are staying on. And I never said I agreed to any bonding ritual. This is a joke, right? Some of the guys at work have paid you to play a trick on me. Ha! Ha! So funny. You can come out now. Where'd you hide the camera?"

"Do you babble often without making sense?" her alien finally interjected.

"Oh, please. How gullible do you think I am? I'll admit you might have had me fooled there for a second 'til you asked me to take my clothes off."

Mr. Blue sighed in exasperation. "I assure you this is quite serious. Now, stop your pointless arguing and disrobe that we may get the ritual over with and be on our way."

Did this alien live on some kind of caveman planet, ordering her about like some harem girl? Hmmm, now that had some interesting visuals. Reining in her naughty thoughts, Diana glared at the source of her frazzled mood. Did he really think that he could simply materialize into her life and she'd become his willing love slave? Hadn't he heard of women's lib?

At his impatient look, she replied sarcastically, "Yeah, well, good luck with that. You might be hot for an alien guy, but I am single and staying that way, and the clothes are not coming off."

Although, on second thought, maybe I should get naked. After all, it's not like I'm a virgin, and to be honest, when will I ever get another chance to play alien probe with a hottie like this?

Blue's ebony brows drew over his clear violet eyes, and when he spoke again, he'd lost some of his arrogance. "You don't wish to be my mate?" The idea seemed to flummox him.

"Look, I appreciate the offer, but even though this must be some kind of weird hallucination or joke, come on, your mate? That sounds like a long-term commitment to me, and well, I just don't think that's going to work. We've just met, after all, and I know nothing about you, not even, for example, your name."

"Kor'iander Vel Menos, but you may call me Kor. I am descended from the Third Moon clan, the primary line, of course, and I have the post of first warrior to the Third Moon regiment," he said with a bow, marred only by the swinging appendage between his legs, which made her blush crimson again.

Gathering her composure, Diana looked him in the eye—no lower. "Nice to meet you, Kor, but I'm still not going to be your mate. Now why don't you go back to where you came from and meet some nice blue-skinned girl and get married? You'll be much happier."

"This isn't how it's supposed to happen," he muttered darkly.

"Sorry, but that's how it's going to be," Diana said primly. Although her shameless side was screaming, *Take my clothes off and have your way with me, you big hunk of stud!*

And then Diana wondered if he'd read her last thought, for, with a curse—or at least she assumed he cursed, as he spoke in an odd guttural language —he strode all six-foot-something of blue naked-ness over to her and grabbed her by the arms. Diana, stunned, didn't even think to scream. She gaped up at him, utterly distracted by the tingling his closeness created in her body, and she wondered if his lips would taste like blue raspberry.

"Now," he barked.

Now what? Diana wondered. But as it turned out, he wasn't speaking to her.

And her lack of action, caused by her overactive hormones, was what led to her being on board her very first alien spacecraft.

Not that she admired it for very long because she felt a prick in her arm and fell—make that crashed—to the floor in a dead sleep.

KOR'IANDER VEL MENOS STARED AT THE SLIGHTLY snoring form of his soon-to-be mate asleep on the floor and shook his head in disbelief.

The Oracle had to be wrong. Of course, that had never happened before, but in this instance, Kor really had to question the Oracle's choice.

Surely, this feisty, argumentative female could not be his life mate? Docile. He'd specifically written docile when he'd filled in his request for a mate. And this is who the spirits of his ancestors had chosen? A celestial jest on their part perhaps?

Her looks at least seemed passable. Perhaps once she groomed herself, she'd even be attractive. The kogi nest that currently adorned her head made him want to shave it for fear of unsavory little critters. As for her shape, the ugly garment she wore did not give a proper indication, although she did seem plump and healthy. Thank the Three Moons. His poor childhood companion Rex'Anor had been given a very slim mate for bonding, and it had taken him many moon cycles to plump her up 'til he'd found her attractive enough to bed.

Kor sighed. And to think he'd been so excited when he'd been called to see the Oracle. He'd felt honored and thrilled to be chosen. *What a joke*, he thought, staring down at his chosen's limp form.

Well, at least there was no one here to witness his ignoble attempt to go through with the mating rituals of his people, somewhat adapted to take in the new reality that they needed to mate with females from outside their species.

The problem with being alone, though, was who in the silvery moons did he ask for help?

"Alphie, please search archives for anything on the subject of reluctant earthling females."

Kor could have sworn he heard Alphie—Alpha 350, the ship's artificially intelligent computer who someone mistakenly had given a sense of humor —snort.

"This is not entertaining. My chosen refuses to acknowledge me as her leader and won't bond with me."

"Could it be because you demanded instead of asking?" came the computer's smooth voice.

"Why would I ask? I'm doing her a great honor

and following ritual. I think maybe I didn't get the right female."

"The coordinates were exact. But perhaps you should have done a little more reading on earthlings, their women to be precise, before ordering her about. On their planet, the concept of arranged marriages is almost nonexistent, especially in the area she resided in. As a matter of fact, many of the Earth women choose to not enter into a pair bond."

"What? But that's preposterous," said Kor, appalled at the thought of thousands of females roaming around without the guiding hand of a male.

"Preposterous or not, that's this planet's custom. And furthermore, I did recommend you read the file on your future mate. But what did you say to me?" reminded Alphie.

Kor grumbled. "I said it would be fairer if we met at the same time without preconceived notions about each other. You could have warned me." When he'd made the decision at the time, it had seemed like the right choice and still would have been had his intended been docile like he'd asked for. *But a feisty mouth might mean a feisty bedmate.* Her bed skills, though, would become apparent only once he convinced his earthling she had no choice but to bond with him.

"You should have listened better," continued Alphie in a matter-of-fact voice. "What's the point of having access to a supercomputer like myself if you don't take advantage of it? Now stop your complaining. What's done is done. There's still time for you to catch up a bit before she wakes. Now, are you ready for the decontamination process? Might as well get it done now while she's still unconscious."

Kor straightened his intended's limbs then sighed and braced himself for the low-level laser cleansing. The process, accomplished painlessly—actually, truth be told, it could be quite arousing—was necessary to ensure that alien microbes did not survive and cause havoc back on his home planet. During the course of the voyage, his soon-to-be mate's body would be cleansed and prepared to adapt to life on his planet, something he just knew she'd argue about too.

Unmoving, she lay as he'd positioned her on the floor, and he decided that perhaps it would be best if he gave her the first of the several inoculations she'd need to ensure her body adapted to the slightly different atmosphere and consumables of his planet. He injected her quickly with only a slight red pinprick left behind to show he'd even touched her. With that done, he also decided he'd better relocate her just in case the sedative wore off sooner than expected and she awoke on the hard floor.

Picking her up, Kor found himself pleased at the soft curves that pillowed against his body, making his blood pound faster through his veins and other places, creating an erection that was impossible to hide in his still undressed state. But with no one to see him except a machine, Kor relaxed and decided to enjoy holding his chosen female without her haranguing him.

The cruiser, thankfully, had a well-appointed cabin, one with a large bed that took into account the new service the males of his planet required. The cruiser's primary use now consisted of fetching female mates from around the galaxy so that the males of his world could mate with them and make sure his people did not die out. *A pleasant task for most*, or so he'd heard, he thought with a disgruntled look at the still sleeping female who had refused to do as he told her.

Kor laid the earthling on the covers and stood back, looking at her again pensively. The garments she wore were truly awful, and given her earlier stance about keeping them on, with a mischievous grin, he stripped them off her. When he'd disposed of them—permanently—he looked at her again, interest making his violet eyes glow and his body firm up in arousal.

Lush curves met his gaze, her smooth, unblemished skin tempting his hands to touch. She had a very full bosom, heavy handfuls with light pink areolas that puckered as if sensing his interest. She had an indented waist, a rounded tummy, and a thatch of ebony curls that hid pinker delights, which he'd explore and taste later when she finally accepted her fate.

Kor found a brush and painstakingly combed out her messy hair, the texture so silky between his fingers that it made him shiver as he imagined her dragging it across his sensitive skin. With her dark hair fanned across the bed's pillows, sensuous full lips slightly parted, and serene face, Kor found himself mightily attracted to his future mate. Perhaps this wouldn't be so horrible after all.

Tempting as he found her, though, he would wait 'til she awoke and completed the bonding ritual with him. He wanted their first joining to be mutually pleasurable, something he'd trained for with great success, according to his teachers. Now if only he could get her to feel the same attraction when she awoke. Then they could mate properly and satisfy the sexual urges that now consumed his body.

However, the sedative he'd given her would last a few more hours still unless she proved resistant, so with time to waste, Kor dressed in loose slacks and a billowy shirt before going to check on their travel status and other ship functions that needed tending. But while he worked, his mind strayed often to the lusciously obstinate female in his bed.

DIANA WOKE SLOWLY, her mind still pleasantly befuddled from the dream she'd had about a handsome blue alien who wanted her as his mate. Diana wished only that the dream could have continued a little longer and that she hadn't been so prickly. She would have liked to touch that smooth blue skin and maybe even taste it. *Oh, the things I would have done to his deliciously muscled body.*

Diana giggled and rolled over onto her stomach, the smooth, satiny sheets rubbing sensuously against her bare skin.

Bare what? I never sleep naked.

Diana opened her eyes and sat up in shock. Her gaze flicked down to see she wore not a stitch of clothing and that the bed she found herself in wasn't her own.

Where on God's green earth am I?

She looked around in consternation, not seeing anything familiar. Panic settled low in her tummy. *Okay, let's not freak out here. Maybe I'm still dreaming.* Diana pinched herself hard.

Owww! Diana glared offensively at the red mark she'd given herself. *Okay, maybe not a dream then.* Grabbing the loose satin sheet on the bed, she draped it around herself and stood up to take a look around.

Smooth, seamless cream-colored walls surrounded her. No door, no nothing to show how to get in or out. *Is this some kind of prison? But I've never heard of a prison like this. And, besides, I've committed no crimes.*

For furniture, there just seemed to be the large bed covered in creamy sheets and pillows, and two chairs that looked like overly large beanbags that had been punched in the middle for a seat.

The floor underneath felt spongy on her bare feet, and Diana looked down at it and frowned. She'd never seen anything like it. It looked and felt like suede with the consistency of rubber, making it very cushy to walk on.

Her dream of the blue alien came back to taunt her. *Surely not. I mean, aliens don't exist, right? But where am I then?*

Feeling a change in the air, Diana whirled, the sheet clasped tightly to her breasts, and saw her blue E.T. standing in a doorway that had just appeared in the wall.

"You?" she exclaimed then narrowed her eyes as understanding sank in. "Where am I? Why have you kidnapped me?"

"We are aboard my spacecraft heading for my planet. As for why you are here, I told you that earlier. You have been chosen to be my mate. I will be your leader, or will be as soon as we complete the ceremony."

"I am not doing any ceremony with you. I demand you take me home right now, or I'll-I'll—" Diana got flustered at this point. *What exactly can I do if what he says is the truth? If we really are in space, I can't just jump ship and walk home.*

"Taking you home is not an option. Believe me, I am not so sure the Oracle made the right choice either. But choose you as my mate she did, so whether you are willing or not, we will be conducting the bonding ceremony."

Not likely. "I can assure you it won't be willing. So, unless you intend to force me, there will be no bonding, mister. Besides, did it ever occur to you that maybe I already have a boyfriend?"

"You mean a mate?" Mr. Blue frowned at her. "Do you have one?"

"No." Diana couldn't help a sulky tone. Stupid jerk had been cheating on her, so she'd dumped his ass. "That's not the point. I could have had someone special, but you didn't even ask."

"Sorry," he said, not sounding the least bit apologetic. "Now can we move past this? You will be my mate and the mother of our children. It has been decided. You need to accustom yourself to this idea so that we may move on."

"Children? Okay, now you're really getting ahead of yourself there. Just who is this Oracle who says I'm supposed to be your bride? I'd like to talk to her. I think she's made some kind of mistake."

"Are all earthling females so argumentative?" he asked.

"Only the smart ones," snapped Diana. "And my name is Miss St. Peters to you, not earthling."

"I will call you whatever I wish."

"We'll see about that," growled Diana. "Now I demand to speak to this Oracle."

"You cannot speak to the Oracle."

"Why not?" Diana asked, chin jutted out stubbornly.

"Must you keep questioning everything?" he asked with exasperation.

"Hey, this is my life we're talking about here. I think I have the right to know what's going on."

Kor—she remembered his name from the dream that wasn't a dream—sighed loudly. "Will you be more agreeable if I answer some questions for you?"

"Maybe."

"Fine then," he said, walking over to sit in one of the funny-looking chairs. "Ask away."

Diana hadn't expected him to give in that quickly, given his previous high-handed behavior, so she collected her thoughts before speaking. "How did I get here?"

"Molecular transportation."

"What?" said Diana blankly.

"My computer dissolved our molecular structure and reassembled it here, on the ship."

Diana's eyes widened. *Beam me up, Scotty.* She patted herself down, relieved to see she seemed to have made it in one piece, including those pounds she'd have preferred to lose.

Shuffling her feet, she got her toes caught in the edge of the sheet wrapped around her body, reminding her of her nude state. "Where are my clothes?"

Kor grinned at her with what she swore was a twinkle of mirth in his eyes. "Gone."

"What do you mean gone?"

"They were ugly, so I got rid of them. Next question?" he said, leaning back, looking pleased with himself.

Diana glared at him. Never mind the fact he was right, her clothes had been awful, that didn't give him the right to strip them from her. *Wait a second . . .*

"You undressed me?" she asked slowly.

Kor nodded his head.

"But that means you saw me naked!" Diana flushed crimson. Somehow this fact had evaded her usually alert mind, and she burned with embarrassment.

"I have to admit that, in that respect, the Oracle chose well. You have a beautiful body, and I look forward to enjoying it."

Diana just gaped at his comment. On the one hand, she felt a tingly little pleasure that he'd liked what he'd seen, but on the other . . .

"There will be no enjoying nothing, mister. I

mean it," she said, stomping her foot when he chuckled.

Kor didn't seem to mind her childish tantrum. He stood and walked over to her, thankfully dressed now, unlike earlier, but even clothed, he still seemed very intimidating—and sexy. Diana backed away, but the cabin wall met her back, and she couldn't escape him when he draped an arm on either side of her body. He leaned toward her, his violet eyes alight with some emotion she couldn't identify. She just hoped it wasn't anger.

Diana lost her ability to speak—a rare occurrence—stunned by his proximity, a closeness that had her body warming in naughty places. His face drew nearer, and when he spoke, his minty breath feathered across her lips, making her nipples tighten and her lower parts flush with heat.

"Oh, I will enjoy taking you, and I guarantee you will enjoy me in return," he promised arrogantly before touching his lips to hers.

[3]

DIANA'S EYES FLUTTERED SHUT AS HE KISSED HER, his full lips surprisingly firm against hers, and she felt an electric shock run through her body. Make that more like a lightning bolt, as his touch made every nerve ending in her body come alive and sing with pleasure. Diana wanted to push him away, but her body betrayed her. Melting instead under his sensuous onslaught, her lips parted on a soft sigh to let his alien tongue plunder her mouth. She felt his hands move to grab her around the waist and pull her closer to his body. This close to him, she could feel the hardness of his arousal pulsing against her tummy, making her damp. Diana sighed into his mouth and moved her hands slowly up to grasp his shoulders, then . . .

An amused voice broke the embrace.

"Kor, while I see you are busy, you are being

hailed by your mother on the status of your mission. Should I tell her to call back?"

Diana, shocked to discover their kiss had been witnessed, found the strength—barely—to push him away. Kor let her flee to the other side of the room, his face thoughtful and his eyes glowing. Diana, for her part, felt shaky and unfulfilled. Wanting . . .

She rubbed her lips, trying to erase the feelings he'd aroused in her, but her body still pulsed, and she quivered when she looked down his body and saw him in the same state.

Kor smiled at her regretfully. "Your questions and the rest of our *discussion* will have to wait. I hope you now see that this is what's meant to be. I shall return shortly."

"But . . ." Diana spoke to empty air as Kor left and the door sealed seamlessly shut behind him.

"Arrgh!" she yelled, stomping her feet. She flounced over to the bed and fell on it, her thoughts and emotions a jumbled mess as she fought arousal and irritation in equal measures. *How did he manage to get me so hot so quick? I don't even know him.*

"Do you require anything?" asked the smooth voice that had interrupted the kiss.

Diana peered around the empty room, looking for the source of the voice but saw nothing. "Who are you? Can you take me home? I think your friend's gone off the deep end," Diana asked, hoping for a way out of this mess.

"I regret that I cannot take you home. But never fear. Your new life will be an enjoyable one with wonders never dreamed of on your planet. As for me, I am Alpha 350, ship computer and the premiere model in artificial intelligence. You may call me Alphie. I can provide you with food, clothing, toiletries, as well as answer some questions you may have on your new life."

Great, a computer. Hopefully this one doesn't go psycho like the one in that sci-fi book. "Okay, I have a question for you. Why me?"

"Why not?" retorted the smart-ass machine.

That's if it's really a machine. Seems to talk pretty human to me.

"Oh, come on. I mean, look at me. I'm not exactly the kind of woman men go all gaga over."

"Please explain. I am not familiar with the term 'gaga.'"

Diana rolled her eyes. "What I meant to say is usually kidnapping for the purpose of marriage happens to pretty, skinny women, not plumpers like me."

"Where Kor comes from, women with girth are considered much more attractive than one who is, as you say, skinny. A too-slim mate is the sign of a poor provider. Was that all you wanted to know?"

Great, a BBW-lovers society, this is getting weirder and

weirder. "I have another question. If Kor is an alien, and you're an alien computer, just how is it that I can understand you? Don't tell me English is the language of the universe."

"Of course not." The hidden voice chuckled. "Kor learned your language through an implant. We'll give you one, too, as part of your integration. It will allow you to understand any language in the universe and, where vocally possible, speak it as well."

Diana, while intrigued at the idea of being multilingual, did not like the idea of an implant. *It never goes well when they get one in the movies.* "We're going to have to talk about that implant idea. Have to say that doesn't sound like something I'm going to enjoy."

"I begin to understand Kor's difficulty."

Diana put her hands on her hips. "Hey, are you implying I'm difficult?"

"Let me phrase this using an expression I discovered when researching your species. If the shoe fits . . ."

"I am not—that is, if the situation were different . . ." Diana sputtered.

"Let me ask you, earthling—"

"Would you stop calling me earthling? My name is Diana." Why she gave him her first name when she'd told Kor to address her formally, she didn't know. *Maybe because he's not trying to marry me and get into my pants.*

"Diana, then, what exactly do you object to? According to my report, you have no close living family. Very few friends. No current love interest. No pets. You hate your job. You hate your apartment. Your romantic fantasy confessed to an online acquaintance consisted of a tall, dark stranger sweeping you off your feet and taking you away from it all. So let me ask you, what has Kor done that you object to so strenuously?"

Diana just listened, dumbfounded, as the computer recited off facts of her life that made her sound, well, pathetic, and lonely actually. "How do you know all these things?" she whispered, shocked.

"I did my research, of course. The advent of computers and the Internet on your world have made it quite simple for an advanced AI system like myself to find out pretty much anything I need to know."

"Have you told Kor all of this?" she asked, hoping the answer would be no. Her life, or lack of one, was none of Kor's business.

"He never asked," said Alphie sullenly. "But that's beside the point. Let me ask you again. What exactly about his choice in you as a mate do you object to?"

"Well," she stammered, "he didn't ask. He just told me, and he's-he's blue!"

Alphie gave a snort of disgust. *How does a computer snort?* "I can't believe you're an alienist."

"A what?" she asked, confused.

"Someone who thinks her species is better than all the others. We see that a lot in earthlings."

"But I never said I thought I was better. You're twisting my words. It's just . . . he took me by surprise. I've never seen a blue man before and certainly never imagined marrying one."

"If he weren't blue, would you be reacting like this?"

Diana thought about it. "Actually, yes, I would still act like this because this isn't romantic. When I dreamt of my fantasy man taking me away, it was because of love, not because some busybody told him to. He doesn't even like me, but he wants to marry me 'cause some Oracle says so."

"Romance? Hmmm, I'll have to research that. Let me get back to you. Bye."

"Wait," Diana shouted.

"What?" asked Alphie.

"Before you take off and do computer stuff, could you maybe get me some clothes? I'd rather not wear this sheet all day. And maybe something to eat. I am kind of hungry."

"Of course." And with those words, a drawer popped open, and Diana walked over to it and pulled out an outfit—a very revealing, diaphanous outfit made of draped layers of what seemed to be scarves stitched together.

"You've got to be bloody kidding me," she grumbled, holding up the flimsy cloth.

"It's what the females of his world wear," said Alphie with a snicker. "Talk to you later."

As he said that, another drawer opened in the wall, and Diana peeked in, hoping for more clothes, but, instead, saw a steaming plate of food consisting of a white-sauced pasta with vegetables and garlic toast. *Well, at least they're feeding me stuff I recognize,* which made her wonder who did the cooking.

Sighing, Diana decided to eat first before tackling the sex kitten outfit. *But I swear to God, if Kor laughs when he sees me looking like a giant fluffy marshmallow, I am going to sock him where it hurts.*

KOR WALKED IN AND STOPPED. For the first time since he'd laid eyes on Diana, he thanked the Oracle. And, yes, he'd finally relented enough, or should he say groveled enough, that Alphie had given him his mate-to-be's name, along with some basic information about her, but not too much. Kor, for some unfathomable reason, looked forward to discovering more about his chosen. He especially couldn't wait to see how she'd look naked with face flushed and her body aroused. That erotic thought presided at the forefront of his mind as he viewed his intended looking radiant as the moon goddess wearing the flowing garments of his people. Her shapely curves, both hidden and revealed by the strategically draped cloth, made her look good enough to eat. As soon as Diana opened her mouth, though, Kor rolled his eyes and lost his appetite.

"I demand you find me some proper clothes," she stated, hands on her hips, glaring at him, not realizing what a fetching picture she made. "I refuse to be dressed like a harem girl."

"I do not know what you refer to, but the answer is no. All the women on my planet are attired thus. I do not see the problem. Your planet seemed to embrace attire of a much more revealing nature than this."

"I look like an idiot."

Kor processed the word and its meaning. His brows rose. "On the contrary, you look quite attractive."

Surprisingly enough, his compliment stopped her next harangue, and, pinking prettily, she said, "I do?"

"Very," he said, crossing the room to stand before her, his towering height making him feel oddly protective, an emotion he was unaccustomed to. "Come," he said, offering her his arm. "The ship is not large, but I thought that perhaps you would enjoy a tour, and perhaps I could satisfy some more questions I'm sure you have."

For once not arguing—had his one compliment disarmed his prickly intended?—she tucked her hand onto his arm, her pale skin looking stark against the vivid blue of his own and sending a surge of lust through him. His aroused body demanded he throw her down 'til those pale hands scratched his back in pleasure.

But no, he had to control his urges and guide her slowly, as one would a Jelaxian mount, those pesky alien creatures commonly used for planetary travel. They were well known for their skittishness, just like his intended. He needed to build up Diana's trust in him. Not perhaps the way he'd envisioned his mating trip but, given her lack of cooperation, a necessary step.

Leading her from the bedroom, he showed her the conservatory where fresh produce was grown to keep space travelers healthy. They toured the lounge area that also doubled as a dining area then, finally, the command center with its large window screen showing the vast, dark space they traveled quickly through.

"Oh my God," she exclaimed, taking her hand off his arm and wandering up to the large display, her eyes wide in her face as she took in the celestial view.

Kor wandered over to the main console and

slowed the ship down so she could better see some of the stars and planets they were passing.

He heard her gasp. "We really are in space."

"Of course we are," he replied, somewhat confused. "Where else would we be?"

Facing him, she looked uncertain, and he had the strangest urge to take her in his arms and hold her tight. *What is happening to me? I am a warrior by trade, she is simply my mate. Why do I feel like this?*

"I guess I still thought this might be some kind of prank or even a dream. But it's not, is it? This is really happening. To me. I'm never going back home, am I?" The last she said in a lost voice, her arms reaching around to hug herself as if she felt alone.

Kor, without thinking, strode over to her and replaced her arms with his own. Hugging her lush body tight to his, he rubbed his cheek and chin against the softness of her dark curls. "You will have a new home, never fear. One I am sure you will approve of. And I will show you such wonders as you've never imagined."

"I'm sure your planet is chock-full of neat stuff, but it's your planet, your people. How is someone like me going to fit in?"

"As my mate, you will be accorded full respect."

"I'm not talking about respect," she said, pushing out of his embrace, a spark of her will straightening her back again.

So much for docile, he thought ruefully.

"I'm talking about friends and companionship," she said, gesticulating with her hands, agitated.

"I will be your companion," he said with a grin. "I look forward especially to sharing the communal bed with you."

"I'm sure you do," she muttered darkly. "But what about the rest of the time? Surely you have to go work or something. What about then?"

Kor held back some of his glee that she finally spoke as if she intended to bond with him. He needed to tread carefully now. "There will be other mates for you to befriend, earthlings like yourself and females of other species who have been mated."

"So I'm not the only one?" she queried.

"No, there are many like you who have been chosen to leave their home worlds and become mates to the males on ours."

"Why?"

"Let us become more comfortable if we are to embark on a history lesson," he said, guiding her back to the lounge area and pressing a button to drop a vid screen from the ceiling. At least instead of arguing she was now showing an interest. He hoped she'd be more receptive to his plight once he gave her a history lesson.

DIANA ALLOWED him to seat her, still somewhat stunned by the reality of her situation.

I'm really on a spaceship flying through the universe on my way to a new world. Holy crap! And by the sounds of it, I'm not the first one.

A giant screen that had dropped down from the seamless ceiling lit up, and Kor stood beside it, pointing to the large planet that appeared in the middle of it.

"This is my home world, Xaanda, or, translated, Planet of Bounty. You'll notice it resembles your planet Earth quite a bit, although we are several times larger. We have a bright sun much like your own and a second, smaller, red sun. Rotating around our planet are three moons, the resting place for our ancestors. But that is a history lesson for another day."

Kor touched the planet on the screen and zoomed in quickly 'til the view shrank to a panorama of a city—a futuristic one by Diana's standards. It gleamed silver, white, and cream with some buildings towering high while others seemed low and spread. Little saucers zipped around busily like bees in a hive.

"This is our capital, Menderiosa, where what you would call a president or emperor resides. We will be living just outside the capital, here, in Jenol." Again he zoomed.

Diana gaped at the astonishing scenes he was

showing her. *It's so pretty,* she thought. "It's all very nice, but you still haven't explained why you took me."

"I'm getting to that. We discovered the ability to space travel quite some time ago, something your people are only just coming into. We've been exploring the galaxy far and wide, bringing back treasures in the form of new plants and animals. We chart the stars and their planets, tracking other sentient beings like ourselves, making contact when deemed ready. We are, however, a violent species, much like earthlings. The world I showed you is divided into six major areas of government. And while we skirmish over borders and rights, we mostly save our aggression for the races beyond our planet who enjoy subjugating. One of these violent races thought to enslave us. They are now extinct."

Diana shivered at the dark smile that came over him when he said that.

Kor continued. "But before we destroyed them, one of them came to our world unbeknownst to us. He brought with him a deadly virus. One that attacked our women and killed them. Those who survived were left barren. Our males retaliated and wreaked horrible vengeance, but our revenge was bittersweet, for the cure to the disease was found too late. Over ninety percent of our female population died, and of the ten percent left, less than three percent could still bear children."

"That's horrible," whispered Diana.

"Beyond horrible. Without the gentle guiding hand of our females, the males became wild, fighting among each other, fighting over the few females left. We were going backward in evolution. Then the Oracle spoke. The Oracle, you have to understand, has always been. Whether it has always been the same being or if the position of Oracle is an inherited one, no one is sure. However, the Oracle is considered the most powerful person on the whole planet. When she speaks, all listen."

"The Oracle is a woman?"

"The Oracle has always been a female, yes. Anyway, she told us during the great turmoil to stop our fighting. If we wanted to rebuild our world, there was a way."

"So you started kidnapping women and forcing them to be your wives."

"No, not quite. See, even though we are similar physiologically, alien matings rarely reproduce. Certain conditions need to be met. One of them is mental harmony."

Diana giggled. "What, they need to be in love?"

Kor frowned at her. "I am not sure I understand that word. We don't have a translation for it in our language. What I am talking about is complete mental balance, where the souls of both join and become as one."

Now it was Diana's turn to frown. "What do

you mean the souls join? You guys believe in souls? Life after death?"

"Yes, but we are digressing. The Oracle said she'd found a way for us to rebuild our population by bringing in female outsiders. At first this idea was scoffed at. We are a proud race, but numbers, mainly population numbers, brought us to our senses. If we did not do as the Oracle suggested, our race would die out."

"So one person is in charge of setting all you men up with wives?"

"Not quite. The Oracle, as you said, is only one, the universe vast. She wisely turned to the spirits of our ancestors to help us in our hour of need."

"You mean you're letting ghosts choose your brides?"

"The spirits of our ancestors are nothing so vulgar as your world's concept of ghosts. They are beings of energy that retain a sense of their corporeal self."

Diana snorted. "Ghosts."

Kor's brows drew together, and she could see him about to argue again, but he held himself back. With a pained expression, he continued as if she hadn't spoken. "The ancestral spirits, not being bound by the laws of physics that we are, can travel the galaxy quickly. With the fate of our civilization at stake, the Oracle asked them for help. While some had been dead so long they'd lost their sense of self and family, many others, especially the recently dead females, still remembered and thus set themselves the task of finding mates for their remaining male family members. As choices are made, the spirits inform the Oracle, who then notifies the lucky male."

"Do the men not get a choice in this?"

Kor squirmed a bit. "The males are given the choice of whether or not they wish to have an alien mate found for them, as the females of our species, even so many moon cycles later, are still too few."

Diana watched him and had a feeling there was more to it than that. "And?" she said, arching a brow and trying to look supercilious.

"Males fill out a questionnaire with one of the Oracle's acolytes, and the questionnaire is relayed to the spirits."

Diana jumped up. "You mean I was chosen from some kind of shopping list you made up?"

Kor's cheeks blushed a mauve color, but instead of admitting he was wrong, he jumped up to defend his actions. "If my ancestors had followed my list, you wouldn't be here. I asked for a biddable female, not someone who questions everything I say or do."

"Well, excuse me, Ken, for not being your perfect Barbie doll," she retorted, hurt that he didn't consider her his ideal female. She was even more pissed that she even cared what this stupid blue alien thought.

"I do not know what you refer to, but before you get all annoyed, let me just say in my defense that I was simply following procedure."

"Blah, blah, blah," chanted Diana. "I'm not listening to you."

Maybe it was the fingers in her ears that sent him over the edge. Whatever it was, Diana found herself wrapped in a pair of strong blue arms, looking up into a volatile pair of violet eyes that swirled with emotion.

"Let me g—" Diana never did finish her sentence, as his firm lips crushed hers and captured her voice. And to her mental chagrin—but her body's delight—she felt that same inferno as earlier go racing through her body, lighting all her senses and making her melt in his arms.

Floating on a pleasurable cloud that consisted only of his lips making hers feel *ooooh soooo* good, she didn't register what he said at first.

"They didn't follow my list, but," he said, tightening his arms when she tried to push away, "I'm realizing that perhaps my ancestors knew what I needed better than I did."

Diana stilled and looked up at him. "Really? Even though I'm not docile and I argue?"

"Well, I could do without the arguing. However"—he grinned at the glint in her eye—"it will sure make our lives more interesting, won't it?"

Giving her lots to ponder, Kor brought a dazed

Diana back to the cabin. To her surprise, he left the door unlocked, a fact she discovered when she learned how to open the door by watching him. Basically she just needed to slide her hand over the wall in the right spot. *So I'm not a prisoner on the ship, at least.*

But instead of roaming, she paced, thinking about what she'd learned. Diana still wasn't crazy about the idea of some ghosts running around the universe with a list looking for gals who could be kidnapped, but in a perverse way, it was kind of romantic. *I mean, think about it. Of all the women in the universe, they chose me. And from what Kor said, they know their stuff. Me, the perfect wife for a hunky blue stud.*

Even better, in his obtuse way, Kor had said he liked her. Diana warmed at the thought.

Then kicked herself.

Hello, Earth to Diana. What the hell am I thinking? I can't seriously be entertaining the thought of bonding with him. He's arrogant, controlling, a kidnapper, not to mention part of an entirely different species. But then again, he's hot, he thinks I'm hot, and he makes me feel better than a cherry-topped, caramel-smothered, vanilla ice cream sundae. Mmm, now I'm hungry again.

"Alphie," she called.

"Yes, dear Diana."

"I'm hungry," she said plaintively. Although most of her hunger seemed to be centered between her legs. No matter, the between-the-lips kind would have to do. She never made important decisions on an empty tummy.

And as she sucked on her spoon, licking every creamy drop of the sundae Alphie managed to conjure up, she thought about her blue suitor and, to her chagrin, how he made her feel.

4

"No, absolutely not," Diana said, arms crossed, shaking her head.

Kor sighed and resisted the urge to rip out his hair. "These shots are necessary to ensure your health and well-being once we arrive on my planet." Not to mention one of them had the implant that would allow her to speak and understand all languages. He'd thought it best not to tell her about it being included in the shots, given her earlier rant about implants turning humans into killers. Earthlings had way too much imagination.

"No way. I am not letting you inject me with some weird alien cocktail," she repeated stubbornly.

"The shots will barely hurt. Please cooperate. We need to vaccinate you."

"Not to mention make your Earth eggs more viable," piped in an unhelpful Alphie.

With a mentally groan, Kor braced himself.

"What?" she shrieked. "You're trying to pump me with fertility drugs? I haven't even agreed to marry you yet."

Kor brightened. She used the word 'yet' instead of 'absolutely not'. *I'm making progress.* Now if she'd just calm down so he could give her the shots.

But Diana was on a rampage, and he watched her through slitted eyes as she railed back and forth about aliens and their needles. Although she did lose him for a bit when she ranted about anal probes. What kind of perverted medicine did earthlings practice anyway?

When she finally ran out of breath, Kor said one word that he'd discovered during his recent research into earthlings and their behavior. "Chicken."

Diana stopped and faced him, mouth open. "Am not," she retorted.

"Yes, you are chicken. All your unreasonable claims of me trying to poison, kill, or maim you are just that, unreasonable. If I wanted to hurt you, I could. Yet I haven't, even though you would provoke just about anybody else. So you know what? Don't take the shots. And when you end up in the hospital with your stomach dissolved and coming out of your rectum, don't complain. I'm just trying to prevent this." Kor had a hard time keeping a straight face when he said this, but his words had the effect desired. She turned to the side and presented him with the smooth flesh of her upper arm.

Kor quickly gave her the shots and then, in another Earth custom, kissed the red mark. "All done," he said, pleased when she flushed at his touch. His feisty intended seemed to be melting toward him. He just wished she'd hurry it up. He didn't want to be the first one to ever return unbonded because his chosen didn't like him.

"Why are our species so alike?"

Her unexpected question startled Kor, so he replied with a question. "Don't your people keep histories?"

Diana wrinkled her nose. "Of course we do, but what's that got to do with how similar we are physically?"

"I'd say we have a lot of differences. I can show you if you'd like?" Kor said with a comical leer.

Diana giggled and blushed. "No, I've seen your difference. I'm talking about how we look and stuff. I mean, we're both from different planets, right?"

"But we share the same creators."

She gave him a perplexed look. "What, you mean to say God made you too?"

"The progenitors of our race were not gods. We are—and I am speaking of both our people—descended from a race of superior sentient beings.

Space travelers that roamed the galaxies seeding populations and starting civilizations."

"You mean we're descended from aliens?" Her eyes grew wide.

"Did it ever occur to you that who is an alien is a matter of perspective?"

Diana thought about this for a second and frowned. "Wait, are you saying you're not the alien, I am?"

"You will be when we reach my planet. But fear not, alienists are few. Rebuilding our species is more important than illogical notions. But forget about that. You want to know where we come from. Many sentient beings are descended from this super race. The differences that have evolved, such as our skin and small biological features, are a result of our different planetary environments. Our bodies' adaptations. This shared genetic heritage is why it's possible for us to mate. Sentient beings that evolved on their own do not share these common traits with us."

"You mean there are real aliens out there?"

"If you mean nonhumanoids, then yes. Alphie has a catalog of charted planets and their inhabitants if you're interested. I especially enjoy the Kergorsiams—their touch has enough hormones in it to make you orgasm on the spot. Kind of embarrassing if you're in public when it happens."

Diana laughed as he intended, and Kor went on

to tell her more tales of alien encounters just to keep her smiling. It beat her yelling at him, and as she relaxed, he inched closer. He just couldn't help himself. He wanted, no, needed, to touch her. Even more puzzling, he wanted her to feel the same way.

Ancestors, what have you done to me?

DIANA GIGGLED as Kor told her far-fetched stories of alien life. *I know he's got to be pulling my leg, but at least he's entertaining.*

After one tale on the mating rituals of the Xian-malons—it seemed odd that you needed to die in order to get married first—she broached the subject of bonding.

"Okay, so you need to explain this bonding thing to me a little better. I mean, it is why I'm here. Mind you, I'm not saying yes. I'm just curious."

Kor, who had gotten closer to her while he talked—disturbingly close—seemed pleased with her question. "What do you want to know?"

"If I understood you correctly before, we get naked, then say some words, and we're, like, married?" *So much for a white wedding.*

"Bluntly, yes, although it is a little more spiritual than that."

"I still don't see why I need to be naked." Although she had to admit that a part of her looked forward to seeing him naked again. *Surely he can't be as big as I remember. Can he?*

"As part of the bonding ritual, the shedding of our vestments symbolizes the leaving behind of our previous life and coming into our new life together as equals."

His words startled her vision of all the smooth blue flesh, and she almost blushed. "That makes sense, I guess. In my world, we wear our fanciest clothes for the occasion. Women especially tend to wear really fancy white dresses, and the men wear tuxes."

"I've seen examples of Earth weddings. It seems rather ornate and ritual-driven, not to mention crowded with spectators. On my world, it is a private matter between two individuals."

Kor leaned even closer when he said this, his lips hovering over hers, making her breath hitch. Feeling her body betray her again, Diana moved away. She couldn't think coherently when he got that close.

"I'm not saying I won't be your mate, but I'd like more time to decide or at least feel like I'm the one making the choice and not some strange oracle." *Although if he keeps getting close to me, it will be my hormones making the choice soon. Damn, he turns me on.*

"I will respect your choice, for now. But keep in mind that we must have this accomplished before we arrive at my planet. While females are held sacred, that doesn't mean that they will allow a non-mated female to walk around. Oracle or not, there are some who will claim you for their own with no regard to your wishes."

Diana didn't like his last remark. She didn't like feeling pressured. She'd bond if and when she chose to. And if anyone thought—Kor included— that they could force her, she'd . . . *Probably not have much of a choice.* She sighed.

It wasn't that she disliked Kor. On the contrary, she found him entertaining, a good listener, patient —very, very patient—not to mention super sexy. But was that enough? They were talking about a lifelong commitment. Or was he? Did they have divorce in his society? And she still worried about adapting. Would she be lonely for others of her kind? Homesick for the things she'd lost? And what color would her babies end up being—light blue? Diana almost giggled at that thought. She must have made some kind of noise, though, for Kor looked at her oddly.

"What is so entertaining?"

Diana thought about lying but then, imagining a blue hued baby—that reminded her of a certain cartoon she watched growing up—giggled and told him, "What color are the babies?"

That flummoxed him, apparently, and he knitted his dark brows. "I don't know. I've never held one, and I honestly don't recall seeing any. I was the youngest of my mother's brood. Alphie?"

"I already heard the question," said the computer, and to Diana it sounded as if he was suppressing chuckles too. "The babies, depending on the parents, run a gamut of colors, actually, but most often they are a mixture of the parents' skin hues."

"I'm going to have a blue baby?" Diana spoke without thinking and then tried to backtrack. "That is, if I decide to—"

But Kor had heard enough, and with a grin, his arms were around her, his lips capturing her mouth and shushing her. *He sure has an interesting way of making me shut up.* She closed her eyes, enjoying what had become a daily occurrence between them. And, despite her protests, she looked forward to his daily embraces.

As he deepened the kiss, parting her lips to slide his tongue inside, she grew bolder as well. Her hands touched the hair at his nape, the texture softer than it looked. As the kiss deepened though, she let her fingers drift from the silk of his hair to grip the defined muscles in his shoulders.

His hands performed an exploration of their own, skimming up her rib cage to lightly touch the underside of her breasts. Diana felt her breath hiccup as she waited for his hands to grab her full globes and squeeze them. They felt heavy with longing, her nipples so taut. But instead, his hands came back down to her waist and slid around her to hug her in close.

Diana felt frustrated and mewled against his mouth, arching her body into his.

Kor chuckled. "Sorry, moon flower, but I will not take advantage of you without the bonding ritual. If you are ready, let me know."

Diana felt like a bucket of cold water had been dumped on her. She jumped up, his unresisting arms falling away.

"I—No," she managed to say in a voice that wasn't too breathy. Then she fled from his laughter, the heat from his kisses still branding her lips, her loins wet enough to wring.

However, horny as she was, she knew one thing for sure. *I'm not ready yet.*

I still have so many questions. So many concerns. And lucky me, I only have a horny blue man and a sarcastic computer to answer them.

The responsible part of her knew she should say no. After all, they had nothing in common.

Oh yeah, like me and my ex, Rick, had so much in common. Rick had been a lawyer by day, asshole by night. She'd dated Rick the gym enthusiast for three months. They spent most of their dates at either his place or hers, ostensibly to watch a movie, but usually they ended up in bed.

And while she could not say she had actually

loved him, she had liked him and thought he liked her too. Turned out she was his closet fetish, a fact she discovered by accident when she asked him why she hadn't met any of his friends. Rick had hemmed and hawed and then finally admitted that her size embarrassed him.

"Excuse me? I thought you said you loved my curves."

"Well, I do in private, but in public, no one wants to be seen with a fat chick."

Diana had thought she'd been pretty restrained when he'd made that comment. After all, she'd slapped him only once. She'd been more pissed at herself for crying when she got home. Who cared what one asshole thought? *So what if I'm plump? I'm also smart, funny, considerate . . .*

Now that she thought about it, Kor appreciated all her qualities, even her rounded shape. So what was her problem? Kor had no intention of hiding her away like a shameful secret.

Or would he?

"Alphie, how are the women on Kor's planet treated?"

"Could you be more specific?" asked Alphie.

"Well, do the women over there have freedom? Are they allowed to go out and do what they want? Do they have to wear veils over their face? Do men decide everything?"

"Yes and no," came Alphie's oblique reply.

"Before the plague, females had almost as many rights as men. Since the plague, some of those freedoms have been curtailed in order to protect them."

"Curtailed how?"

"Simply put, females must be married when they come of age, and widowed females must likewise be taken under the care of a male guardian. This is for her own safety, though, as the lack of females makes the males a little more violent in their courting methods."

Diana kind of found that idea archaic-sounding for a supposedly advanced culture. It did sound, though, like the issues were mostly safety ones. And Kor certainly hadn't tried to restrain the way she spoke to him. How bad could it be?

"Anything else I should know?" she asked. "Like, can he dump me if it doesn't work out?"

"Mate bonds are for life. A male mate, especially of the warrior class like Kor, would die before allowing you to come to harm. You will be well taken care of."

But will I be loved? she wondered, still confused as she went to sleep in the large bed, alone.

5

"KOR," SAID HIS MOTHER IN A FIRM TONE, "WHAT do you mean you have not bonded yet? You are almost home. What are you waiting for?"

"She hasn't said yes yet, Mother," said Kor, restraining an urge to run his hand through his hair, a sign of agitation his mother was sure to recognize.

"What? Who cares if she hasn't said yes? She was chosen by the Oracle. Now do your duty and bond with her."

What did his mother think he'd been trying to do? By all the silvery moons, he thought he'd had her the last time they'd kissed. She'd been ripe for him. He could sense it, smell it. His body still twitched in remembrance. Yet, she still hesitated. He'd never understand females.

"I'm trying," grumbled Kor under his breath.

But his mother, of keen ears, heard him.

"Well, try harder, son. Have you not explained the plight of our world?"

"Of course I have. But she insists that we date." Dating, an unfamiliar term that Kor had researched and found to mean, on her planet, some kind of extended courtship.

"Date? Oh my, I haven't heard that term in a long time," said his mother with a chuckle. "They found you an Earth girl. How marvelous. But that changes nothing. Give her what she wants and be done with it."

"I'm not even sure what she means by a date. I've been courting as best I can on board."

"Then take her somewhere off ship. Somewhere romantic."

Romantic, another term Kor didn't quite comprehend. Did he not lavish attention on her already? What more did Diana need?

Kor chatted with his mother a few moments more before saying goodbye and switching off the communication console. He leaned back in his seat, thinking.

According to Alphie's research and his mother, he should take her somewhere pretty and flatter her, make her feel attractive. Didn't his kissing and touching her every chance he could count? He needed to make her feel comfortable in his presence. By the power of the moons, this dating business seemed complicated. No wonder the bonding ritual had been invented. A pity his mate couldn't see the beauty of it.

Kor pulled up on-screen a map of the system they were currently flying through and grinned when Alphie circled one particular planet in red.

"Thanks, Alphie," he said, jumping out of his chair. He'd found the perfect spot to make Diana his.

"COME WITH ME," Kor said mysteriously, interrupting her virtual game of chess with Alphie.

Diana barely glanced at him, intent on her next move. But her body sure knew he was there. *Treacherous body.* She'd barely slept the night before for thinking about him. At least she'd come to a decision. She'd bond with him before they got to his planet, but only when the time seemed right, which, judging by her reaction to his presence, would probably be the next time he kissed her. However, she had no intention of telling him that. A lady should always play hard to get if she wanted her man to appreciate her.

Kor leaned into her line of sight with a pleased look on his face, like a little boy who had a surprise and couldn't wait to reveal it.

"Come with me," he repeated.

"Where?"

Kor shook his head with a smile and didn't answer. Diana found herself intrigued at his mysterious, almost playful air and rose from her seat. Tugging her hand, Kor led her to a bland room she had never seen before.

"Close your eyes."

"Why?" Diana asked suspiciously. *Is he going to kiss me again? Yay!* Diana frowned at her subconscious glee at this thought. *Just because I'm going to marry him doesn't mean I have to be so eager,* she thought. *Remember, make him work for it.* But even with that admonishment to herself, her body tingled in anticipation. The man, alien, whatever you wanted to call him kissed like a god, and she couldn't wait to taste him again.

But he didn't kiss her. Instead he spoke. "You asked for a date. I think that was the term you used. So I had Alphie find a place for us to go on a picnic. According to your Earth histories, that is considered romantic."

Diana smiled. *He's been doing research? For me? Maybe I'll kiss him first this time.*

"Now close your eyes, no peeking," he said, standing close behind her, his hands on her waist, that simple touch enough to set her pulse racing. Diana shut her eyes tight and waited.

Nothing happened.

"Open your eyes," he said, his breath teasing the lobe of her ear.

Thinking something had backfired, Diana opened them, expecting to see the bland beige room again, but instead a colorful vista appeared, to her shock.

"Oh my freaking God," she exclaimed, trying to take it all in.

Kor, pleased at her reaction, smiled before tucking her hand into his arm and leading her down a pink grassy hill—although she'd never imagined a grass that would tickle like silk on her ankles.

Bet making love on this would feel . . . Diana almost gasped at the direction of her thoughts. She seemed to be inundated with naughty thoughts that kept multiplying and centered around her blue suitor. *Remember, make him work for it. This is just part of his diabolical plan to make you succumb to his delicious body. I can't give in too easily.* But God, he was making it hard.

"Where are we?" she asked, crouching down to stroke the pink tendrils at her feet that she could swear sighed in the wind with pleasure.

"Ambresia. A planet that has no resources, no sentient life, no real value other than it's pretty and gentle."

"I'd think a planet like this would be mobbed with folks. Or are there, like, ferocious alien-eating monsters or something?"

"There are those who've tried to build here, but the planet overtakes the structures overnight. It's like the planet itself is sentient and prefers to remain untouched. As for monsters, unless you count cute, cuddly creatures who mob you for petting, then, no, nothing to worry about."

Diana sat down on the pink lawn and looked up at Kor with a smile. She had to admit he'd found the perfect spot, not to mention he looked so yummy standing there, loose white shirt rippling lightly in the gentle breeze, his snug breeches ending mid-calf, his feet bare like her own. Her eyes caught his, and she stared, transfixed, at his violet orbs, aware that once again they were glowing, something that happened, she noticed, when he became aroused. *And what do you know? It happens every time he gets close to me*, she thought gleefully.

Blushing—and feeling heat coursing through her body—she dropped her gaze. So, of course, he chuckled. Alien jerk, he knew how he affected her.

Hearing him moving around, she watched as he spread out a blanket, a checkered red-and-white thing reminiscent of home—Alphie, she supposed. Then he unpacked a type of cooler filled with food —little bite-sized pastries, fruit both familiar and not, a bottle of something that sweated, along with crystal glasses. He'd come prepared.

Diana moved onto the blanket and sat lotus-style before helping herself to tidbits. Then, curious, she asked him more questions about the planet as they ate, the atmosphere—not to mention the company—relaxing her completely. She wanted to blame the fresh air and sunshine for the way her body came alive, but she knew better. *Oh, why lie? I love being with Kor. For an alien, he sure knows how to make me feel good.*

Diana, stomach happy, lay on her back, her head pillowed by one arm. Kor moved to lie on his side beside her, head propped on one hand, watching her. Diana could see his eyes glowing again, and she felt her body tingle, aching for him to touch it. *Wanton*, she chided herself. But who was here to care? *And, to be honest, it's not like I miss my old, boring life. In fact, I've been happier and more alive these last couple of days than I've ever been. So why fight it?*

Diana made the first move and lifted up her free hand to gently run a finger down the side of his face. Kor closed his eyes, and she could have sworn she felt him tremble. She rolled onto her side to face him and, this time, lightly touched his lips with her finger. He parted them for her, and she felt the edge of his tongue wet her fingertip before his lips closed around her digit and sucked it.

Diane felt such a jolt of longing shoot through her that she let out a surprised cry. His eyes opened, blazing now with arousal. She felt his hand reach up and touch her face like she'd touched his. He mimicked her action, and when she felt his finger part her lips, she nipped it and then sucked it.

"Oh, Diana," she heard him whisper, his hand

sliding to the back of her head to twine itself in her hair and draw her face toward his.

Diana's eyes fluttered shut, and she held her breath at the feel of his lips, feather-light, slide across hers. Diana trembled at this delicate touch, her whole body awake and taut with erotic tension. He rolled her onto her back and lay partially on her, his heavy weight so welcome. The hand in her hair had traveled down her body, lightly touching her neck before tracing a path between her heaving breasts. When his hand cupped one round globe, Diana arched and moaned, a moan that quickly turned into a cry of pleasure as his lips, which had been softly teasing hers, moved to wetly embrace the tip of her breast.

Beep! Beep! Beep!

The annoying sound that would not stop had Kor pull his head away from her body and the delicious things he was doing to her nipple through the fabric of her top.

Diana pulled at him to come back, and with a groan, he came back down to crush her lips with his own. But Alphie's intrusive voice dowsed them like a cold shower.

"Kor, I hate to interrupt, but this is important."

Kor, with a heavy sigh, rolled onto his back. "Alphie, I am going to unplug you."

Diana giggled as she traced patterns on Kor's chest, her body still aroused, hoping Alphie would go away so they could continue their sensuous exploration. And once they got naked, what the heck, maybe get bonded.

"Kor," came Alphie's unrelenting tone.

"Fine," grumbled Kor, standing up and giving Diana a hand. "Let me take care of this, and then, perhaps, we can resume where we left off," he said to her with a hard kiss.

Bemused, Diana wandered down the hill to the water's edge while Kor dealt with whatever it was Alphie had deemed so important. The violet-hued liquid sparkled in the light of the three red suns. A rustle on the other side had her looking up quickly, only to see the cutest floppy-eared pink bunny ever! Of course, the bunnies back home had only two ears, not four, and their tails weren't as big as their heads, but still, the little critter was adorable as it regarded her with big eyes.

Looking back at Kor, Diana saw him talking up to the sky—Alphie no doubt trying to give him pointers—and she shrugged. She wouldn't go far. Besides, having Kor come find her could be fun. In the movies she'd watched back home, a lifetime ago, a man chasing a woman usually tended to end in torrid outdoor fun.

Diana hopped across the stones that glittered like diamonds in the water—*could they be giant diamonds?*—and landed on the other side.

The little bunny creature stared at her, whiskers

twitching. *Oh my God, it is so cute!* Diana crouched and put out her hand, but this movement startled the fluff ball, and it bounced off. Diana giggled and followed it, not too worried because Kor was, after all, just behind her and he had told her that nothing dangerous inhabited the planet. *Well, unless you count him. He looks like he could be plenty dangerous—yum!*

The pink bunny hopped behind the thick trunk of a tree, a gnarly, twisted mauve specimen that looked like something Dr. Seuss had dreamed up. Diana rounded its trunk and stopped in astonishment. She'd found her bunny but wished she hadn't as it twisted in the grip of a large, hulking brute who, even from three steps away, stank to holy heaven.

"What have we here?" He leered at her.

"Nothing," Diana stammered, her heart suddenly racing in fright. "I'll just be on my way now. My friend is waiting." Diana whirled to run back to Kor but came face-to-face with a broad chest wearing a studded bandolier. Swallowing because she already knew it wasn't Kor, she looked up to see an ugly, ogre-ish face that grinned at her, the black spaces of missing teeth and the two intact sharp incisors giving him a sinister look. He reached out callused hands and grabbed her upper arms tightly.

"Let me go," she said, her voice wavering in fear.

"I don't think so, me pretty," he said, his fetid breath washing over her. He tightened his grip on her while someone behind her pinched her rear.

That was when Diana screamed really, really loud.

6

"This better be good," grumbled Kor.

"Stolen vessel spotted on the other side of the moon. Could be some contraband inside. Shall we disable it?" said an eager Alphie.

"Not now, Alphie," said Kor, distracted, watching Diana saunter down to the water. He turned away from her, trying to control his urge to chase her down and make her his. *I am a warrior. I have control over my body.* Kor repeated this mantra to himself, but his body didn't seem to be listening.

"Come on, Kor. She won't even know," the computer whined.

Frustrated with himself for not being able to resist her allure and with Alphie for continually interrupting, Kor almost snapped. "Alphie, if it were any other time, I'd say go after it, but I am so close to getting her to bond, I can't risk it."

"You are no fun," said Alphie in a distinct pouting tone.

Kor, about to respond, instead jolted into action when he heard Diana let out a piercing shriek.

Looking around, he realized she'd wandered off out of sight, not something to be worried about on this gentle planet and one of the reasons he'd chosen it. But Alphie's inopportune call made him think of the stolen vessel hiding behind the planet's moon. Under normal circumstances, Kor would have hunted the stolen vessel down because of possible pirates. Could Diana have run into some of the vessel's crew? Or had some cute and cuddly critter jumped out to scare her?

He heard her shriek again, followed by gruff, snorting guffaws of laughter.

Pirates! He'd found the stolen vessel's crew—or, rather, Diana had.

Kor cranked up the speed and ran down to the water's edge. He leapt over the babbling brook to land with sure feet on the other side. Up ahead, he could see the hulking figures of the space pirates—not to mention smell them on the breeze—and he felt his heart stutter. And here he came to challenge them weaponless. Thinking with his groin instead of his head, he'd left his daggers and blaster back on the ship, a fact he now cursed.

"Unhand my mate," he bellowed, seeing Diana

struggling, her face fearful as they bounced her among them like a child's ball.

"She bears no band of mating, so she's free for the taking," said a one-eyed brute with a smirk, and then, instead of waiting for Kor to wipe the smug smile off his face, the pirate thumped the communicator on his chest, and they were gone.

Kor skidded to a stop and cursed. "Alphie!" he bellowed.

He'd no sooner said the ship computer's name than he found himself onboard.

"Follow that ship discreetly. And I want the plans for their vessel. I am getting Diana back." Kor bubbled with a dark rage at the effrontery of these beasts who thought to take what was his. And, for that, they would pay. "And while you're at it, explain to me how in the silvery moons you managed to miss their life signatures when you scanned the planet."

"This planet gives off inconclusive readings because of its sentient nature. I will have to revise my programming in the future to take that aspect into account. I apologize, Commander. It won't happen again."

"It had better not. Now status!" barked Kor, more mad at himself than Alphie.

"Ship plans located, Commander," said the computer, all business now. "Enemy vessel still located behind the moon. Now what?"

"Now," said Kor in a menacing tone, "I rescue Diana and punish her kidnappers." *Very painfully*, he thought.

DIANA'S MIND SPUN. Things had happened so rapidly. Only seconds ago, she'd watched Kor running for her, his face grim and his eyes flashing. A moment later, she found herself in a dank room that smelled bloody awful. Her captor let go of her, and Diana rubbed her arms where he'd gripped her, trying to erase the slimy feel of his touch. Diana looked about frantically for a place to run— any kind of refuge—but found herself surrounded by loud, hulking creatures. The crew of dubious origin—although judging by some of their porcine features, she could guess—leered and grunted at Diana. The unpleasant aroma of unwashed alien and something even more rancid tickled her nose as they swarmed around her. The foulness in the air made her stomach churn.

Diana tried to take shallow breaths, which were not much better, as she could almost taste the filth. *I wonder if they'll let me go if I puke on their feet?* But judging by the grime on their boots, that had been tried before, and she didn't think they cared.

Grubby fingers pinched her chin and turned her face from side to side, inspecting her like a potential buyer. Diana clenched her teeth and reminded herself she was outnumbered and that it would be best not to antagonize them 'til she knew what they wanted. But even knowing that, she had an insane urge to kick her captor in the shin or other sensitive parts. *I wonder if he'd squeal like a pig?*

The lug pinching her chin stepped back and gave her a partially-toothed grin. "I can't believe the stupid Xamian didn't bond with this fine piece. A virgin with plump flesh like hers will fetch a pretty price in the market."

Diana couldn't help the laughter that bubbled out.

"What's so funny, girl?" asked her captor, narrowing his eyes at her.

"I hate to disappoint you, but I'm not a virgin." Too late Diana realized she should have kept her mouth shut, as several pairs of eyes now swiveled to look at her with interest. "I—um, can I take that back?" Diana wanted to kick herself. *Dummy!*

"Not a virgin. Well then, there's no reason not to test the goods before we sell them then."

"What? No testing the goods. Not a good idea," Diana stammered, panicked.

But the brute in charge just pinched her boob with rough fingers, making Diana wince. "Well, my crew, it seems we're going to be entertained tonight." A flurry of grunts and snuffles accompanied this announcement. "But first let's get out of this space system in case the moon warrior decides he wants her back."

Diana found herself rudely thrust into a cell with the door slammed shut and locked. She ran at the door and pounded on it with her fists, screaming, "Let me go! Right now. You can't do this to me." Dead silence answered her. Pacing the confines of the room—it didn't take long as it measured only about four feet by four feet—she looked for a way to escape or, barring that, something she could use as a weapon. The scratched and stained walls were seamless and the room devoid of furniture of any type. She couldn't even find a crack big enough to squeeze a mouse through. Diana sank to the floor and huddled her knees to her chest, the seriousness of her plight finally sinking in.

I can't believe I went from almost making love to the man of my dreams to being the intended victim of a gang rape by smelly ogres. She wished she could rewind time and not been so prickly with Kor. Had she bonded with him in the first place, they would have never gone to that planet, and she wouldn't have been kidnapped.

But at least she wasn't alone. Oh no, she had misery for company.

KOR, using his people's advanced technology, teleported onto the pirate ship with them none the wiser. They'd messed with the wrong Xamian. Alphie had managed to locate a schematic for the stolen vessel, and Kor had memorized it. He'd arrived in an obscure part of the engine room that he doubted they manned. On silent feet, he edged out around the ship's energy core, disappointed to find the room clear.

Kor had been angry since Diana's abduction, and he really wanted to hurt something to help ease some of his temper. Alphie thankfully hadn't tried to talk him out of this insane rescue attempt. For one, he knew what Kor's answer would have been —no. Besides, Alphie was well aware of Kor's training in the guard. After all, it was his high rank and commendations that had made him eligible for a mate in the first place. Only the best were rewarded.

Kor peered out of the doorway of the engine room into the corridor and found it still empty. He padded down it on silent feet, anticipation rising when he heard the murmur of voices around the bend.

Drawing his blades—only idiots used laser weapons on board a sealed vessel in space—he dropped into a roll and went around the corner, his unexpected arrival allowing him to gut the two crewmen before they even had a chance to realize death had arrived.

Kor wiped his blades on the tunics of the

downed creatures—although judging by the filth staining the cloth, the blood might have been cleaner. Impatient to find Diana, Kor carved a path of violence through the ship, pausing only briefly once to question a crewmember on the where-abouts of his mate—an interrogation that involved a lot of squealing. Discovering the captain planned to enjoy Diana first before handing her over to the crew, Kor made his way quickly to the captain's quarters.

Kor intended to be on hand before anything happened to his chosen. The only taste the captain would be getting tonight would be that of his own mortality.

Kor crouched in the captain's quarters, his eyes glowing in the darkness and his teeth bared in a vicious grin. In a grim silence, he waited to execute the beast who'd dared lay hands on his mate.

Stupid, stupid, stupid. I have got to be the dumbest earth-ling to ever leave her planet. Absolute brilliance telling them you're not a virgin. Hey, why not send out invitations for rape?

Diana huddled dejectedly in a corner of the cell with tears prickling her eyes as she thought long-ingly of Kor and his strong arms.

It's my fault I'm here instead of with Kor. If I'd only

been a little less stubborn and done the mating thing with him, we wouldn't have even been on that planet. Hell, it's not like I don't want him. He's nice, gentle, thoughtful, not to mention the hottest thing since wing night at Kelsey's. But I just had to fight it, and now instead of making love to a hunky blue alien, I'm gonna be . . .

Diana hiccupped, in tears and frightened. She really deserved a Darwin Award for this.

Diana heard the lock in the cell door turn and looked up hopefully. A foolish part of her had entertained a faint hope that Kor would come to rescue her like a damsel in distress from a romance novel. But seeing the big ogre the others called captain enter, she slumped dejectedly. Kor would be insane to try to rescue her. After all, what could one blue man do against a horde of nasty brutes? He'd probably just go to the Oracle and ask for another mate—one not so reluctant and argumentative.

"Get up," grunted her captor.

Diana sat in complete apathy, hoping he'd just leave. That turned out to be a slim hope. Harsh fingers dug into her forearm and dragged her up.

"Let me go," she cried, terrified into action. Diana pulled at the meaty hand grabbing her, but the grip of iron didn't budge, and she found herself being dragged from her cell. Diana struggled, kicking at her captor and twisting in his grip, but her kidnapper just chuckled, the rattling sound of phlegm making her feel ill. *I'll die if he touches me.* She shuddered.

"I like a wild one in bed," he wheezed with a leer, his fetid breath steaming in her face, making her gag.

Diana's heart froze at his words while deep despair flooded her. *Oh God, someone please save me. Please.*

Too soon they reached a door that the captain opened, and he flung her roughly inside. Diana, eyes awash in tears, stumbled into a hard body inside, and she sobbed as arms of steel wrapped around her. Diana opened her mouth to scream but stopped when she felt her nose twitch at the clean scent of the chest she'd landed against, a fresh scent she recognized.

"Kor!" she exclaimed, looking up with relief. *He came for me!*

Kor gave her hard smile, his arms tightening around her briefly before he set her behind him.

"You shouldn't have taken what was mine," said Kor in a deadly low voice to the captain, his words sending a thrill to the core of Diana's being.

"Prepare to die," snarled her repulsive captor.

"Not today. Today I avenge the honor of my betrothed," said Kor, who suddenly held a silver dagger in each hand, their blades encased in a shimmering light. The captain, chuckling evilly, pulled out a long dagger of his own and, with a bellow, charged at Kor. Diana backed up fearfully, looking for a place to hide in the small room, for Kor would surely move aside to avoid that deadly-looking rush.

But Kor stood his ground and provided her with a shield using his own body. The brute hit Kor with a grunt, but Kor, like a wall, remained unmoved. A few lightning flashes as Kor moved his deadly blades, and the fight, as quickly as it had begun, was over.

The captain fell with a gurgle to the floor, and Kor wiped his slimy blades on his prone body before sheathing them on his belt. Then he turned to Diana and opened his arms.

Diana flew into them, sobbing with relief. Clutching at him, she pulled his head down to kiss him frantically. "Thank you for saving me," she murmured against his mouth. His arms crushed her against him as he devoured her lips.

Diana, her relief over her safety and his assuaged, leaned back. He let go of her reluctantly.

Then she yelled at him. "Are out of your mind? You could have been killed!"

Kor looked stunned for a moment then grinned. "You mean you'd care?"

"No." Then at his pointed look, she muttered, "Maybe a little."

"You're mine whether you've said the mating words or not. No one touches what is mine."

Diana felt goose bumps at his words. His words were possessive but, God, so hot! She threw herself in his arms again, her lips hot and wet against his.

She felt her feet leave the floor as he swept her up into his arms.

He lifted his head long enough for her to see they were back on his ship and for him to say, "Finish it, Alphie, and see that we're not disturbed."

Then his lips came back to crush hers, and Diana clung to him, relief and desire making her determined not to let him go 'til she was truly his, body and soul.

KOR HAD NEVER FELT such relief as when he'd found her safe. And revenge had never tasted sweeter. His little earthling, even without the ritual, had come to mean so much to him already. He might not understand the scary, dangerous feelings she aroused in him, but he did know they now seemed to rule him.

Her sweet capitulation, instead of reducing this feeling, had actually increased it. *Mine*, he wanted to shout to the world. *All mine*. And he intended to claim her—no more arguments or interruptions.

He laid her on the bed, his body painfully aroused at the sight of her swollen lips and heavy-lidded eyes. He stripped himself quickly, feeling his cock jerk and dance in anticipation. Diana licked her lips watching him, and Kor shuddered, imagining those lips and that pink tongue licking other things. He removed Diana's garments quickly, something she didn't protest. Nay, she lifted her hips and helped him, and when she lay before him nude, his heated gaze visually devoured all that creamy flesh that begged for his touch.

When he would have covered her body with his, though, she raised a hand to stop him.

"I want you, Diana," he whispered, "and I know you want me too." He slid his hand up her calf to her thigh, feeling his breath almost stop at the way her body arched and writhed at his simple touch.

"Oh," she gasped, her face flushed. "I want you too. But first . . ." She lost her train of thought as he teased an ebony curl at the V of her thighs. "Oh, Kor, damn it, I can't think. Do the bond thing quickly, would you, before you drive me mad."

Kor was tempted to take her first and do the bond after. But he just knew what his mother and the Oracle would say about that. And they'd find out somehow. They had ways of ferreting out a male's shameful secrets.

At least they were already both naked, and the ritual itself was simple.

"Kneel," he told her, dropping to his knees on the spongy floor. Diana, in all her naked splendor, knelt before him, and Kor almost asked her to postpone this 'til later. His body ached for her in a way he'd never thought possible.

"Put your hands against mine," he said, holding up his two hands, palms facing her. She placed her pale hands, so much smaller and more delicate than his, against them, the vibration of their bodies' energy, their souls, sizzling at the touch.

"My life, my soul, I pledge to thee."

Diana, without prompting, repeated the words huskily. "My life, my soul, I pledge to thee."

"Forever joined for eternity."

Looking into the whirlpools of her eyes that tumbled with emotions, Kor heard her repeat the words, and when she said "eternity," like hot and cold colliding, he heard a thunderclap as their souls merged. He heard Diana gasp as their spiritual signatures, each a distinctive energy, swirled together and forever more into one. The euphoric sensation became so intense it made them both cry out. Then the flare of their joining died down, and all that remained was desire.

Somehow they found themselves on the bed again, skin to skin.

His erection pulsed and hung heavy between his legs. He could smell her arousal and, when he touched the apex of her thighs, feel her wetness on his fingers. But he wanted her more than ready. He wanted her wild.

With just the tip of his cock, he rubbed it against the nubbin that hid just below her curls. Diana arched, and Kor grinned in male pride. But her arching also drew attention to another splendid part of her body that he had fantasized about, her luscious breasts.

Kor, bracing his body on his forearms so as to keep up the sliding motion of his swollen head against her clit, leaned down and captured one pink tip in his mouth, his teeth lightly grazing the already erect nipple. Diana panted and thrashed, her hands reaching to grab him by the hair and push his mouth down more firmly onto her areola. Kor obliged and opened his mouth wide to suck in more of that perfect globe. He swirled his tongue around the taut nub, and applying suction to the mouthful he had, he pulled his head back 'til his lips snapped off and left her breast quivering. He then switched his attention to the other breast, laving it with the same devotion, a sweet torture that had his beautiful mate moaning.

The tip of Kor's erection slid slickly back and forth still across her taut clit. Too close to the brink himself now, he stopped the torture and pushed his engorged head between her nether lips, an action she approved of judging by how fast her legs locked around him, driving him deep inside, 'til the tip of his shaft nudged her womb.

Kor let out a moan at the exquisite feeling. Her

slick muscles tightened around his shaft, squeezing him, and Kor almost lost it. He pulled back then pushed as deep as he could to sheathe himself, and Diana arched high off the bed. Kor retreated again and then slid himself hard and deep, the tip of his erection curving to find her sweet spot. Diana let out a short scream when he found it and stroked it. And, once found, he'd never lose it again. With long, measured strokes, Kor pushed in and then pulled out, each thrust hitting her hidden spot, making her keen in pleasure, the sound building in intensity until, with a loud scream, she came to the edge of the abyss of pleasure and fell into it. Kor quickly joined her, shouting her name when, at the feel of her muscles orgasming around him, he found himself losing control and finding his ultimate pleasure deep inside her.

And, for the first time since he'd crossed the threshold into adulthood, he saw the universe explode.

7

Diana felt her body tremble as it came back down from the intense orgasm she'd just experienced.

Apparently size did matter. Or did he just have more skills than the human lovers she'd had in the past? It had seemed almost like his cock had a G-spot sensor, one that ensured he hit it each time he pumped into her.

Whatever the case, Diana felt like purring, and judging by the look on Kor's face, he wanted to thump his chest and strut. He had a right. That had been amazing. Diana laid her head on his chest and listened to the steady sound of his heart beating. His arms snuggled her tight. And to think she'd come so close to missing all this.

"I didn't think you'd come back," she whispered, cradled in his arms. Now that the bliss had mellowed and reality returned, she had to ask.

"I will always protect you," he vowed with such sincerity that Diana felt her heart tighten. Perhaps the term 'love' might not exist in his vocabulary, but it seemed possible the emotion existed under a guise of other actions.

"But you could have been killed." The thought of him dying terrified her still.

He shifted position until he could cup her face tenderly between his big hands, his callused thumbs gently rubbing her swollen lower lip, his eyes pools of light as they stared into hers. "You are my mate. I will not allow you to come to harm."

Diana thought about retorting, *I've only been your mate for a few minutes*, but instead, she let the sincerity and pure maleness of his words wash over her. Her body shivered with arousal and renewed need. She saw that same need mirrored in his eyes, and even more titillating, she felt it against her thigh.

God, is he ever hung. I wonder what he tastes like. Feeling reckless and suddenly possessed of an insatiable curiosity, she slid down his body, her lips and teeth grazing the taut skin of his abdomen 'til she reached his hairless groin, the skin here smooth and soft, not to mention so temptingly lickable.

Diana felt her body flush with desire when she saw him already erect and getting bigger the longer she stared at it. She reached out a hand to grasp his erection, eager to play, but as soon as she touched him, she found herself distracted by her wrist.

"What is that?" she asked, staring curiously at the smoky gray band around her wrist, a band she couldn't feel, and when she tried to touch it with her other hand, her fingers went right through it to her flesh below. She let go of his shaft and played with her new piece of smoky jewelry.

"It's our mating band."

"Our what?" she said, looking up from the bracelet that kept changing shape.

"Mating band. With females being so scarce, a way was needed to ensure that males did not just claim any female they found. In the early days, once our madness had settled, there were many arguments and misunderstandings caused by females being claimed twice, sometimes even three times. Once again our ancestors came to the rescue with a solution. When a pair bonds now, a small piece of our ancestors forms itself into a bracelet on the female. This band cannot be removed, except by death, and can identify a female's mate should a challenge arise."

Kind of like a wedding ring, just not as sparkly. "And what do the men get marked with?" she asked, looking over his body for a mark to show he'd bonded to her.

"Marked? No, the males do not get a band."

Diana sat up in the bed and frowned at him. "Well, that doesn't seem fair."

"No one's trying to steal us," he teased.

But Diana found herself annoyed with this indication, once again, of a male-dominated society.

Kor, as if sensing her mood, smiled and raised his hands in mock surrender. "If it bothers you that much, then I will let you shackle me. You'll have to settle for metal instead of a spirit band, but . . ."

Diana tuned out his voice as she watched his wrist in fascination. Kor stopped talking and looked down at his wrist as well, and Diana giggled at the stunned look on his face.

"Well," she said, holding her spirit-banded wrist up beside his now-matching one. "Looks like your ancestors just heard me and agreed. Now we match."

Kor, however, looking at the gray band he now sported, didn't seem as happy about it as she did, though.

"What's wrong?" teased Diana. "Now everyone will know you belong to me."

"I suppose," he said slowly. "But I'm the only male I know of with this mark."

"I'll give you another mark," said Diana impishly.

Suddenly she felt frisky again. She pushed him onto his back and straddled his abdomen. While she leaned forward, her heavy breasts brushed his chest and her hair fell in a curtain around his face. Diana could see his eyes beginning to glow, and her lips curved into a sensual smile. Hovering over, leaning close to his lips, she stuck out the tip of her tongue and licked his lower lip before tugging it down with her teeth. His hands came up and pushed her hair back to cup her face. But Diana laughed and shook her head and his hands free. She grabbed his hands and pushed them up over his head. She bent over his face and teased him with the sight of her breasts hanging so temptingly close, close enough that his warm breath made her nipples tighten.

When she let go of his hands, he went to grab her boobs, but Diana grabbed his hands and pushed them back up above his head. "Keep them up here," she mock-growled.

"Or what?" he drawled, his eyes heavy-lidded with desire.

"Or I won't do this," she said, sliding down his body, his erection a hot poker that pressed against her as she slid down its length. When she straddled his thighs, she smiled wickedly at him as she grabbed his jutting member.

"Is this good enough?" he said, locking his hands together and tucking them under his head.

"Perfect. Don't move," she warned.

Finally she could look at him like she'd been aching to do since she'd met him. She perused the long, lean length of his blue body with its well-defined muscles, and she licked her lips. His body lay before her like a feast, and all she wanted to do was eat it.

Her frank appraisal made his cock grow even harder in her grip. Stroking his silky length up and down, she marveled at the size and color. Dark blue like the rest of him, when engorged, the tip blushed a deep purple color. Diana leaned forward and flicked her tongue against his swollen head, gratified to hear him groan. It was time to make him lose control.

She bathed his shaft with her tongue at first, licking it up and down before swirling her tongue around the head. Then she took him in her mouth, his girth a tighter fit than she'd ever attempted, but so worth it when he closed his eyes and let out a gasp.

She worked his cock up and down with her mouth, her cheeks hollowed as she sucked him. With one of her hands, she gripped the base of his shaft. She used her other hand to play with his heavy balls. He really seemed to enjoy her touch on those, so she cradled them in her hand and squeezed them, a move that made his hips arch.

Diana worked his shaft wetly with her mouth and hands, his obvious pleasure making her own pussy wet with desire. Unable to contain herself, Diana sat up and positioned herself over his shaft.

Rubbing her cleft with his engorged tip, she threw her head back in pleasure before sitting herself down hard on it, impaling herself.

Oh God, that feels good.

His long, thick cock filled her so tightly, the throbbing length so deep inside her, she convulsed a little in pleasure.

Distracted by the sensations his shaft inside her made her feel, she didn't protest when she felt his hands on her hips, helping her to rise and fall on his member, each movement down its length sending a shock of pure bliss through her that made her mewl in pleasure. She could feel her body tightening and coiling around him, lost in a vortex of pleasure that rapidly gained in intensity the faster they pumped their bodies together 'til, with a scream, she felt her muscles convulse around him, spasming with the intensity of her orgasm. He echoed her shout, driving himself one last time deep inside, his shaft shooting molten liquid inside her.

Diana collapsed on top of him, her body glistening with sweat, her breath erratic. He hugged her tightly, his breathing just as irregular.

And as Diana felt her body slow down, a heavy languor overtaking all her limbs, making her slip into sleep, she thought she heard him whisper, "Mine, forever."

[8]

KOR AWOKE SLOWLY, THE UNFAMILIAR FEEL OF A warm, naked body pressed against him an instant— and pleasant, indeed—reminder of the previous day's events.

She's mine. This possessive thought made his lips curve into a smile, and he hugged her close. As if it had a mind of its own, one of his hands found the heavy globe of her breast and squeezed it. Even in her sleep, she squirmed and sighed at his touch. Kor felt himself getting hard.

"Ahem," came the ever-present Alphie, using his uncanny ability to interrupt at inopportune moments.

Kor sighed and rolled onto his back, letting go of Diana's breast with regret.

"Your mother is calling again. Shall I put her on

the view screen in here?" said Alphie with altogether too much mirth.

"No!" Kor shot out of bed and scrambled for his clothes. While he hopped about in an undignified manner to yank them on, he heard Diana's sleepy voice from behind him.

"I have to say I never expected the day after getting married to be greeted by a blue moon."

Confused, Kor turned to ask her what she meant, finally sliding his pants up over his blue buttocks, but he had no need to ask as it dawned on him what she meant when both she and Alphie burst out laughing.

Pretending affront, Kor stalked out of the cabin to the command center to take the call from his mother—again. The matriarch of his lineage deserved his respect, but these daily multiple calls were getting tiresome. Not to mention he'd had different plans about what he'd be doing when he woke up beside his mate for the first time.

"Mother, what can I help you with today?" he asked, sitting in his chair and drumming his fingers impatiently.

"Judging by your disheveled look, I'd say you finally did the deed. About time."

Kor shook his head at her blunt statement and laughed. "Yes, it's done. Does this mean the calls are going to stop? I just left my mate and a warm bed to attend to you."

"Oh, you poor thing," said his mother without the least hint of remorse. "I'll see you in a cycle when you arrive home. In the meantime, get started on making me a grandchild. I want to be able to brag about one to the ladies at our next moon gathering."

Kor shook his head and signed off. *Children, well, there's a way to make a warrior avoid the pleasures of the flesh.* Sure, he'd thought about it, in a very abstract kind of way like, yes, eventually he'd have some. However, his mother's words suddenly made the prospect seem imminent. *By the silvery moons, Diana could already be pregnant. We certainly gave it a good attempt last night. I don't know if I'm ready to be a father. I'd kind of hoped to enjoy my mate for a while.* But enjoying her meant possibly impregnating her, as birth control was unheard of since the plague. Kor suddenly had a vision of Diana, her belly rounded with child, his child, and from somewhere deep inside him, a wave of protectiveness rose at the thought. *My mate, my child. My family.* Feeling more positive about the idea, he rose and left the command center to find Diana.

No time like the present to get started on the future.

IN THE CABIN, Diana lounged on the bed, her body

pleasantly sore and even still a bit aroused at the thought of the previous evening's pleasures.

Kor is a phenomenal lover! The way he uses his tongue, his body. Diana felt like sliding a hand under the sheet to stroke and ready herself for his return, but her tummy growled impatiently.

Resigned to take care of other bodily needs first, she draped the sheet around herself and stood up.

"Alphie, you there?" she called.

"I am always here."

"I'm hungry," she said, almost plaintively, rubbing her tummy.

"Well, we can't have that," said Kor, striding in, looking deliciously rumpled.

Diana licked her lips looking at him. Suddenly she felt a whole different kind of hunger. Kor wagged a finger at her.

"First, real food," he said, his eyes glowing. "Then we play."

Diana liked the sound of that. Looking around, she spotted her dirty veil outfit from the day before and wrinkled her nose. Kor, seeing where she was looking, picked up the garment and, pressing the wall, opened a chute where he dropped it.

"So am I going to breakfast naked?" she asked, boldly dropping the sheet. She felt her nipples pucker as his look turned smoldering hot. With a groan, he looked away and stripped off his shirt then tossed it in her general direction.

"Quick, put this on before I forget about eating and we both die of starvation."

Diana smiled as she slipped the loose shirt smelling of him over her head. *It's always nice to know you're wanted.* The only problem now was he stood there bare-chested, and Diana so wanted to rub and lick that delicious blue skin.

"By all my wiring, would the two of you stop looking at each other like you're a five-course moon feast? Go. Eat. Now."

Grinning like a kid caught being naughty, Kor grabbed Diana's hand and brought her to the lounge, where a meal had already been laid out for them.

While they ate, Kor supplied a steady stream of conversation, which Diana didn't hear a word of. Between chewing her toast that almost tasted like home and sipping her orange juice, which tasted freshly squeezed, she wondered what Kor really thought about the human mate he was now bonded with. He certainly enjoyed her body, and she his. But did they have anything else in common?

"I thought after our meal that perhaps you'd like to get clean."

The word 'clean' caught Diana's attention, and with a look down at herself, she suddenly realized just how filthy she must be. Her daily washes with the moist cloth Alphie had provided did not replace the need for a real shower or bath. *I am such a dirty girl. Hell, I didn't even think about bathing I was so worried about getting his clothes off and having my way with him again.*

"I'd like that," she said. "Do you keep water on board for showers and stuff?"

"Water?" Kor looked shocked at her suggestion. "Water is much too precious for us to waste on such a thing like bathing, especially on board a ship. I know your society still uses water like it's a renewable resource, but that will soon change. Our society adopted strict water conservation measures quite some time ago. We've come up with new methods of washing and cleaning, and not just our bodies, but clothing and dishes too."

"What, no more baths?" said Diana mournfully, thinking of her decadent love of hot water and bubbles.

"I think we have some alternatives that you'll quite enjoy. I'll show them to you when we reach my planet. Now, are you ready for your first space cleansing?"

Dubious, but willing to try, Diana took his hand and followed him back to the bland room he'd taken her to before when they teleported down to the bunny planet.

"Strip," he told her, dropping his loose pants and standing there naked as a blue jay. Diana almost giggled when she thought of this. He did have a big blue bird, after all.

Biting her lip so as to not giggle, she stripped off her shirt and stood there naked, feeling a little self-conscious. After all, Alphie, the computer with no boundaries, was probably watching, but hey, having an audience did make it more exciting.

"Okay, now what?" she asked, waiting.

Kor placed his hands out toward her, palms out, and Diana lifted her hands to place them against his. As with every other time she touched him, Diana felt a tingle run through her. Apparently he did too, judging by the lifting appendage below.

Then, whatever the cleansing process was, it began. Diana felt a staticky energy that tickled and sizzled across her skin, starting with the soles of her feet and moving up.

"Oh," she exclaimed when the energy cleaner reached her buttocks.

"Spread your legs," whispered Kor, whose eyes had begun to glow.

Diana spread them and felt the electric tingle on her nether lips, an erotic sensation that made her quiver, to her embarrassment.

"This can't be clean," she gasped. "It feels too dirty."

"If you mean pleasurable, then yes," said Kor, leaning forward to nip at her ear.

The energy wave continued its way up Diana's body. Her nipples puckered at its ghostly touch, and her hair floated around her head in a halo.

And then the beam came back down her body again, and Diana's awakened nerve endings shivered and her body arched forward to touch Kor's. The electrical jolt as their skin touched made her moan. She felt his hands grasp her buttocks and squeeze them. The hardness of his cock poked at her belly, and Diana reached a hand down to grab him. He jerked in her grasp, a living, pulsing, thick pole that she wanted to feel inside her.

Kor bit her neck and sucked the skin, an erogenous zone that had her knees buckling, but he held her in a controlled descent to the floor, its cold surface chill against her fevered skin. He pushed her legs up 'til they rested on his shoulders, exposing her to his sight, and Diana felt herself gush wetly at his smoking gaze. He licked a finger and rubbed it against her clit, and Diana cried out. With her legs still pushed up, he sank down 'til his breath feathered against her inner thighs and brushed softly across her wet lips.

Diana pleaded with him, arching her hips. "Please, Kor."

And he obliged, his hot, wet tongue flicking at her swollen nubbin while he slid two fingers inside her. Diana moaned incoherently at this point. The feel of his tongue laving her and his mouth sucking her tender flesh while his fingers pumped in and out of her was too much for her sensitized body.

She could feel her muscles tightening, and her

pleasure built itself up quickly, a symphony of notes that was about to end in a big climax, 'til he suddenly pulled away.

Diana cried out. "No, please."

But he replaced his fingers and mouth with his rock-hard cock, his thick length sliding easily into her dampness, and with her legs pushed up, he drove himself deep into her. Every stroke seemed to unerringly jab that sweet spot on the underside of her womb, creating a sensation so pleasurable she moaned each time he hit it. It didn't take long for her to reach orgasm, the intensity of it rippling through her body while her muscles clenched him tightly in waves of bliss that had her gushing wetly.

She felt him come inside her, a hot spurt of liquid and a spasm that shook his whole body as he joined her in heaven.

He collapsed on top of her, breathing hard. Diana giggled under his slumped body.

"I'm afraid to ask what you find so amusing."

"Well," said Diana, running her fingers down his dewy back, "I think we need another cleansing. We got dirty again during the first one."

Kor grinned. "Yes, that's an unfortunate side effect when you cleanse yourself nude with your mate."

"What? You mean we can do this clothed?"

"If you keep the clothes on, then the erotic feeling

is much reduced, and you will emerge just as clean, as the cleanser works at a molecular level. Actually, doing it clothed will clean your clothing as well."

"Wait, you mean we didn't have to get naked to get clean?"

"No, but I think this was much more pleasurable for us both, don't you?"

What could she say? Her alien had a point. But that kind of erotic subterfuge needed to be punished. And once they made it back to the cabin —clean this time—using her lips and teeth, along with some knot skills she'd learned in Girl Scouts, she made sure he apologized, or at least she assumed his mumbled response was an apology. It was hard to tell since he had his mouth full at the time.

Sated again, he groaned when she brushed her fingers down his chest. "Mercy," he said with a laugh. "I need time to recuperate."

"Pity," she murmured. Her body felt pleasantly sore, and she snuggled into his body, enjoying this newfound intimacy. "Okay then, since you're not up for another round, then maybe you can answer a question instead."

"What?" he asked, lazily twisting her ebony curls with his fingers.

"What happened to the aliens who kidnapped me? They won't come back to hurt us, will they?"

"Oh no, they've been taken care of permanently," he replied grimly.

"But how?" she asked, leaning up on an elbow to frown at him. "We've been together pretty much the entire time since you rescued me."

"But I haven't," said a smug Alphie from a hidden speaker. "Those pirates were no match for the firepower we've got on board. They are now just galactic dust."

Diana knew she should have been shocked at the violent reaction, but instead, she felt satisfaction knowing those pigs wouldn't be kidnapping and raping anyone else. What did shock her was how she'd forgotten about the nosy computer. God only knew how much he'd seen or listened to in the last little bit.

"Any more questions?" asked Kor.

Diana knew she should just shut up and bask in the afterglow, but her mouth had a way of running away before her brain could catch up. "Actually, I want to know more about this Oracle. Like what did she tell you about me? Did she just hand you a slip of paper with my name on it or what?"

KOR CHUCKLED. His mate had such an interesting way of putting things. But he knew her curiosity needed sating.

"First I had to be found worthy."

"How did you do that?" she asked, snuggling into the crook of his arm, her thigh draped over his while her hand lightly stroked his chest.

Distracted, Kor had to form his thoughts before he could answer her. "With so many males and few females, even considering the other races we've been drawing on, not all can be blessed with a mate. Thus a reward system of sorts was established."

"You mean I'm a prize?" she huffed indignantly.

"The very best," said Kor, silencing her with a kiss.

Mollified, she signaled for him to go on.

"Males can distinguish themselves through hard work, courageous deeds, those kinds of things."

"Let me guess, you did something courageous."

"You could say that." Actually, Kor had yet to fail on any of the missions he'd been assigned. "Once you become noticed, then you are tested physically to ensure you have no genetic abnormalities."

"Oh, I'd say you passed that with flying colors. Nothing wrong with this body," she murmured against him, her nails scraping down his chest lightly, a highly erotic sensation that made him shiver.

The three moons blessed me indeed.

"Then we filled out a questionnaire."

"Yes, the famous shopping list," Diana grumbled, but she stayed snuggled to him, and Kor let out an inaudible sigh of relief.

"Then, after moons of waiting, I was called."

Kor had pretty much forgotten about the whole mate application. It had been so long since he'd filled it out. And, after all, not all who applied had mates chosen for them. Thus his surprise, when he'd been told he had an audience with the Oracle, had been great. He'd bathed and dressed ceremoniously for the occasion. After all, the whole course of his future could change on the basis of that one meeting.

Arriving at the temple, he'd been blessed by the acolytes before being led to a dim and smoky room. Small, soft hands had pushed him down to his knees 'til he knelt on a woven mat, with his head bowed, waiting for the words of the Oracle, his inner turmoil masked by his iron control. A part of him waited eagerly for the honor of being chosen to have a mate while his warrior side yearned to run and remain free to enjoy his bachelor ways.

The sweet, smoky scent of incense swirled in the air around him, making his head feel light, his senses deadened. They said the incense helped the Oracle keep from being overwhelmed by the visions. It just gave him a headache.

Finally, he heard a whisper of movement, the slide of silken robes across the stone

flagstones, and he found himself holding his breath.

"Welcome, son of the third moon. The spirits of your ancestors have spoken."

And? Kor didn't speak aloud—he liked his head on his shoulders—but he could have done without all the dramatic buildup and suspense.

"For a long time they wavered in choosing your destiny, judging your worthiness. As a warrior, you've proven your bravery and loyalty. As a son, you've been exemplary to your parents."

Kor felt like rolling his eyes but resisted.

"The decision has been made. You have been tasked to collect your life mate from the planet Earth."

Yes, he'd been chosen! No more warrior life for him. Instead, he'd get to enter the coveted ranks of the mated. A much safer—albeit more boring—life with many perks, including sleeping in a soft bed every night. The biggest benefit, though, was getting his very own mate instead of relying on a Galaxian whore in a brothel.

Kor bent his head lower. "Thank you, Oracle. The wish of my ancestors is my command."

"The full coordinates for the location of your betrothed will be given to you. Prepare for departure immediately. And good luck."

With those odd parting words, the Oracle left, and he'd departed the smoky temple to prepare himself for his last voyage as a single male.

Trust Diana to latch on to the last part of the Oracle's words. He should have omitted them in the retelling.

"Good luck? What did she mean by good luck?" said Diana, sitting up, her splendid full bosom heaving.

Kor smiled lazily at his new mate, his vigor renewed and ready for action. "Can you do that move again?"

"What move?" she asked, brow creased.

"Like this." Kor palmed her breasts and made them jiggle, his eyes latched onto their motion in fascination.

Diana gaped at him for a second then laughed. Her throaty mirth was contagious, and he joined her, turning what could have been a serious moment into one of fun—then exploration as he used his fingers to find all her ticklish spots and attack them.

"No more," she panted.

She changed her mind quickly and begged for more when his hands caressed her intimately. Once again, he joined his body to hers and exploded when he felt her sheath convulse around him.

Mine.

DIANA PACED THE COMMAND ROOM, NAKED—LUCKY him. They'd just tested the captain's seat springs. They were satisfactory, but the seat itself could have used another inch or two in width.

"What do you mean we arrive in a few hours?" she said, flinging her arms up, making her boobs jiggle in a hypnotic manner that never grew old.

"Well, the ship has been heading there since we left your planet, so it was only natural we'd arrive eventually," he said, baiting her.

She whirled and glared at him, her ebony locks flying, looking so desirably annoyed he wanted to take her up against the view screen with the backdrop of the stars at her back. But judging by her look, perhaps now was not the best time to attempt that. He braced himself for her outburst.

"That's not funny, Kor. I am not ready yet. There's still so much I don't know."

"So you'll learn," he said, shrugging. "My mother will be happy to help you." At the word 'mother', Kor saw her cringe, and in a moment of understanding—a rarity for males anywhere in the universe where females were concerned—he suddenly realized what was really bothering her. "You're afraid to meet my mother."

"Am not," said Diana too quickly.

Kor quirked a brow at her.

"Maybe a little. What if she doesn't like me?" she wailed, pacing nervously. "I mean I'm sure you told her how difficult I was to mate with and I argue all the time and . . ."

"My mother will like you fine," said Kor, finally getting up and wrapping his arms around her tight. "She'll especially like the fact you're willing to stand up to me."

Diana grumbled something under her breath that he didn't quite catch—something about mama's boys that he didn't understand the meaning of. Instead of arguing further, Kor decided to give in to his earlier thought and the one surefire method of making her forget her ire. He kissed her and let his hands slide down her body to cup her buttocks. Unable to resist the temptation, he gave them a squeeze.

When she responded and ground herself

against him, he lifted her up and pressed her against the glass screen that displayed the space they traveled through. As he pounded into her willing flesh with the stars and the galaxy at her back, Kor once again found himself exploding like a supernova. He'd lost count of the times they'd done this and marveled that each time could be as powerful and fulfilling as the last.

And, for the moment at least, he'd made sure his argumentative mate, who lay breathless in his arms once again, forgot what reality would soon bring.

THE MOMENT HAD ARRIVED—OR rather they had arrived at Kor's planet—and Diana's stomach felt like a herd of butterflies had taken up residence. She clutched Kor's hand tightly, her face taut with tension while she prayed she wouldn't throw up on anybody's shoes.

Kor pulled her death grip loose and hugged her in his arms. "Why are you so nervous?" he asked.

"Hmm, let me see," she said sarcastically. "I'm going to a new planet full of woman-hungry aliens, where the only thing familiar will be my face in a mirror, not to mention meeting your mother for the first time. Gee, nothing to worry about at all."

"I know how I can get you to relax. Let's go

back to bed," he whispered in her ear before licking it.

Diana gasped. "Kor, that's not funny. How can you think about sex at a time like this?" *Well, that's a dumb question. After all, he is a man, and to be honest, hiding under the covers sounds mighty good right about now.*

The jerk, of course, chuckled. "What?" he said in mock innocence. "It's the first thing I intend to do as soon as we get into our new home. Actually," he said, dipping his face down to nibble her neck, "I was thinking we'd *explore* the place, room by room, 'til we make it to the bedroom. A welcome present to celebrate our future."

"Oh, Kor," Diana whispered, feeling her tension melt at his naughty suggestion. She molded herself against his body as his lips found hers.

"Ahem."

Diana felt her cheeks burn as Kor lifted his head to face their audience. Embarrassed, she buried her face in his chest. As usual, she forgot everything around her when he kissed her. Damn his magic blue lips.

"Mother, I should have known you wouldn't wait for us," said Kor wryly.

"You were taking too long," said a tart voice with humor. "Now aren't you going to introduce me to your mate?"

"Mother, I'd like you to meet my mate, Diana. Diana, my mother, Ele'Anor Vel Menos."

Diana, biting her lip nervously, turned from the comfort of Kor's chest to greet her new mother-in-law, a woman who, if not for her very light blue color, would have appeared human in every way, right down to her brown hair and eyes. She also didn't appear old enough to be Kor's mother, making Diana wonder just how young they made their women marry.

"A pleasure to finally meet you, daughter. I see you're both getting along better now than the last time we spoke," said his mother pointedly at Kor, who smiled sheepishly.

"I meant to call, but," he said, shrugging, "we kind of became busy."

Diana felt her smile freeze on her face. *Oh yes, we've been busy, all right, christening his ship in every position imaginable.*

The knowing look in Kor's mother's eyes didn't help Diana's embarrassment.

"Oh goodness, child, don't look so mortified," said Ele'Anor with a laugh. "I was once in your position too."

Diana didn't understand and said so. "What do you mean? You were obviously born here."

Ele'Anor chuckled. "Wrong. My birth name is Eleanor Jones. I was also taken from Earth as a mate, just like you, many moon cycles ago."

Diana blinked. "But you're blue."

"As you will be after you've spent some time

here. The suns on this planet project their own version of UV, one that, instead of causing a tan, turns our skin a bluish tone."

Diana stored this disturbing piece of info away for later when she and her new husband were alone. Kor had some explaining to do, and she might even let him try after she vented on him. *Why did he not tell me his own mother was human? And blue? I don't want to be blue. I like my peaches-and-cream complexion. I wonder if I can get a heavy-duty sunblock to prevent it?*

While Diana pondered what UV rating she'd need, Kor, with an arm around Diana's waist, guided her off the spacecraft she'd finally gotten used to into a bustling terminal. Reminiscent of an airport back home, humanoids of varying shades of blue with a bit of mauve, yellow, and green thrown in wandered around with piles of luggage while video displays flashed words and numbers.

"Your accommodations only came through yesterday," said his mother over her shoulder. "I managed to get some basics sent over, but you'll have to do some shopping to pick up the rest."

"Is there a bed?" asked Kor mischievously, not even grunting when Diana elbowed him in the ribs.

"Of course there is. I had that delivered first thing."

Diana wanted to die of embarrassment as Kor and his mother chuckled at her prudishness. Diana had grown up in a household that did not talk about sex and certainly never joked about it. This was so unnatural. *So alien.*

"I've also booked Diana's appointment with the family physician for a full workup."

"I don't need a doctor. I feel fine," interjected Diana.

"Even so, it's best to get checked out in case the ship diagnostics missed something."

Diana swallowed her arguments. *I get the feeling I might not win.*

Reaching a busy curbside with little saucers zipping down and up to pick up and drop off passengers, Kor's mother stopped her talking and walking to give them both a quick hug.

"I know you're anxious to see your new home and christen it," she said with a wink that had Diana staring at her toes again.

"How about you both come over tomorrow evening for dinner? Your father will be there too."

With a wave, Ele'Anor left them, hopping into a waiting saucer that zoomed off as soon as it sealed its door shut.

"My mother can be somewhat overwhelming," said Kor at the still-stunned look on Diana's face.

"You think?" said Diana sarcastically.

Kor laughed and kissed the tip of her nose, which made Diana warm and lose some of her ire. With a hand in the middle of her back, he guided her to a waiting saucer and ushered her in.

"Are these things safe?" asked Diana nervously, looking at the plush interior for a seat belt of some sort.

"Very," said Kor with a chuckle. "They are piloted by computers and have been accident-free since before I was born."

Somewhat reassured, Diana relaxed and watched the zipping scenery outside, only to turn away as the blurring speed they were moving at made her feel motion sick.

"What's your dad like?" she asked, trying to take her mind off the stomach she'd left behind a few miles back.

"Not as talkative as my mother, so you needn't worry about him embarrassing you."

"So he kidnapped your mom too?" Apparently abduction ran in the family.

"Yes, but she didn't argue as much about it as you did."

Diana stuck her tongue out at him then giggled at the look on his face. "Why didn't you tell me your mom was human?"

"Would it have made a difference?"

Diana thought about it for a second. Would it have made things easier? "No, it wouldn't. But if she's human, how come you're so oblivious about our culture?"

Kor shrugged. "My mother embraced her new life here and left her old one behind. She didn't want me to feel less than Xamian, so they didn't even tell me I wasn't a full-blood 'til I'd reached an age where I could understand I was no different from anyone else. And as Mother also explained, there was no point in her teaching me about a culture that I would never be a part of."

Diana frowned, for she had a different perspective, it would seem, from Kor's mother. When she and Kor had children—a thought that didn't make her want to faint in shock anymore—she fully intended to tell them about their human heritage and mother's birthplace.

"I take it you don't agree," he said, noting her silence.

"I think being multicultural is a blessing and should be something to be proud of and not hidden. Just think, had you known more about my people, your mother's people, then perhaps we wouldn't have had such a rocky start." Kor just tilted a brow at her in response, and Diana laughed. "Okay, I might have still given you a hard time, but at least you would have better understood where I was coming from."

"You fought against a fate chosen for you. I have no problem understanding that. What I don't understand was how you were able to resist me." Kor said this so seriously that, for a moment, Diana just gaped at him. Then she noticed the twinkle in his eye.

Kor burst out laughing, and Diana joined him, pleasantly surprised by this more relaxed and humorous side of Kor that she hadn't seen much of onboard the ship.

When the taxi-style saucer stopped, Diana didn't have a chance to look out the window, as suddenly Kor's hands covered her eyes.

"No looking yet," he ordered, helping her out of the vehicle. "Welcome to your new home," he whispered, standing behind her.

He dropped his hands, and Diana opened her eyes and stood for a moment in shock, staring at the residence in front of her.

This is our house, she thought, looking at it a little teary. *And I love it already.*

A cross between an igloo and a Mexican adobe, the house looked like a dome with a circular door and porthole windows. The exterior looked like sand blocks interlocked together. The walkway leading up to a rounded door looked to be made up of thousands of glittering crushed stones. The only thing that took away from the cuteness of her new home was the fact that her front lawn seemed to be dry dirt—purple dirt, mind, but still dirt. Judging by the neighbors around her, though, Diana realized she could plant and landscape depending on her taste. *I can have my own garden.*

But Kor seemed little interested in the front

yard. Sweeping her up into his arms, he strode to the front door of the house.

"Kor, what are you doing?" giggled Diana, torn between embarrassment if neighbors were watching and arousal.

"Alphie says it is an Earth custom to carry a new mate over the threshold of her home."

"It is," she said breathlessly, "but I never read the part that said the husband would be groping me while doing it."

"I adapted it," he growled in her ear. "Being around you, surrounded by your sweet scent, gives me the inspiration to please," he before he nipped her lobe with his teeth. They barely got the door shut before he began caressing her in earnest. Pushing her up against the wall, his strength holding her steady, he fumbled with his pants. In hurried times like these, Diana welcomed the loose garments the women of this world favored, as he simply swept the fabric aside and slid himself into her willing body.

Diana wrapped her thighs around his lean waist, locking him deep inside. His hands cupped her plump buttocks, and he squeezed her smooth flesh as he pounded her. His breathing came jaggedly against her lips as he alternated licking and sucking her lower lip. Diana held on to him for dear life, thrilled at the strength he exhibited and the sensations his rough lovemaking evoked.

She'd never had a lover so impassioned for her, so impatient to take her. The feeling made her blossom. *He makes me feel so beautiful and wanted.*

When his grip tightened, Diana knew he'd reached the brink, and she closed her eyes, waiting —not long. With a bellow, he buried himself deep between her thighs, the tip of his member touching her womb and that other spot that made her scream in response as her body convulsed around his. Wet, trembling waves spread through her, making her momentarily black out in pleasure overload.

As she slowly regained consciousness—a hard task with her body languorously refusing—she smiled. *Elusive G-spot, my ass. Funny how it took an alien to find it unerringly every single time.*

Kor kissed her on the forehead and, still holding her by the cheeks, carried her into the next room and groaned.

"What is it?" asked Diana, unwrapping her legs from his flanks.

"No furniture," he said, disappointment clear in his voice.

Diana remembered his plan to seduce her in every room of the house. Her eyes widened—surely he hadn't meant all in one day.

Before they could explore any further, a knock sounded, and they looked at each other.

"Who could it be?" she asked, hurriedly

straightening her clothes and hoping she didn't smell of sex.

Kor shrugged as he did up his pants. He took her by the hand, and they went to answer the door as a couple. Diana had to hold back the giggles. Two reasons—one, she still had sticky thighs from their quickie in the front entrance, and two, these were their first guests they'd be meeting in their new home as a married couple. I'm a Mrs. now. Diana couldn't help the little giggle that popped out, and Kor looked at her oddly before pressing a flat square that slid the front door open. Diana made a mental note of its location and purpose. It wouldn't do to get stuck in her own house.

A mismatched but smiling couple stood outside. Diana looked up to see a towering blue giant with a platinum crew cut and then down again to see a petite, curvy thing with a bouncy blonde ponytail.

As soon as the blonde saw them, she smiled and thrust something at them, which Diana accepted with a grin, because judging by Kor's face, he had no idea what was going on.

"Welcome to the neighborhood," said the perky blonde. "I'm Lisa, and this big guy here is Ror'Andorian, my hubby. I just call him Rory, though, for short. We live in the house right across the street. I'm so glad to see new folk moving in. This neighborhood is still pretty new, so not all the houses have folks in them yet, and gosh, it's so nice to see another Earth girl here."

Diana giggled at the stunned look on Kor's face and the forbearing one on Rory's as Lisa babbled.

Finally managing to slip in a word edgewise, Diana said, "Nice to meet you, Lisa and Rory. I'm Diana, and this is Kor. He's got a longer name, too, but I'm still not sure how to pronounce it, so I won't try. Thanks for the casserole."

"No problem," said Lisa, beaming. "Nothing like a taste of home, well, kind of, with adapted ingredients, to say welcome. I know cooking is an option around here, but, well, I like to keep busy."

Cooking an option—Diana wondered what that meant. Having few cooking skills herself, she looked forward to finding out.

The giant rumbled finally. "My mate is overeager and filled with joy to see another of her people move in. Perhaps when you have settled in, you would join us for a repast."

"That would be our pleasure," replied Kor.

With a nod, the giant Rory picked up his petite wife, who it seemed might have kept talking all day, and carried her squealing with laughter back across the street.

Kor shut the door and looked at Diana with a shudder. "Well, thank the silvery moons that the Oracle didn't deem her my perfect mate. I think I would have gone deaf."

Diana laughed. "Oh, she's just energetic and a bit lonely for something familiar, I think. I have a feeling she and I will get along famously." And Diana found herself greatly relieved that she wouldn't be alone trying to figure out this new world.

"Now where were we?" murmured Kor. "Ah, yes." He scooped up Diana and strode through the house. "We were looking for some furniture."

Diana barely got to see their new home, as Kor had only one thought in mind—finding the bed. And when he found it, he made sure they put it to good use, twice.

[10]

HOURS LATER, SEXUALLY SATED AGAIN, DIANA heard her stomach growl to her intense mortification, a sound that Kor, who snoozed lightly beside her, thankfully didn't hear. Diana crept out of the room and decided to finally check out her new home. She wandered down the hallway outside her bedroom and found two more bedrooms, somewhat smaller than hers but each with a window overlooking a virgin backyard with a lone yellow tree. *I see a garden and a patio in our future. And maybe even a swing set for the kids eventually. While I'm at it, I might as well put on an apron, heels, and pearls and call myself Martha Stewart. Jeesh, could I get any more housewifey?* Diana couldn't seem to stop the flow of thoughts and ideas that kept popping into her head. Apparently her mind had accepted her new status and was already looking ahead. As for her heart, thinking of her blue hubby, Diana knew her heart had already been lost.

Trying to ignore her almost epiphany, she kept exploring and found the bathroom, thank goodness, a bright white room that she put to use immediately, emerging feeling more refreshed. She hadn't seen a tub, though, a fact that made her a little sad.

Padding down the hall again toward the front of her home, she noticed the casserole dish still sitting on a shelf by the front door, and she grabbed it, continuing her exploration.

A step down to her right, and she twirled around the large living area. *This room is huge!* The floor had been patterned in a colorful mosaic of stars within stars, prettier than anything she'd ever seen, and the lack of curtains over the large window made this room bright, something Diana vowed not to change.

She crossed the airy room and went up a few steps into what had to be the eating area, with a small bistro-style table and two chairs. Then she found the kitchen. At least she assumed it to be the kitchen, judging by the cupboards she found filled with exotic bowls, plates, and glasses. A long counter stretched in a U shape around this room, smooth and unblemished, making her wonder where the sink and stove were.

Opening one tall cupboard, she found the fridge or, as she'd heard Kor call it, the cooling unit.

Diana eyed the casserole dish in her hand and debated whether to put it away for now or heat it. *Let's see what it looks like first.* Diana pulled off the cover and made a face. This didn't look like any casserole she'd ever eaten. With something purple shredded on top, green layers, and a lumpy white sauce, Diana wondered if this was an extraterrestrial version of lasagna.

Diana's stomach growled again, and she realized that a hungry tummy couldn't be a picky one. She hadn't found any other food, so picking up the dish, Diana looked around for an oven and ran into her first roadblock.

What the hell constituted as an oven in this pristine place? She put down the dish and began opening and closing cupboards, looking for the elusive stove. Surely they cooked their food somehow.

"What are you looking for?" asked Kor, standing in the kitchen doorway, looking rumpled and sexy wearing just loose trousers and no shirt.

"Cooking dinner, or trying to," she mumbled, opening another door to find tall vases.

"You know you don't have to," he said, gliding into the room to wrap his strong blue arms around her.

"Why? Are you cooking?" she asked, smiling up at him.

His brows shot up, and he laughed. "Me? No,

why would I do that when we have a brand new Culinary 6000?"

"A what?"

"Let me show you instead," he said with a sexy grin. "Name a food you'd like to eat."

Diana thought for a minute, chewing her bottom lip. Then her eye was caught by the purple casserole. "Lasagna."

Kor grabbed two metallic blue plates from the cupboard and said, "Meal request. Earth lasagna for two." A slot slid open in the backsplash that bordered the counter, and Kor slid the two plates in. The slot shut, only to reopen almost immediately with a ping. Kor pulled out the plates, now steaming with—and here Diana blinked—what looked like lasagna.

"What is that, like, the world's fastest food delivery ever?" she asked in disbelief.

"No, just the most current food synthesizer."

Diana looked at her steamy plate and sniffed the steam coming off it. "You mean this isn't real?"

"Yes and no. Samples of dishes have been analyzed at a molecular level and entered into an enormous database of foods. Using this molecular knowledge, the synthesizer recreates the meals. It is not always as exact, or should I say the food isn't quite like something made with true ingredients. However, especially with foreign foods whose ingredients can't be found, it's an adequate substitute."

Diana's tummy growled again, and she shrugged. Fake food or not, she was hungry. Then she thought of something—actually two things. "The food on the ship, was it synthesized too?"

Kor nodded. "That was a Culinary 5000, an older model."

"Does it make garlic bread too?"

To her delight, it did, and while not as good as Gino's back home, it tasted a heck of a lot better than anything she'd ever attempted to cook. *Well, at least we won't starve,* she thought happily. Diana also made a mental note to see if she could get a menu of things the Culinary 6000 could provide. A whole new gustative horizon beckoned her healthy appetite.

When dinner was over, Diana picked up the plates and carried them over to the counter to wash them but again stopped, stymied. "Where's the sink?" she asked, perplexed.

Kor, with a chuckle, took the dishes from her. He opened a drawer she'd thought was empty, dropped them in, and shut it. Thirty seconds later they heard a ping, and opening the drawer, Diana almost wept, for there were the spotless dishes. No more dishpan hands for her. Heck, she didn't even have to rinse them or scrape food off.

I think I'm going to like this world. Already they have taken two chores I disliked and turned it into a dummy-proof and laborless miracle. I love it!

But now what to do? Diana's body felt too full from eating to make love, and she wondered what married folk did here for entertainment.

"How about a walk?" suggested Kor.

Diana eagerly agreed. She dressed quickly in a clean veil outfit that Kor produced for her from a hidden closet in the bedroom. From another hidden closet in the front hall, Kor pulled out a silvery cloak for her and a black jacket for himself. Holding hands, they walked out of their home into the cooler evening air, and for a moment, Diana held her breath and stopped, absolutely stunned by her first view of a night sky so different from her own.

For one thing, three pale moons shone in the sky above her, two small and one large, each an antique white that glowed. And the stars! My God, the times she'd managed to see the ones back home— an hour or so drive out of town—they'd seemed plenty, but out here, they took over the night sky, blinking and twinkling and shooting, a constant ever-changing tableau.

"Is the sky always so busy?" she asked, craning her head to watch a particularly bright star zipping across the sky.

"Some say we live at the very edge of the universe, where worlds, stars, and even galaxies are constantly being born and dying."

"What do you think?"

"I think the sky isn't half as interesting as you are."

Diana blushed in the dark, both surprised and pleased by his compliment. "I forgot to ask on the ship. Does your planet have the same time setup as us? You know days, hours, minutes."

"Yes and no. We do have days divided into cycles. Our cycles correspond to the movement of the moons in the sky and are similar to your concept of hours, but longer. Like your planet, we also work and play when the sun's shining and relax and sleep when darkness falls at night."

"I feel like a child trying to learn to read time again," Diana grumbled.

"Why not ask Alphie to teach you the things you need to know?"

"Isn't Alphie still on the ship?"

"All of our planetary computer systems are all conjoined. The Alphie persona I deal with is one specially adapted to interact with me and is accessible to me wherever a computer can be found. And, by that extension, accessible to you as well. So, in space or on land, we can be subjected to his debatable form of humor."

Diana found herself quite happy to know her computer friend would still be around. She'd quite enjoyed Alphie's sarcasm and wit. "But how do I talk to him?"

"Just say his name in our home or on any vid comm to speak to him."

"Vid comm?"

Kor unclipped a small box from his waist and showed it to her. Similar to an iPhone, with a screen but no buttons, Kor spoke to it. "Alphie, can we have a vid comm delivered for Diana by tomorrow?"

"Sure thing," replied Alphie, his familiar voice coming out of seemingly nowhere.

"Thanks, Alphie," said Diana, amazed at the technology Kor kept showing her.

"I don't understand one thing, though," she said after Kor put the vid comm away. "If you need that to talk to Alphie, then how come when we were on Earth and those other places, you could talk to Alphie without it?"

"Ah," said Kor, grinning. "Noticed that, did you? When in space, especially when visiting planets other than our own that aren't as technologically advanced, we use an implant in our ear to speak with the ship computer. This prevents our technology from falling into hands that might not be ready for it."

"Why not just use the implant all the time?"

"Well, for one thing, the implant can only speak to us and hear what's going on, as well as pinpoint our location. The vid comms can do much more than that. I'll show you when you get yours."

"Sounds good. But you know what I'd rather see right now?"

"What?"

"You naked in the bathroom for some *cleaning*." And with those daring words, Diana, with a laugh, turned around and ran back up the street to their house. She laughed even harder when her new husband, with his longer stride, scooped her up as he ran past, not stopping 'til he held her naked body panting in the bathroom.

It took two attempts to get clean, but damn, it was worth it.

THE NEXT MORNING DIANA, clearing off the dishes from the little table, nearly wet herself when a slot by the floor opened up and a whirring robot zipped out.

"What the hell is that?" she exclaimed, resisting an urge to hop up on a chair and tuck up her feet.

Kor barely glanced up from his vid comm, where he browsed the news. "It's the house cleaner."

Diana, realizing this little tin bucket on wheels was considered normal, watched it zip around on the floor and, yes, sucking up dirt. Jane Jetson, eat your heart out. Diana had her own collection of robots that did it all.

Kor put aside his vid comm and looked up at her. "I was thinking perhaps we'd go shopping today. Alphie says Earth women enjoy that type of excursion."

"I'll get dressed," said Diana, already hurrying out of the room. She couldn't wait to see what wonders could be found on this planet.

In no time at all, they found themselves in front of a large edifice with wide glass doors.

"Is this like a mall?" she asked, looking up at the building that lacked signs.

"I'm not sure what you mean. Inside, we will find a collection of vendors with goods that we may select from."

With an arm around her waist, he guided her inside. Diana looked around in curiosity, for, instead of a venue lined by boutique fronts, they instead found themselves facing a counter with a screen sitting on top.

A face appeared on the screen, startling Diana. "Welcome to the Emporium. Please state your name."

"Kor'iander Vel Menos and mate."

Diana frowned at him. "I have a name, you know."

"Yes, but no money to spend. The purchases we make today will be deducted from my credit account, hence the use of my name only. I've already sent in a request for you to have your account set up with funds of your own to spend."

Diana blinked in surprise. "You did?"

"Let's just say I had a feeling."

"You thought right. And once I get settled in, we'll have to talk about what I can do to bring in some more money to help out." Seeing him about to open his mouth and probably spout something hugely male and arrogant, she shook her head. "Nonnegotiable, buddy. Until the kids come along, I want to do my part. Humor me, okay?"

With a nod and a sigh, he agreed. A door opened to the side of the counter, and a slick-looking blue guy walked out.

Kind of looks like a used car salesman back home. Diana had to bite her lips so as to not giggle. They followed him into a windowless room with just one large plush bench in the middle. Kor seemed to think this was normal, but Diana's brow creased as she looked around. *I thought we were shopping for furniture.* At the salesman's urging, they seated themselves on the bench.

"What would you like to see first?" asked Kor.

Diana chewed on her lip. "Um, couches."

The blank wall in front of them immediately showed them a large picture of a sofa. Diana shook her head. The couch looked stiff and uninviting.

Kor spoke up. "Deep-cushioned, medium-backed, with armrests and . . ." He looked at her. "What color?"

Diana thought of their bland living room. "Red," she blurted.

The image on the wall changed to eight couches that looked a lot more comfortable in varying shades of crimson. One in particular caught her eye, and she pointed it out to Kor.

Kor tilted his head at the salesman, and Diana had to restrain a gasp as the couch she'd selected suddenly materialized right in front of them. Kor helped her up and went to look it over, an incredulous Diana by his side. They bounced on the cushions, and Kor, to Diana's blushing embarrassment, yanked her onto his lap to make sure it was comfortable for snuggling. Then, to make matters worse, he demanded she lie across it so he could see how she looked. Diana thought about arguing, but the light in his eyes had her captivated, and besides, it seemed their slick salesman had seen it before, as he paid them no mind.

Finally Kor said, "We'll take it." Then he whispered in her ear, "I can't wait to see you naked on it later." An instant erotic rush infused her, and she knew her cheeks were burning bright.

Diana picked out the rest of their furnishings, only hesitating a few times wondering how much it would all cost, but Kor just smiled and nodded at her to continue 'til they had furnishings and accessories for the whole house.

Shopping done, they went for food, but what a restaurant. The building floated above the clouds with windows all round in the dining area. Diana kept forgetting to eat so dazzled was she by the pillowy soft beauty of the sky around them.

At Kor's chiding laughter, she ate a few mouthfuls of food then found herself distracted again when she noticed how many humans sat at tables throughout the dining room. Only a few of the women were blue. The rest spanned most of the nationalities from Earth, it seemed. And then there were a few who didn't look human or Xamian.

She leaned over and whispered to her husband, "The pink lady over there? Is she an abductee too?"

Kor winced. "I wish you wouldn't use that term. But yes, she is a chosen one as well from a planet in another star system."

"How come I haven't seen more wives like her? It seems most of us are from Earth."

"Their species doesn't seem to adapt as well to the mating ritual. Their females tend to be very dominant."

Diana giggled. "Don't like being told who to marry, do they? I didn't see that stopping you."

"You didn't have a four-foot dagger to prove your point."

Diana perked up with interest. Now these were some ladies who sounded interesting.

She pestered him with questions, which he patiently answered. After their meal, they visited some more shops, a few with delicacies that couldn't be reproduced from other planets. The hour growing late, and the dinner with his parents fast approaching, they finally went home. Fatigue made her yawn until she walked into their living room and saw their big, new red couch. Remembering Kor's words from earlier, she flushed with heat.

Kor came up behind her and nibbled the soft skin of her neck. "I want to see you naked on the couch. Now."

Diana shivered. "Don't we have to get ready to go to your parents'?"

"Not 'til I have you," he growled in her ear. He nipped her earlobe, and Diana shuddered. "I've been thinking about being with you all day." He punctuated his words with a rub, the hardness in his groin evident against her backside.

Diana's knees trembled as she walked over to the new couch. Turning to face him, she undid the clips that held her clothes together, and they fell in a silken heap on the floor. With glowing eyes, he regarded her, and her nipples puckered at his look. Sensual longing filled her veins. She draped herself on the couch, one leg bent with her foot on the floor, exposing her to his view. His eyes immediately turned smoldering, which, in turn, made her wet. With quick strides, he came to her, his impatient hands ripping his own clothing away 'til he covered her, skin to skin. He kissed her roughly, his sinuous tongue darting inside her mouth and seeking her own. His fingers found the juncture of her thighs and toyed with her, sliding into her moistness easily. She moaned and arched against him. As impatient as she, he sheathed himself between her thighs, his curved organ unerringly finding her sweet spot and stroking it. Diana wrapped her legs around him as he turned her so that he could kneel on the floor and grip her by the waist. He pumped her, his smooth, hard length welcomed by her wet cleft. She looked up and gasped. Kor watched her intently, his eyes aglow. With his wild black hair ruffled from her hands and his vivid blue skin, he resembled a demon lover. *My demon lover.* His magic touch and cock didn't belong to reality, the pleasure he gave too intense and surreal. As she screamed her pleasure, it came to her that she loved her blue alien, so different from her and yet totally devoted to her happiness and pleasure.

But did he feel the same way?

———

DIANA FUSSED with her hair and tugged at her

karimi, the official name for the garment all the women wore.

"Are you ready?" called Kor.

"Almost," she said and bit her lip. *What am I so nervous about? I already met his mother. This is just dinner. And meeting his dad for the first time.* Diana sucked in a deep breath, still not understanding why she felt so nervous. Kor stuck his head around the doorframe. His eyes brightened with appreciation.

"You look beautiful. Maybe we should stay home," he said, coming into the bathroom and placing his hands on her waist to pull her in close.

Diana pushed him back. "Hands off. It took me an hour to get my hair to cooperate, and I am not letting you mess it up 'til we get home from your parents'."

Kor smiled at her mischievously. "Come on, Diana. They won't care. My mother might even applaud the fact that we're taking this grandchild-making business so seriously."

Diana laughed and slapped at his groping hands. "You are incorrigible. Don't worry. I'll remember this and make you pay later."

"Promise?"

Diana just smiled wickedly in response. Their afternoon tryst had been wonderful, but where Kor was concerned, she never seemed to get enough.

She finished her preparations, and a short time later, a saucer deposited them at a house similar to the one they owned but on a grander scale, made of glossy white blocks.

The front yard exploded with color as various plants fought for supremacy with blooms of every imaginable hue. Diana, delaying the inevitable, stopped to smell several of the flowers.

Soon, though, she found herself ushered into the brightly colored home of her in-laws. Ele'Anor greeted her warmly, and then Kor was introducing her to his father, a stocky dark blue man whose hair leaned more toward gray but whose smile was warm and welcoming.

To her surprise, Diana enjoyed herself. Ele'Anor pestered her with questions about Earth and then regaled Diana with tales of Kor as a child. It seemed he'd had a fetish for being naked as a child, and his mother had documented his many streaking escapades. Kor took the teasing good-naturedly, his pose relaxed and his smile warm as it lingered on her.

When the evening came to an end, Diana and Ele'Anor made plans to meet the following week. As they settled into the saucer to take them home, Kor pulled her onto his lap and hugged her.

"What was that for?" she asked.

"For being you. My parents approved of you."

"I quite liked them." Diana still felt surprised at this fact. *Isn't it tradition to hate one's in-laws?*

"Do you think you can be happy here?" he asked, his voice serious.

Surprised, Diana turned in his lap to see his face. His expression looked grave. She brought her hands up and cupped his cheeks. "I think I will be very happy here," she replied and kissed his lips.

And she meant it.

She should have known that, even halfway across the universe, Murphy's Law would exist and, of course, decide to ruin it.

11

KOR WOKE HER EARLY TO CLAIM HER BODY sexually, his actions slow but his kisses and body so hot. She watched him as he dressed in his uniform, and Kor hated that he had to leave her to return to his duties. Her eyes teased him with sultry lowered lashes, and she'd let the sheet slip, exposing her bountiful bosom.

"Don't look at me like that," he growled.

"Like what?" she said, slowly sliding a finger down between her breasts, a seductive move that made his cock twitch.

"Like you want to undress me and eat me."

"But I do," she said, her eyes alight with mischief.

Kor cursed then kissed her hard. "Keep those thoughts for later. I must check in with my regiment."

"Fine, I'll just play with myself while you're gone." Diana howled at the look of pained anguish that twisted his face, and an erection he hoped would subside before he arrived at headquarters.

Kor had been away for many cycles and would have a lot of catching up to do. But the thought of leaving Diana alone made him wish he'd asked for more time off. It frightened him to realize how much he'd come to care for his mate since he'd found her. She consumed his thoughts. His actions now all seemed geared to pleasing her. He especially enjoyed seeing her smile. When her face lit up, his whole being became imbued with . . . what? Kor had to wonder if perhaps he'd fallen for the elusive earthling emotion, love. What else could explain the insanity that had overtaken him? The worst part, Kor couldn't speak to anyone about it. What if what he felt was abnormal? Maybe he'd caught an alien sickness, one he never wanted to be cured of. He wondered if he could broach the topic with his mother, but his mother told his father everything, and Kor didn't want to face his father and find out that there was something wrong with him. Something that would make him unfit as a mate. What if he was sick in the head and they took her away?

He would allow no one to touch Diana. She was his. Whatever this feeling was that he couldn't control, he'd keep it to himself.

ALONE FOR THE first time since their arrival, Diana prowled her new home looking for something to do, but she couldn't even find one speck of dust to clean. Their robot maid had already done all the work. Sighing, Diana dropped onto the cushioned couch that had arrived yesterday and now held a position of prominence in their living room—and a fond memory that still made her blush.

Now what do I do with myself? I wonder if they've got any Earth books I can read. But then Diana remembered something the robot hadn't done yet, the front yard.

She could get started on making their own statement in the blooms and design she chose.

Rummaging through her closet, she cursed, realizing the only thing she had to wear were the stupid veil dresses. *I can't garden in those.* Diana thought about knocking on Lisa's door across the street to see if she had anything appropriate but then had a better idea. She raided Kor's closet and found a dark-colored shirt and pants to wear. The shirt clung a little snugly to her overly-endowed bosom, and the pants hugged her bottom like a second skin, but Diana deemed them adequate for gardening.

Twisting her hair up in a loose bun, Diana felt ready to tackle the dirt.

Diana had her hands deep in the dirt and her round ass up in the air when the shadow fell over her. Startled, she looked up quickly and, of course, lost her balance and fell over, strands of hair coming loose and flopping into her eyes.

A firm, callused hand helped her up, and Diana, flinging her hair back, said, "Thank you," then had to stop herself from jerking her hand away from the stranger who still held it. Facing her with cold eyes and a leer was Kor's almost-twin. But where Kor's skin shone a healthy blue and his smile made her heart warm, this unknown male in front of her evoked the opposite with his sickly green-colored skin and chillingly clear eyes with slitted yellow irises.

"Well, well, what have we here?" he said in a gravelly voice that gave her goose bumps, and not the good kind. "You must be the whelp's new mate."

Diana, screwing the niceties, yanked her hand out of the stranger's grasp, his touch making her feel ill at ease, and she had to restrain an urge to wipe her hand. "Can I help you?" she asked coolly, not liking at all this stranger's manner. It made her skin crawl the way his transparent eyes roved over her figure.

"Aren't you going to invite me in?" he said, smiling, not a reassuring look on his face.

"No," she replied bluntly. *Whoever this guy is, he's bloody creepy.*

"Now is that any way to treat your new brother?"

Diana tried not to react to his words. Surely Kor would have mentioned a brother, but she couldn't dispute this stranger had familial ties to Kor, given their resemblance.

"Sorry, but Kor never mentioned a brother."

"Then let me introduce myself, Kil'iander Vel Menos. Elder brother of your mate. You mean he hasn't mentioned me?"

"We've been busy," said Diana, trying not to blush as she thought of what they'd been busy with.

"I'm sure you have," he said with a smirk that made her feel like washing in scalding water. "Now be a nice sister and show me in, why don't you?"

Diana hesitated, not wanting to be rude, but, at the same time, unwilling to go into the house alone with him. *There's something not quite right about him. And it's odd Kor hasn't mentioned him.*

"Maybe you could come back later when Kor is home, and then you can catch up with your brother at the same time."

But Kor's brother didn't seem to like this idea. His sickly eyes began to glow, although Diana was pretty sure the effect didn't come from lust, and she began to wonder about running away when a cheerful voice broke the impasse.

"Diana, are you ready?" said cheerful Lisa, her neighbor from across the way.

Relieved at the interruption, Diana smiled and stepped around Kor's scowling brother, glad for the distraction. "Of course," said Diana, playing along with astute Lisa's act while keeping a wary eye on Kil, who did not look happy at being interrupted. "Just let me wash up."

"Going somewhere?" growled Kil.

Lisa turned her perky smile on him and, to her credit, didn't blanch at his scowl. "Hi there, I don't think we've met. I'm Lisa. My husband, who should be out in a second, is Ror'Andorian."

The mention of Lisa's husband's name seemed to register with Kil, who took a step back from the ladies.

"Don't let me interrupt your plans, humans." Then, in a lower tone that sent a shiver up Diana's spine, Kil said, "I'll be back at a later date to resume our conversation, *sister.*"

And with that, he stalked off, leaving behind a slightly scared Diana.

"Wow, is he ever creepy. Sorry if I barged on over, but things looked pretty intense. Who is that jerk?"

"Kor's brother, apparently. He just showed up here and kept wanting me to take him in the house. I'm sure glad you came over when you did. I don't think he would have taken no for an answer."

"No problem. Now what do you say we actually go shopping? I've seen the most gorgeous flowers for both our places."

"Sure," said Diana, needing the distraction. "Just let me change and wash off the dirt."

Diana only wished she could wash off the icky feeling Kil had left behind. That and the shadow of fear he'd cast on her new life.

"I MET YOUR BROTHER TODAY," Diana finally told Kor after they'd made passionate love when he came home, skipping dinner to taste her.

Kor froze in the process of pulling on his breeches. "What did he want?" he asked, his face carefully neutral.

"He wanted to come in and get to know me. I'm afraid I might have been a little rude. He kind of took me off guard. I told him to come back when you were home."

Kor's face turned glacial, and he grabbed her tightly. "Don't ever let him in when I'm not home. Do you understand?"

"I don't intend to let him in. Like I said, he was creepy, but I don't understand. Isn't he your brother?"

"Half brother, and very dangerous. I'm sure you noticed how he differed from others around here with his greenish-cast skin."

Diana nodded her head. How could she not notice, especially his freaky eyes.

"His mother was pregnant with him when the sickness struck. She survived only long enough to give birth, but the disease had affected the baby. It affected all babes in the womb during that time. Most died in childbirth, but a few, like my brother, survived, even if his mother didn't. But they're not quite right. And it goes deeper than their skin tone or eyes. They're violent, uncaring . . ."

"So he's a psycho?" said Diana, shivering, hugging her knees to her chest tightly.

"I'm not sure what you mean by that, but if you're trying to say dangerous, then that is accurate. He is not to be trusted, ever."

"What am I supposed to do if he shows up, though?"

"Call me right away."

Diana rolled her eyes. "Oh, that's going to work real good. Hey, Kil, hold on a second before you kill me while I call your brother."

"I'm sure it won't come to that. Kil hasn't really done anything yet to prove he's lost it. I'll have my father speak to him and have him stay away."

Diana shivered, though. Someone was definitely walking across her grave, and she didn't like it one bit. And she'd just bet his name was Kil.

AFTER DIANA WENT TO SLEEP, Kor called his father, who answered brusquely. "What is it?"

"Kil visited Diana today."

Kor's father's face aged in a moment, his strength of will sapped by those simple words. "Did he hurt her?"

"Not this time," Kor replied tightly. "But he frightened her. You need to do something about this, or I will."

Kor's father looked suddenly haggard on the view screen, and he rubbed his aging blue face with a big hand. "I'll talk to him. If I he shows up again, let me know, and I'll talk to the institution."

Kor felt a moment's regret that it had come to this, but truth was they should have done something about his brother a long time ago. There was something not right about the plague children, and it went far beyond their different skin tones and looks. Their entire psyche seemed damaged. Kil had remained free of the madness longer than most of his ilk. However, Kor finally gaining a mate, it seemed, might be the catalyst that finally pushed him over that edge, the violent edge all of them seemed to hit at one point. After a few horrible cases, they'd finally learned that, painful or not, these special cases needed to be institutionalized, for their own good and the safety of society.

Although perhaps there was still hope. Perhaps Kil would listen to their father and keep his distance. Kor hoped so for both their sakes. Kor had lost most feelings for his brother long ago. It was respect for his father that made him keep trying.

But Kor would not allow Diana to be harmed. He'd kill his brother first.

12

Diana sat nervously in Lisa's living room, whose turn it was to host the monthly mates' tea. Diana had giggled when Lisa told her about it.

"Tea? Seriously?"

Lisa had laughed too. "I know it sounds dumb, but apparently this is a long-standing Earth-wife tradition. A way of bringing us together to help us cope with our new lives and to find friends so we aren't so lonely for home."

"Does it work?"

"I guess, although to be honest, most of the chosens didn't leave much behind. It's like their ancestors look for women who have no real close family or friends. Someone who would welcome a fresh start."

A chiming sound ended their deep discussion, and for the next while, a parade of women of varying styles and personalities came through, but the one thing they all had in common, make that two things they had in common, was they were all plump—nothing smaller than a size twelve, it seemed—and they all adored their husbands. All, that is, except for one woman who arrived late.

She kept to herself, and when Diana tried to introduce herself, the pinched-faced woman said she had no interest in making friends with someone who had caved to the male doctrine.

Someone had her panties in a twist, and Diana frankly found her too depressing to make an attempt to find out why.

Although she wished later that she had.

A subdued Lisa came knocking the next day.

"What's wrong?" asked Diana, ushering her ashen-faced friend in.

"You remember Claire?"

Diana thought back to the luncheon and remembered the sallow-faced woman who had made disparaging comments about everything, it seemed.

"Yeah, what about her?"

"She killed her mate then killed herself!"

"What?" Diana sat down, shocked. "But how? Why?"

"She's been here almost a year and has made it quite plain she wasn't happy about it. Rumor is she found out she was pregnant and lost it. She took a dagger to her husband when he came home and then drove it into her stomach."

"I don't understand." Diana could only imagine her ashen pallor as she felt the color leave her face. "The way Kor explained mating to me, the spirits find soul mates, people who should be compatible in every way."

"And they might have been," said Lisa, shaking her head sadly, "had Claire allowed herself to get past the fact that he was an alien and that he kidnapped and forced her into marriage."

Diana could understand Claire's turmoil, having fought against that very aspect herself in the beginning.

"Didn't anyone try to help her?"

Lisa shrugged. "I'm not sure. I didn't know her that well. For all her talk about hating aliens, she kept a lot to herself. I think she only showed up to the teas because her husband made her."

"Does that type of thing happen a lot?"

"What, you mean the killing thing?"

"That and the fact that some of the chosen mates aren't happy."

"The murder-suicide cases are few from what I understand. Unhappy mates aren't too common, but they do exist. I do know, in some cases, that it takes a bit longer for them to adapt and accept their situation before they find happiness. Sometimes the birth of the first child is the catalyst."

"There's got to be something better we can do. I mean, I know this whole scenario is kind of freaky, especially for us modern gals from Earth, but still I have to say I'm glad Kor found me."

"And I love my Rory. But I know what you mean. I wish we could do something extra to make it easier for the girls. But what?"

What indeed? Diana felt the gears in her mind turning. There had to be something they could do.

WHEN KOR CAME HOME for dinner, Diana threw herself on him and clung to him desperately. He hugged her tightly.

"What's wrong?" he asked with concern. "Did Kil come back?"

Diana shook her head against him then, her voice breaking, told him, "Claire killed her mate and herself. She was pregnant, Kor. How could she do that? I know she was unhappy, but why?"

Kor said nothing, just scooped Diana up and carried her to their living area, where he sat down with her cuddled on his lap. Diana shook in his arms and cried. She couldn't have even said why. She'd barely known Claire. She obviously didn't feel the same way about her marriage as Claire had. But Diana cried anyway. Cried for the loss of the life she knew, cried for the loss of the child who wasn't wanted, cried because she loved her husband but he would never say the words back because his culture didn't have a word to say love.

And Kor, understanding her need to release, it seemed, just held her. He said not a word as he stroked her hair and kissed her temple. He wrapped himself around her, giving her the shoulder she needed, and when she'd finally cried all her tears, Diana felt both relieved and embarrassed.

"Sorry," she mumbled against his neck. "I don't know what came over me."

"Death is always a shock," Kor said. "Even with strangers, the sudden ending of life, especially in such a horrific way, can be threatening, even frightening. It reminds us of our own mortality."

"And the what-ifs," said Diana unhappily.

"In this case, there are no what-ifs, Diana," he said, tilting up her tear-streaked face. "You met this woman once. If anyone should have done something, it was her mate. He must have noticed her unhappiness, but instead of addressing the issue, he chose to ignore it. As did the rest of his family."

"But there was no help for her," said Diana. "Not really. Claire wanted to go home. She hated her life and husband. How many other women out there feel the same way?"

"You cannot save the world," said Kor. "And it's not our problem. We are happy, and that's all that matters."

They made love, or—as Kor liked to say—mated. And when she lay beside him after, her body cooling from the intensity, Diana reran their conversation in her mind.

But I want it to be my problem because, even if I'm happy, don't I owe it to others, women like me who've had so much change in their lives? I'm not asking to save the world. Just help prevent tragedy. I need to do something. I can't wait for this to happen again.

13

Diana rubbed her tummy and smiled as she pictured what grew inside. Her visit to the doctor with Lisa had confirmed it. *I'm pregnant.* Diana almost giggled as she pictured the headline back home, boldly displayed in a newspaper title. *Woman Gives Birth to Blue Alien Baby.*

The physician who'd examined her had been unable to confirm the sex yet—that would have to wait a few more weeks—but the baby so far seemed healthy with a strong, rapid heartbeat, and Diana herself felt great. She couldn't wait to see Kor's face when she told him. She'd even set the romantic scene for her announcement. She'd picked flowers from her garden, not too many because her garden still was in the baby growth phrase but enough for some color. Then she perused her electronic cookbook looking for dishes that Kor's mother had mentioned were his favorites so she could order them with her built-in culinary chef. And finally Diana dressed in a soft pink veil gown, a color he said made her skin look rosy and edible, something he seemed to delight in.

She hadn't found candles, though. This planet had abolished them long ago as too much of a fire hazard, so Diana had to content herself with dimming the lights instead and playing some soft instrumental music she'd discovered when listening to music with Lisa.

Standing back to survey her work, she clasped her hands together, pleased. *Now if he'd only hurry up and get home so I can tell him. Heck, maybe we'll skip dinner and go straight to dessert.*

When the doorbell rang, Diana wondered who it was and skipped to the door to answer, eager to get rid of them because Kor would be home soon. A quick peek at the security screen showed Kor's mother, her face tear-streaked, on the steps.

Diana felt an icy chill descend over her as she slid the door open. "What's wrong?" she asked woodenly.

"It's Kor. He's . . . he's . . . There's been an accident," stuttered Ele'Anor. "He and six others were caught in a cave-in trying to rescue some miners. Their communicators aren't responding, and they can't locate them with the thermal scanner." Kor's mother broke down crying, the tears flowing copiously while her shoulders shook.

"No," said Diana, backing up. "He's not dead. He can't be. I made him dinner," she said inanely.

Ele'Anor's devastated face denied Diana's certainty.

"No," Diana whispered. Then more loudly, she cried, "No. No. *No!*" Diana screamed the last part. She needed to get out of there to go find him. *I need to show them how wrong they are.*

Ele'Anor's face turned even more ashen as she stared at something over Diana's shoulder. Diana pivoted and stopped, frozen, the flickering images on the video screen drawing her attention. Morbidly riveted, she could not turn away as she watched the video showing Kor and his men entering the caves. She jerked when she saw the mountain quiver and a billow of smoke come rushing out of the cave entrance. Heart leaden, she stared woodenly at the images of the men they flashed on the screen, those who had entered and gotten trapped and who were now presumed dead. When they flashed Kor's face staring at her from the screen, she fainted.

Diana dreamed. In her dream, the doorbell rang, and when she answered, it was Kor, his arms full of flowers, his beautiful blue face smiling. Arms full of blooms, she dreamt she told him about the baby, their baby, and he swung her around joyfully. Laying her down on a fragrant bed of flowers, he made love to her, gently. And when they both climaxed, he looked her in the eyes, his laden with such sadness, and said goodbye.

Diana awoke screaming, her life now a living nightmare.

A parade of people—alien and human—streamed through her home, trying to comfort her. But Diana walked about in a daze. She refused to believe what they all seemed so certain of. *How dare they presume he's dead? He can't be dead. I'd know if he were. I'd feel it.*

Diana rubbed her lightly swelling abdomen and knew with a certainty that had no rhyme or reason that Kor lived. Just like she also felt sure that what happened to her mate was no accident. It didn't take long to figure out who was responsible.

When the crowds finally dispersed to leave the widow alone to grieve, he finally showed up, as Diana had known he would. She, of course, did not answer the door—she wasn't that stupid—but something like an electronically locked door didn't stop him.

Using thieving methods, he came into her home and found her in the kitchen area brandishing a knife.

"You killed him," Diana spat, not yet revealing the truth that she knew he'd failed, even if Kor still remained missing. She just needed to be strong long enough for him to make his way back to her.

"Kill my own dear brother?" Kil mocked her, his blank eyes wide and hands raised. "How could you say that? After all, we're family." He shook his head at her then fixed her with a predatory glare. "It's a tragedy, but find comfort, *sister*, because I have come to reassure you that you and the baby have nothing to fear."

Diana stumbled back from him, her grip on the knife slick with sweat. Her heart thumped faster than a rabbit's in the raptor's sight. "How-how do you know about the baby? Kor didn't even know yet."

"I know everything about you." He sneered. "Computers are a wonderful thing, especially when you can manipulate them to give you the information you seek. You have no secrets, Diana St. Peters, formerly of Earth. I even know how you scream when my brother ruts with you."

"You've been watching us?" she whispered. Diana felt ill with the knowledge that her tender moments with Kor had been witnessed by someone so foul. It made her feel dirty.

"I quite enjoyed the show, but I'll enjoy even more being the starring actor. You see I shall take my dear brother's place as your husband, a comfort to you, I'm sure, in this confusing time. And no one, not my father nor the Oracle, can gainsay me, for you see, it's the law."

"You lie," said Diana, fear clutching her at the certainty in his tone.

"Why would I lie? I've planned this moment since I heard of my brother's mating. I have to say the fact you are already with child is unplanned for, but a baby will be very useful, I think, in ensuring your good behavior."

"Never," Diana snarled, suddenly angered at the implied violence toward her still-unborn child. "I'd rather wed a snake. Get out of here. I don't need or want you."

"That's not your decision. As head of the family now, it is my duty to ensure you're cared for. After a suitable mourning period, you will become my mate. You won't have a choice. It's the law."

"What are you talking about?" She feared she knew, vaguely recalling some laws for Kor's planet, but she'd not paid deep attention, never assuming they would apply to her.

"Females are much too rare still to allow them to remain unattached and roaming. So the law states that females, once they reach the age of bonding, with the exception of a mourning period of three moon cycles, must bond with a male deemed suitable by the head of her family."

"No." Diana shook her head. "I'll marry someone else if I have to."

"As the eldest son in the family, the matriarch is sure to select me as your new mate. So get used to the idea. Oh, and don't even think of running, or I'll really make it hurt."

Kil left her with ice running through her veins and a choking fear in her heart. How could she escape? There had to be someone who could help her. Someone who could bend the law. But who?

14

Diana didn't even register the splendor of the Oracle's palace, too intent on her mission, a purpose that the acolyte in front of her was impeding.

"I want to speak to the Oracle," said Diana, tapping a foot impatiently. "Now."

"But," said the flustered, veiled attendant, "you do not have an appointment. One cannot just show up and expect admittance. It's simply not done."

"I don't care. I need to talk to her. She's the reason I'm on this goddamn planet and more miserable than I've ever been in my life. She owes it to me to at least speak to me."

"Go home, and we will relay your request. If the Oracle chooses—"

A voice interrupted. "She does choose," said the

heavily veiled figure that appeared from seemingly nowhere.

The acolyte gasped and dropped to the floor, head bowed.

"You can take me to see her?" asked Diana.

"I am her, child. Come and walk with me. Let us speak of what disturbs you so."

The Oracle, a slight figure, gowned head to toe in layers of veils, turned and walked to the bronze doors, which opened before her as if by some unseen signal. Diana scurried after her, surprised, in fact, that the Oracle had agreed to see her.

Catching up to the quick-walking Oracle, Diana held her tongue, unsure now that she'd found her what to say.

They met no one as they passed through the various ornate rooms until, finally, through some glass-paned doors, they exited the palace into a splendid garden. Life and color abounded in the form of foliage, blooms, and the buzz of insects. The sounds were so mystifyingly similar to Earth that, for a moment, Diana's eyes flooded with tears as she remembered home.

Then she remembered she'd never see her home again because of this person, this so-called Oracle.

"Why?"

"Why what, my child?" asked the Oracle, her

face serene as she sat on a cleverly carved bench that blended into the scenery.

"Why choose me? Why show me love only to take it away?"

"I didn't take your mate away, and I did not choose you either. The spirits did that."

"So whose fault is this?" exclaimed Diana. "I didn't ask to be kidnapped and fall in love with an alien. And now he's gone, and his brother, that sick thing, says by law he can claim me for my own protection. It's not fair. I don't want this anymore. I want to go home. I want to forget."

"You are right. It isn't fair, but let me ask you first. Is Kor truly gone?"

"What do you mean?" asked Diana, her voice almost a whisper as her flicker of hope sparked hotter. "Is he alive?" Diana, over the last few days, had found her own certainty wavering.

"Look at your wrist, child."

Diana looked at her wrist, the smoky band around it a constant reminder of Kor.

"The mating band is still there, is it not?"

Diana, about to say yes, stopped as understanding washed through her. "The band would have disappeared if he died. He's not dead," she almost shouted.

"No, but the danger from Kil'iander is still quite real."

"I'll just tell him Kor is alive. He'll have to leave me alone."

"Will he?" said the Oracle questioningly. "Or will that knowledge merely make Kil'iander more rash?"

"I don't know. Surely he wouldn't . . ." *Oh, but he would. I've seen the way he looks at me. And the way he talked about Kor's accident. I know it wasn't an accident. Kil had something to do with it, but I can't let him know. I've got to hold him off 'til Kor gets back and can deal with him. Kor's alive. Oh, thank God.*

The Oracle spoke softly. "I see understanding. Just be patient, my child, and all will turn out well."

"For me this time, but what about the others?"

"The others?"

Diana forged ahead. "I understand your people need us to help continue your race. It's a necessity, but the way we are treated, it has to change."

"Change how?"

"Well, for one thing, you can't just abduct women and expect them all to be hunky-dory about it. Secrecy is one thing, but forcing a woman, that's wrong. There must be a way that we can give them a choice without revealing your secrets."

"I see."

"And if a woman's unhappy with her mate, she needs to be given help. Not impregnated like the only thing important is her ability to reproduce." Diana mentioned Claire's story to the Oracle.

Maybe if someone had stepped in to help her, the tragedy could have been averted.

"Anything else?"

"Yes, this stupid law of widows being the property of the brother or next male heir, it's got to stop. You don't want single women running around, fine, but you can't just let them be taken against their will."

"I agree."

Diana, about to argue, heard the words and felt her face slacken in surprise. "You agree?"

"Absolutely. In the beginning of the rebuilding, these laws were needed to avoid chaos and violence, but many moons have passed, as have those restrictions. It is time to give the women of this planet back some of the freedoms they enjoyed before the tragedy. And I think you should be one of the women who helps us reform the laws."

"Me? But I'm not even a Xamian."

"All the more reason. Earthling females amount to the largest percentage of our new female population. Who better to help lead the charge to change? Think about it. You will not do it alone. I, and others, will stand to help you."

Diana closed her mouth thoughtfully. What if she could help? Make a difference? It was certainly something to ponder once Kor was safe at home. *Please let him come back to me.*

Diana watched the newscast and cried. They'd found him. Kor was alive! He looked battered and worse for wear, but he lived, and that was all that mattered. Diana smirked as she imagined Kil's reaction to the news of Kor's resurrection.

Diana answered the vid comm and saw a jubilant Ele'Anor.

"He's alive," she squealed, and Diana, too overcome, just nodded, her own eyes wet.

"Do you want me to pick you up on the way to the hospital?"

"Yes, please."

Diana switched off the screen and, smiling, dressed in her best karimi. She paced, waiting for Ele'Anor, elation bubbling through her. When she heard the knock, she flew to the door and opened it, expecting to see her mother-in-law, but Kil hulked menacingly on her step instead.

Diana's smile faltered for a moment before she injected steel into her voice and spine. "You need to leave. Kor is back."

"His return changes nothing. You will be mine."

Diana felt a flutter of fear at his snarled words. But even Kil wasn't stupid enough to try something here and now. Although perhaps a reminder would be a good idea. "Ele'Anor is on her way to pick me up. You've lost. Now please leave."

"No." With brutish hands, he grabbed her and dragged her to his waiting vehicle. Diana struggled and screamed once before one meaty hand slapped over her mouth, choking the sound off.

This can't be happening. Someone will see what he's doing and stop him. Someone please help m—

Another cuff on the side of the head and Diana slumped, unconscious.

[15]

Kᴏʀ ꜱᴜꜰꜰᴇʀᴇᴅ ᴛʜᴇ ᴀᴛᴛᴇɴᴛɪᴏɴꜱ ᴏꜰ ᴛʜᴇ ʜᴇᴀʟᴇʀ, barely. He felt a desperate urge to see Diana.

His mother came in a rush of veils, her face a mask of panic. "Kor!"

"I'm fine, Mother. Now calm down. Where's Diana?" he said, peering around her robust form, looking for his mate.

"I can see you're fine. It's Diana who's not. He's taken her, Kor."

"What? Who's taken her?" Fear and anger gripped his heart in equal measures.

"Kil. Lisa, your neighbor, saw him."

"Where did they go?" asked Kor, ripping the tubes that were rehydrating him from his arms.

"I don't know. Kil has somehow slipped the video relays."

"I need some clothes," said Kor, realizing his state of undress when he pulled back the covers.

His mother, ever one step ahead, opened her bag and dumped out pants and a shirt.

"I don't have boots," she said, shrugging apologetically.

Kor quickly dressed and cursed the fact that he didn't have an earpiece so he could contact Alphie. His mother, though, had her vid comm, and Kor quickly got in touch with him. Racing out of the hospital, heading to the spaceport, Kor hoped only that he'd arrive in time.

———

ANXIOUSNESS KEPT Diana tense as she paced the confines of the room Kil had locked her in. Judging by the less than pristine conditions around her, she seemed to be aboard an older style spacecraft, one with a door that shut manually and locked from the outside.

Diana cursed and railed and kicked at the walls and door to no avail. The only person aboard was Kil the psycho.

Diana sank to the floor and drew up her knees to lean her head on. Closing her eyes, she felt the tears leaking from the corners as she thought of Kor, who waited for her in the hospital. A wait that would never end. *Not to mention a child he will never know*, she thought, hugging her hardened tummy.

"Psst," came a whisper.

Diana brought her head up off her knees. "Who's there?" she whispered back, a tiny thread of hope in the sound.

"It's Alphie. Lucky for you I've been keeping an eye on Kil here, and I made sure to hop on this ship before he shut down communications."

"Can you stop the ship from taking off?" she asked hopefully. Alphie could control all the electronics on a ship. He could save her.

"I wish," said the disgruntled machine. "He deliberately chose an older manual model."

"What's that mean?"

"It means, while the ship has a basic computer system and whatnot, all ship procedures are done by hand, from navigating to doors to everything."

"So what can you do?"

"I managed to send out a message just before he closed down the comm units. Actually, by the sounds of it, smashed them. I've activated a low-level beacon that I hope he won't notice that should help Kor to track him."

Diana found herself torn. On the one hand, she wanted to be saved by Kor and reunited with him. But on the other, a confrontation between the brothers could mean Kor's death.

One thing she knew for sure, if and when Kor saved her, she wouldn't deny her feelings for him anymore. She'd tell him she loved him, even knowing he could never feel the same way. She would love enough for the both of them.

DESPITE THE BUZZING of the comm unit on his hip, Kor ignored it. He had more important things to attend to. Whoever called would have to wait as he strode towards the docking bay that held his aircraft.

But what if it was news of Diana?

Not breaking his stride, he flipped the unit open and found a message from Alphie, of all people—er, machines.

Kil has Diana on board craft S0014533. Charted course the third moon. Will attempt a low-level radiation beacon.

Murderous heat lengthened his stride. In short order, Kor boarded his spacecraft, a place rife with memories of Diana. And in short order, he'd replace those with new ones, because he would get her back.

Programming in the coordinates Alphie fed him, he prepared to follow his brother even if it wasn't he most rational choice. The smart thing would be to wait for his father to arrive with some of the clan warriors, but his brother had Diana. *My mate.* It didn't take much for him to just imagine how terrified she had to be. She could even be injured. *For all the fear and dishonor he has caused, he dies.*

THE CRAFT LANDED WITH A THUD THAT reverberated throughout the vessel. Diana looked around, desperate for something to defend herself with, but the stripped room she'd frantically searched earlier still contained a whole lot of nothing.

Determined to at least try, though, she stood to the side of the door and waited, her palms slick with sweat. When Kil opened the door, Diana swung her clubbed hands at his head. To her surprise, he staggered, and she darted out the door. She took two steps before the steel vise grip of his hands closed around her arms and ribs, the strength in him enough to lift her off the floor. Diana wanted to scream in frustration, and she did when Kil chuckled maliciously in her ear.

"There's nowhere to run, little Diana."

Kil threw her hard over his shoulder, digging it painfully into her stomach. Diana cried, her silent tears running down her face, even as she pounded uselessly at his back. She heard the cranking of metal, followed by a hissing sound as a seal was broken. Cool, musty air wafted into the ship. The dusty, dead breeze tickled her nose and made her sneeze. Kil's heavy tread clomped down the metal ramp from the ship's doorway onto a gray, pebbled surface.

He righted her and dropped her to the ground in a heap, and she scrambled back from him, eyes darting around 'til, in shock, she stopped moving. Kil had dragged her onto a nightmare landscape. Judging by what she could see, he'd brought them to one of the gray moons she'd learned about, littered with tombs and mausoleums.

Diana felt a crazy urge to giggle. *Lucky me, I cross an entire galaxy only to get killed in an alien graveyard, and other than the location, it looks like something you'd find back home. Who'd have thought tombstones, flowers, and stone vaults would be a custom that spanned the galaxy?*

"Why did you bring me here?" she asked, eyes darting around anxiously, hoping to see Kor while praying he stayed away.

"I think it only fitting that Kor die surrounded by the same spirits that denied me. Let them see what their choice has wrought."

"You're insane. You mean you're letting a bunch of dead people make you do this."

"No, I'm doing this because I want to. The location is just for fun."

"So why the accident?" she asked, stalling for time. "Why not just kill him?"

"I thought about it. But then it occurred to me. Why not take everything he has? Wouldn't that just drive his spirit mad? Killing him meant I'd have to leave or be killed myself. After all, his stupid spirit would have tattled to the Oracle. But if I arranged an accident, one that couldn't be traced back to me, well then, his spirit would have no proof, and I'd win. I'd truly hoped the pirates would be less inept."

Diana gasped. "You told them where we were?"

"Of course. Figures they'd get distracted by a female instead of doing the job I paid them to do."

"You're sick."

Kil smiled at her, his sickly eyes alight with maliciousness. "Yes, I am. Sick and tired of seeing that whelp get what should have been mine. No more. Now he dies. And then, while his helpless spirit watches, I am going to take you on the ground beside his body. I'll show all the spirits what I think of their choice."

He's completely insane. She stared up at him and realized something else. There would be no reasoning with him. He existed as a rabid animal, and there was only one thing you could do when something got that unpredictable and violent. Put it down.

Would Kor be able to kill his brother, though? Assuming of course Kor showed up to save her.

Oh, who am I kidding? I know Kor will come. Hasn't he told me enough times I am his? Not to mention he'd never let his brother get away with this. Sibling rivalry thrived among the stars.

"There will be no defiling. This is where it ends."

The beating of her heart tripled when she heard Kor's cool, calm words, and she wanted to run to him when his figure, somewhat gaunter than she remembered, appeared. The accident had taken its toll on him. But that didn't stop him from narrowing his gaze on his brother.

Kil advanced and pointed a laser gun at her, its red guiding light centered on her tummy. "Brother, so kind of you to join us," said Kil, sweeping a mocking bow while keeping his eyes trained on Kor. "I was just telling your mate here how much I was going to enjoy taking her again. Oh yes, I quite enjoyed my taste of her on the ship. Quite the little screamer, isn't she?"

"You pig," she spat. "You—"

. . .

"Quiet, little Diana, or I'll poke another kind of hole in you," he said, wagging his gun menacingly.

Kor shook his head. "I know you haven't touched her, Kil. Another sad fact of the plague is the children born during it are impotent. You're as useless as a eunuch."

With a scream of rage, Kil spun the gun on Kor, firing. And missing. Kor had already moved, and Diana heard the whistle as one of his daggers flew through the air and hit Kil high in the shoulder.

As if that would stop him. An evil grin tugged at Kil's lips. "I don't have to kill you to hurt you. I'll just kill your mate."

Kil swung to Diana, and then it was as if everything slowed down. Diana could see his trigger finger pulling back, and she wanted to close her eyes so she wouldn't see her death coming, but she couldn't. Instead, she watched, wide-eyed, unable to even scream. Thus she saw only too clearly the smoky hands that shot up from the gray soil, the fingers elongated and curved at the end like claws. The emerging cocoon of smoke and shadow wrapped around Kil, and, horrified, he looked down. He opened his mouth to scream, and the dark mist flowed into him. Kil's eyes bulged in terror.

With a slight tremor in the ground, Kil began to sink, the soil beneath his feet suddenly liquid. Eyes wide with panic, Kil was absorbed by the spirits in the graveyard. Diana's gorge rose, and she turned away, feeling, a moment later, Kor's arms around her as he scooped her up and held her shaking body.

"Are you all right?" he asked, finally releasing her enough so she could breathe.

"Shouldn't I be asking you that question?" she retorted, pushing away from him to look him over for signs of injury. Other than a new gauntness from his forced diet underground, he looked fine, better than fine, actually.

Diana burst into tears.

SEEING HIS MATE, his beautiful moonflower Diana, burst into tears caused a fluttery sensation in Kor's chest. *Why does she cry?* What ailed her?

"I thought you were uninjured," he exclaimed, scooping her up and jogging back to the spacecraft he and Alphie had appropriated.

"I am," she sniffled.

"Then why the tears?" he asked, confused,

slowing his pace as he came into sight of the waiting vessel.

"I'm so happy you're back," she sobbed. "I didn't think I'd ever see you again. And I was so scared and lonely."

Kor listened as she recited all of the things he'd found himself feeling too. He didn't understand it. Were these emotions normal with one's mate?

"I'm back now, and Kil's gone. You don't need to be afraid anymore."

Kor walked up the ramp to the ship and carried Diana straight into the decontamination center. Stripping her soiled clothes from her, he ran his hands over her body to reassure himself that she was unmarked.

Of course, even something simple like that aroused him. It had been many cycles since he'd last been with his mate.

Kor felt possessed of a powerful urge to join with her. He needed to feel her clasped around him, screaming his name. Reassured she sported no injuries, he began caressing her smooth skin, even as the tickling sensation of the decontamination lasers made Diana's flesh tremble. He buried his face in her stomach, kissing it. Then, laying a trail of light caresses, he made his way down her soft skin to the thatch of curls that hid her sex.

He parted her with his fingers, and Diana

sighed. Noticing her trembling legs, he lay her down on the pile of their discarded clothing and parted her thighs. Her pink wetness invited him, and Kor, parched for her taste, buried his face into that sweet heaven. He used his tongue to lick the ambrosia that was hers alone. His cock swelled thickly at the mewls of pleasure and tremors in her limbs. He continued to tease her with his tongue, unwilling to move from her.

HE DEBATED for a moment when he felt her muscles tightening, letting her orgasm against his mouth, and he tasted the nectar as it flowed from her, but his body ached terribly. *I need to be inside her.*

SLIDING up the length of her body, being sure to kiss her erect nipples, he buried himself deep inside her. He sighed at the hot, slick feel of her sex clenching tightly around his spear, the heaven he needed after the nightmare he'd been through.

HE PUMPED HIS SWEET MATE, her pliant flesh moving with him, squeezing him tight, and driving him to the brink 'til, with a bellow, he came, shouting her name. She wrapped her legs tight around him and echoed his cry as she orgasmed, her wet flesh pulsating and prolonging his own pleasure 'til he thought he would die in her arms.

COLLAPSING beside her on the hard floor, Kor vaguely realized where they were. While they'd satisfied their carnal need, the cleaning process had finished.

SCOOPING HER BONELESS BODY UP—A sure sign she'd enjoyed his attentions, Kor thought with a grin—he carried her to the cabin where they'd first joined and become mates.

WHEN HE LAID her on the soft mattress, Diana opened her eyes and smiled at him, her eyes heavy-lidded and her lips swollen.

"I'M SO glad you're home," she whispered huskily. "I love you, Kor. I know you don't have a word for love in your people's language, but I know that what I feel for you is real. I don't ever want to be without you. I'm so glad you're back. Me and the baby I carry," she said, stunning him as she grabbed his hand and placed it on her abdomen.

Kor felt the new hardness through her flesh, and

he stood speechless long enough that Diana got an anxious look in her eyes.

"Aren't you happy?"

Calling himself stupid for causing her to doubt, he lay down beside her and held her in his arms and spoke the words he found in his heart. "My people might not have the word 'love' in their vocabulary, but even without that word, this is how I feel. You are mine. And, in return, I belong to you. I would cross the universe to be with you and die a painful death to protect you. The thought of being without you causes fear where fear was never known. When you smile, I can do anything. When you cry, I would fight the world to make it stop. What is this, then, if not this love you seem to speak about?"

WHAT INDEED, thought Diana, her eyes wet and her throat tight. All this time she should have seen it, recognized it, not gotten caught up in the Hallmark version of love that required those three specific words. Love was an emotion, not a word. And if love could be seen, it would look like Kor. If love could be felt, it would feel like Kor.

As she snuggled next to her mate—*yes, mine*—Diana smiled. It might have been ghosts and an

Oracle who initially brought them together, but it was love, an emotion that transcended the boundaries of space and differences of their species, that bound them now. Forever.

ALIEN MATE 2

1

Lex stood in the bland transport and decontamination room, his naked body tense with anticipation as he waited for the Alpha 350 to teleport him to his intended's location. When nothing happened, he shifted from one foot to another. "Computer, is there a problem?"

"You know, we've been travelling together for a few days now. Could you not call me by something less formal? Your friend Kor calls me Alphie," said a voice from seemingly nowhere.

"You are a machine," Lex stated for the umpteenth time.

"An intelligent one," said the shipboard computer with a sigh.

Lex clenched his teeth. The AI unit on this vessel—artificial intelligence, his ass, more like pain in his ass—kept acting inappropriately. *A machine that wants to be my friend.* He almost snorted at the incongruity. Lex had already noted in the service log the need to service this model.

"Please cease with the idle chatter and transport me to my intended mate that I might bond with her and return her to our world."

"Bit of a problem with that," announced the AI with a hint of glee.

"What now?" Lex said, unable to hide the exasperation in his voice.

"The teleporter seems to be malfunctioning."

"Impossible. Try again." The molecular transportation unit had worked as expected at their last planetary spot, so he saw no reason why it wouldn't be working now.

"Try again? Are you joking?" said the computer with a realistic note of incredulity. "You want me to use a malfunctioning teleporter on you? What, you don't like your body parts where they are?"

Lex winced at the vivid image the AI's words painted. "What do we need to fix it?"

"*We* can't. We'll need some of the techs back home."

Frustration made him tighten his hands into fists. "Unacceptable. I'm here to collect my mate. I will not return without her." Lex never failed to complete his missions.

"I was afraid you'd say that," mumbled the

Alpha 350. "In that case, we'll need to land, and you can disembark manually."

"Make it so," said Lex, crossing his arms over his chest imperiously.

"Um, shouldn't you put some clothes on first?"

"What for?" asked Lex, his brow creasing. "I need to be nude to bond with my mate."

"Yes, but you'll need to find her first," said the AI with a long-suffering sigh. "You can't seriously think you can wander around naked and not be noticed. It's bad enough your skin is blue, but a giant, naked blue male wandering around a human city is sure to get noticed."

Lex frowned. The computer had a valid point, one he should have realized had he not been so anxious to complete his mission. "I will dress myself while you locate a suitable landing area."

"You do that."

With what sounded suspiciously like muttering —something to the effect of big blue aliens with more brawn than brains, which Lex chose to ignore, the Alpha 350 revved the engines in preparation to penetrate the atmosphere surrounding the planet known in their database as Earth.

While the computer took care of the minor details involved with landing, Lex clothed himself in a silvery jumpsuit, the material specially made to adapt to all types of weather conditions. He added a pair of supple black boots to protect his feet, and just in case the inhabitants of this Earth proved hostile, he slid a dagger into a waist sheath and another into his boot.

Checking on their progress—still descending into the earth's atmosphere—Lex pulled up a picture of his intended, Amanda Beckwith, a blonde, blue-eyed alien doll. The only image the AI had been able to find didn't show her figure, but Lex sure hoped she sported a well-rounded shape like he'd asked for when selected by the Oracle to enter the ranks of the pair-bonded. It was considered a high honor in his society to be chosen to mate, even if the females had to be fetched from other planets. Arranged pair-mating was a necessary survival tactic forced on the males of his world to compensate for the lack of females in their society, a lack cruelly caused by a deadly virus that had decimated the female ranks many moon cycles ago. Now, only the worthiest were chosen to help repopulate Xaanda, and Lex had acquitted himself well in battle for that honor. A decorated warrior, he'd finally achieved the reward for all his hard work and looked forward to the new life he would undertake with his biddable, if alien, wife.

"We're almost there," said the Alpha 350, interrupting his thoughts.

Lex strode down the corridors of the spacecraft to the exit hatch, the AI's voice giving him last-minute instructions that he only partially listened to.

"Remember to stay out of sight. The humans here are known to capture and medically experiment on unknown species."

Lex would like to see them try.

"Try and move about at night, where your skin coloring is less likely to be noticed."

"I don't intend to be here that long," Lex muttered. His plan was to find his mate quickly and rendezvous with his ship for a prompt departure to his home world.

"If, by some chance, your communicator malfunctions, I'll meet you at the gypsum crystal fields on this planet's full moon a few days from now."

That warning caught his attention. "Why would the communicator malfunction?" asked Lex.

"Just humor me," said the AI. "The teleporter shouldn't have malfunctioned either, yet it did. So remember, on the full moon, meet me at the gypsum fields. Now, your mate can be found at 351 El Paso Drive. Remember to stay out of sight. This location is very close to an Earth military establishment, and while I've fooled their radars, I can't blind their eyes, so be discreet."

Lex absently nodded, anticipation roaring through him. In and out. His superior warrior training would outclass these humans who were barely more civilized than barbarians.

With a soft thud, the craft landed, and the hatch

hissed open. Lex descended the ramp and stood on the alien soil, breathing deeply. The air, so like that of his own world, smelled of dirt and plant life. Their similar atmospheres made the deportation of the female earthlings viable, that and the fact that they were descended from the same group of space-farers who had seeded life throughout the galaxy.

"Where to?" he asked aloud, glad he'd brought on this mission the advanced earpiece communi-cator that allowed the AI unit to reply back, unlike some other models used on not-as-technologically-advanced planets.

The computer's tinny voice spoke in his ear. "You need to hike a few miles due west. I couldn't land any closer without being seen."

Lex jogged off in the direction of his intended, his groin tightening in anticipation. Soon, he'd be among the ranks of the mated and indulging in his lusts whenever he wanted. No more galactic brothels for him. He—and his libido—couldn't wait.

A few hours later, his breathing ragged, his clothing torn, the baying sound of the animals with vicious teeth still echoing in the darkness behind him, he soundly cursed this planet and the savages who inhabited it.

A fence appeared seemingly out of nowhere in the lightening gloom that signaled the sun's rising. He nimbly climbed the barrier and dropped to the other side. He quickly scanned the darkness, looking for threats. All clear. He loped off toward the shadows of the building he could barely perceive. He planned to hide amid the humans in an unused location, perhaps steal some of their clothing, and mask his scent. Well, that was the plan until his foot didn't hit the hard ground. He stumbled into open space and plummeted into an invisible pit of liquid that sucked him down.

His last thought before losing consciousness was he should have listened to the stupid computer who'd recommended they abort when the chase first started.

Too late now.

2

". . . GEORGE, WHO HEARD IT FROM HIS COUSIN Juanita on the base, swears, this time, it's real. Aliens have landed, and they're not friendly."

The word "alien" caught her attention. Maya turned to the petite Latina woman who spoke. "What's going on at the base?"

Eager to tell her story again to a new avid listener, Marcia spoke quickly. "Apparently their radars didn't catch it, but this object, unknown object," she said with a wide-eyed whisper, "landed by the white sands. My cousin says the military sent out a detachment, and they found a circle like the ones you see in them crops. The dog unit was called in, and last I heard, they were chasing some giant alien, and he's heading toward us!"

Several of the listeners crossed themselves, and excited babble broke out. Maya shook her head.

She knew better than to listen to gossip. How often had so-and-so's cousin, sister, or uncle made the same claim, when the truth usually ended up being something benign? The last false alarm had been caused by drug runners whose plane had run out of gas and they'd done an emergency landing. That night had also involved a chase, and aliens had been caught, but they were of the illegal immigrant type, not extraterrestrial. But Maya couldn't help listening to the stories nor stop that little flutter of hope that maybe this time it would be for real. Her parents had, after all, raised her to believe.

Seeing the bulky form of Andre, the night-shift manager, waddling into the room, Maya slammed her locker shut and hightailed it out of there using the back door before he snagged her to do one more thing. Alamogordo's stupid yearly balloon festival had almost arrived and, with it, hordes of tourists who, for some reason, always ended up with an urgent need for food or cleaning at three in the morning. She knew she should be thankful she had a job—especially one with awesome benefits like hers—but right now, tired, her feet aching, and with a headache pulsing behind her eyes, she just wanted to crawl under the covers of her bed and pray she won the lottery.

Yeah, right, I'm more likely to run into a hot alien who wants me for my body. Maya snorted at the ridiculous thought.

Sneaking through a service entrance, she took the shortcut past the pool deck, a copy of the key that unlocked the gate on the other side—without the hotel's knowledge, of course—a quick route to the employee parking lot and the piece of crap known as her car.

The dawn hadn't yet started lighting the gloom, but even in the dark, she heard the rattle of the fence as if someone climbed it and then, a moment later, the distinctive sound of someone or something hitting the surface of the pool with a splash. *Keep on walking*, she told herself. *Don't get involved*. The early morning swimmer was probably a drunk on his way back from a night of debauchery, but if whatever was in the pool ended up being human and drowning, then she'd have a hell of a bigger headache, especially if the cops got involved. No one ever believed the Hispanic girl. *Stupid gringos*.

Sighing, Maya headed toward the deep end, where she'd heard the sound. Peering at the dark, lapping water, she almost wondered if she'd imagined it, but then a series of bubbles rose to the surface, and with a curse, she kicked off her shoes and dove in. With sure strokes she'd learned from years of swim lessons, she arrowed down to the bottom of the pool and waved her arms around in the sightless murk, encountering nothing. Her chest grew tight, and she'd prepared to go up for air when a flailing limb touched her. Grabbing it, she kicked up, dragging a form that had grown limp, her lungs screaming at the added strain. She broke the surface with a pained gasp. Treading water, she pulled at the body she'd found 'til it bobbed up beside her. Wrapping an arm around his upper body—there was no mistaking the wide male chest—she towed him to the shallow end, where the steps would make it easier to pull him out.

Maya wanted to call for help, but her breath stuttered in and out of her chest painfully from exertion. Nothing like a life-or-death situation to remind her she really should get into shape. Wheezing, she concentrated on lugging the big male body clothed in a slick, formfitting material onto the pool deck. When she had most of his body horizontal, she turned him onto his stomach and pumped his back, forcing his lungs to spew out the water he'd inhaled. She flipped him back and, hiking her work skirt, straddled his chest, trying to remember her first aid training.

Do I pump his chest or give him mouth to mouth? They kept changing the first aid rules, and tired, she decided to do both. First, she did some quick compressions to his chest and then leaned down to listen for his breathing.

Nothing. She compressed again, not liking the bluish pallor to his skin that the lightening sky revealed. When he still didn't respond, she thought,

What the hell. She pinched his nose and latched her lips over his, blowing air.

The chest she straddled expanded. She turned her head to let him exhale, counting, and then placed her lips over his again to breathe.

With no advance warning, she found herself flipped onto her back. The wet stranger pinned her body underneath his and pressed his groin—a very aroused groin—against her. She couldn't make out his features in the gloom, but she caught a glimpse of glowing violet orbs and white teeth before his mouth claimed hers in a kiss that shocked her wet body from head to toe.

¡Dios mío!

[3]

Lᴇx ᴅʀᴇᴀᴍᴛ ʜᴇ ᴋɪssᴇᴅ sᴡᴇᴇᴛ ʟɪᴘs ᴡʜɪʟᴇ ʜɪs ʙᴏᴅʏ covered a luscious body made for pumping. It took him a moment of fuzzy bliss to realize this was no dream. The smart thing to do would have been to break off the passionate embrace with the human, but he didn't want it to stop. No longer confused, even though his shock at falling in that liquid pool had been great, he briefly wondered at his unexpected reaction to the woman underneath him, for there was no mistaking what he felt—desire—and it raged like a wild beast through his body. He might have lost consciousness, but he was definitely awake now, well, a certain hard part of him, that is.

Sharp teeth bit his lip, and with an exclamation, he pulled back from the kiss.

"Get off me," said a female voice that, even in irritation, lilted musically.

Lex didn't move right away, his body reluctant to leave the soft haven it nestled on. The body under his thrashed, and a knee came perilously close to his male parts. Rolling off the female, who, despite her kissing of him, no longer wanted his attentions, Lex wondered if perhaps he'd finally gotten lucky on his forsaken mission.

"I don't suppose your name is Amanda Beckwith?" he asked.

"Mierda!" exclaimed the earthling. "I save your life, let you maul me, and now you have the nerve to ask me if I am another woman? Bah, I don't know who this Amanda is, but she is welcome to you."

The human's words and attitude were fiery, and Lex, who hadn't lost his initial erection, hardened even more, a fact that he didn't understand since he preferred his women respectful and obedient.

"Sorry. I am unsure of your customs." Lex waited for the Alpha 350 to prompt him on what he should do next, but he heard nothing. Actually, come to think of it, he hadn't heard the AI since he'd plunged into the liquid.

The female just glared at him as she picked her damp self off the ground.

Lex groaned, not just because he'd lost his link to the computer but because he finally got to see the plump body of the feisty female, and by all the moons, she was curvaceous perfection. The damp white fabric of her clothing clung to and outlined full breasts, the nipples visible and erect against the cloth.

"What is wrong? Are you injured? Do you require medical attention?" Her words displayed concern, but her tone implied annoyance.

Lex lied. Somehow he didn't think telling her that she had the body of a moon goddess that he longed to worship—with his tongue and cock—would go over well, given her rather violent reaction to his earlier kiss. "I can't contact my computer."

She turned to look at the rectangular pit filled with fluid, surely a trap for the unwary and a great defense mechanism.

"You dropped your laptop?" she finally queried as she slipped on some shoes and picked up a bag.

"Your comment makes no sense, earthling. My lap is still on my legs. I speak of the communicator for my vessel. It must have been damaged in my plunge into that vat of foul liquid. I have no way of contacting my ship's computer. This is a complete disaster."

"You are loco." She laughed. "Figures, a man who kisses a chubby maid like me would be out of his mind. Since you are obviously fine, or as fine as someone like you can be, I will be leaving, señor."

The voluptuous earthling turned to leave just as the sound of baying animals sounded, their rabid voices carried on the rising dawn air.

"Wait," he called out. When she did not stop, he strode after her and grabbed her arm, spinning her.

She opened her mouth but then said nothing, her eyes widening as she stared at him in shock.

"¡Dios mío. You're—you're blue!" she finally exclaimed.

"Of course I am," he said with a frown. "What other color would I be?"

———

WHAT COLOR INDEED? Maya reached a hand up to smear what obviously had to be blue makeup, but his smooth skin did not change hue, and a tingle ran down her body at the touch of his smooth, beardless face. With the sun rising brightly, she could now see him more clearly, and if he wasn't an alien, then he wore a damned good disguise. His skin shone a beautiful dark blue, and his hair, cut short, was a startling white. He had strong masculine features, with hard lips and vivid violet eyes—eyes she remembered glowing before he'd kissed her. She stepped back and looked him over, the silvery material of his jumpsuit already dry and clinging to an obviously muscled frame.

Well, alien or not, he's sexy. Even without the dip in the pool, her panties would have been wet. *So why did I bite him when he kissed me?* An even better question—*is he the alien that has the military in an uproar?* She hadn't forgotten the rumor circulating in the break room.

"Who and what are you?" she asked.

"I am Lex'indrios Vel Romannu," he said, standing tall. "I am descended of the Second Moon clan, the secondary line and fourth class warrior for the Second Moon regiment."

An impressive title but one easily made up. "Are you really an alien?"

He grinned at her with impossibly white teeth. "I'm not, but you are, earthling."

Maya felt her lips quirk. Point in his favor. Who the alien was really depended on the perspective. "Okay, let's say I believe you for a second. Why are you here?"

"Why, to fetch my mate, of course. The Oracle has decreed that Amanda Beckwith shall be my intended."

Maya bit her tongue so as to not laugh at his declaration, even as a sense of disappointment swept through her. *Why can't I be someone's intended, especially someone as hot as him?* But back to his words, if—and that was a big if—what he said turned out to be true, then he was in for a surprise when he told this Amanda person about their arranged galactic engagement. Then again, she thought, eyeing his muscular frame and handsome features, a lot of girls would jump at the chance to be with him, blue skin or not. *Count me in. I wouldn't mind taking him for a spin in my bed.* Maya couldn't help the heat that spread through her body at the thought.

Lex of the impossible name looked over his shoulder nervously as the sound of dogs approached. "Is there not a more secure place we can continue this discussion? The beasts that track me are relentless."

The approaching canine cacophony lent even more credence to his tale, and Maya found herself too intrigued to ignore him. Not to mention the spirits of her parents in heaven were probably screaming at her to hide him. She led him through the fence, using her copied key, and across the parking lot to her beat-up excuse for a car.

He stood looking dubiously at her rusted heap. "Is this vehicle deemed safe for transportation?"

Maya blushed at his remark, which in turn made her angry. *How dare he belittle my car! It's not my fault I can't afford anything better. Idiota.*

"Don't make fun of my car. I bought it myself at least. And, besides, I don't see you with any other means of transportation, do I?" she said sassily with her hands on her hips.

Through gritted teeth, he apologized. "I did not mean to sound disrespectful. I thank you for your aid."

Mollified, and even somewhat amused at forcing the apology, Maya climbed into the car, biting her lip so as to not giggle as he folded himself into the car gingerly. She started the car with a coughing sputter and drove with her eyes glued to the road, trying to ignore the very masculine presence of the large man—or was he truly an alien?—beside her.

Not entirely convinced of his story, and determined to scrub at his skin a little harder, she had still reserved judgement. *What about his glowing purple eyes when he kissed me?* Probably a refraction of light, she tried to tell herself. But what if his tale were true? *What if he is an alien?*

Maya had grown up with a belief, almost a religion actually, that extraterrestrials existed. Her parents had worshipped at the shrine of UFO sightings, fanatic believers whose idea of a family vacation involved packing up the old VW van and driving across the lower states to places of interest. They'd visited the famous Area 51 and stood with faces pressed against the chain-link fence. They'd camped out in lounger chairs, with telescopes and marshmallows with other UFO watchers, waiting for their own close encounter of the third kind. She even knew all the human-meets-life-from-space movies by heart. Her parents had scoffed at *E.T.,* even as they coached her on what to do should an alien ever visit her.

But the absolutely freakiest part of her whole encounter with this giant blue alien? It reminded her of the story her grandmother had told her over and over again 'til her death a few years back. A story about a tall blue warrior, descended from the stars. An alien male who came and took her grandma's sister to be his wife. An alien who took a nubile female for his own and left for the stars, never to be seen again.

Mother of all galactic coincidences, or could this be a prank? But who would know or remember an old woman's tale, let alone act it out? *If this is a joke, I am going to string him up by his cojones.* But if it wasn't . . . A vivid image of herself cradling those same cojones had her squirming in the vinyl seat, making her glad they'd reached her little house with its plot of dirt outside of town. Even in the dark, the place looked sad, kind of like her life.

It needs sprucing up, she thought, looking at it with a critical eye, but working nights six days a week, not to mention the fact that she blew most of her budget on movies or books, made that unlikely. And, besides, she kept hoping she'd leave it all one day, move on to a better life and never look back.

"This is your home?" He spoke, his velvety voice sending frissons down her spine, pleasurable ones.

Embarrassment made her cheeks color, but she held her head high when she turned to him and responded, "Yes. It's not much, but it's mine."

Saying not a word, just flashing a grin that made even more heat pool between her thighs, he unfolded himself from her car and stretched, the smooth silvery material of his jumpsuit doing nothing to hide the rippling muscles.

Maya just about drooled, and that baffled her. She didn't usually behave like a cat in heat. It just went so contrary to her usual aloofness around men. Yet watching him with avid eyes, she was pretty sure she had a minor orgasm at just the sight of his well-toned body. He had a sinuous grace and masculine vitality that screamed sex. Hot, pounding, sweaty sex. Just, unfortunately, not with her, no matter that kiss he'd given back when he'd regained consciousness. Now awake and aware, he'd be looking for that mate he'd spoken about, probably some cute, skinny thing who had never had to shop in the big girls' section.

Maya sighed. Her weight didn't bother her most of the time. She might not be the skinniest girl, but she had a nice curvy figure, a very hourglass one that got more than its share of slaps on the ass and boob grabs. But come on, a galactic babe like him? Why would he settle for a plush Latina when he could have a Barbie doll?

Annoyed that he made her wish for a different body—and life—she slammed her car door harder than needed, startling him.

"We'd better get inside before someone sees you." Not too likely given her location and neighbors, but still, she preferred not to take chances. She had some questions she wanted to ask before she decided if she believed him or not.

And a cold shower she needed to take. *A long, frigid one*, she thought, clenching her fists at the sight of his gorgeous ass walking into her house first. *Dios, give me the strength to resist this alien.*

LEX FOUND himself swirling with a confusing mixture of emotions, the most prominent one being lust. The woman who'd rescued him looked nothing at all like his picture-perfect Amanda with her blonde locks. Yet this female, whose name he hadn't yet gotten, with her wild brown curls, smooth, tanned skin, and mouth-watering curves, made him want to forget the Oracle, forget his intended. He wanted this feisty beauty. In her soft, pillowy curves, a male could lose himself and never want to leave. He couldn't blame confusion on his near-death experience anymore either. He knew full well she wasn't his for the taking, and yet he wanted her with a desire that almost frightened him with its intensity.

Could the Oracle have made an error? Had his ancestors not looked hard enough? And since when did he doubt his betters? Part of what made Lex a good warrior, and the reason he'd become eligible for a mate, was his unquestioning of orders. His superiors gave him a mission, and he did it. Simple. Why now this sudden urge to buck tradition? Unacceptable. Lex always completed his quests, and while this earthling appealed to his baser instincts, his focus still remained finding his mate.

As he wandered into a small room cluttered with worn furniture and earthling detritus, he wondered, though, what to do next. The loss of the AI's instructions meant his mission had failed even before it had begun. How would he find his intended now?

"Sit," ordered the goddess of the lustrous brown eyes, pointing to a lumpy sofa. "And start talking."

Sitting gingerly until he ascertained the cushions would take his weight, he leaned back and perused her, an act that made her flush and sent the blood rushing to his groin. Despite her violent reaction of earlier, he could tell she was not immune to him. They had a sizzling chemistry that distracted—and enthralled—him. Leaning forward, he made his turgid state less noticeable and tried to bring his mind back on track.

"If I may ask, you have not yet told me your name."

"Didn't I?" she replied, frowning. "Sorry. I guess I was kind of distracted by the whole alien thing. My name is Maya, Maya Romero."

"I thank you for your timely intervention in the pool of deadly liquid, Maya." Lex gave credit where due, even given the disturbing fact that a female had saved him, which went against everything he'd been taught as a warrior.

"Deadly liquid?" Maya giggled, an enchanting sound that made him pulse even larger. "That was a swimming pool. It's only deadly if you don't know how to swim." When Lex frowned, still not comprehending, she explained. "A pool is filled with water and chemicals to keep it clear, and people swim in it. Umm, move their arms and legs to keep their bodies afloat. It's a form of recreation on Earth and a way to cool off on a hot day."

Appalled, Lex sputtered, "You use water for recreation? Is your race completely crazy?"

Maya crossed her arms under her ample breasts, which had the effect of pushing them together and out, a sight that made him speechless for a moment. "Listen here, señor. I don't know where you come from, but here on Earth, we have *lots* of water. And if we want to swim in it, we will," she said huffily.

"On my world, the use of water is strictly prohibited it is so scarce. Not to mention necessary to ensure a healthy planetary survival. I can't believe you would treat such a precious resource so recklessly."

"Whatever. *Dios.* See if I save your ass next time," she muttered under her breath, but Lex still heard every word, although he had difficulty following when she mixed up her languages.

"Why is it you speak in two languages?"

"I am Hispanic. Spanish is my mother tongue."

"I thought you were an earthling?" *Or is Maya yet another unknown breed of alien?*

MAYA LOOKED AT HIM STRANGELY. "*Ai*, you must be alien to be so ignorant. I am human, or earthling, if you prefer, but my people are called Hispanic, or Latina. We tend to have dark hair"—she pointed to her halo of curls—"and tanned skin. Don't tell me everyone on your planet is blue like you?" And she wondered if the blue extended to *all* his body parts.

"No, we have different shades depending on the purity of the bloodline and the occasional other color depending on the mixing of alien genes."

Maya shook her head at the remark that skirted the edge of racism. "I'm not even going to touch that one," she said, shaking her head. "Now, it's time you explained exactly what you're doing here. And you'd better tell the truth, or I'll call the military police myself. You said something about marrying some human girl?" Actually Maya wouldn't turn him in. Somewhere between the hotel where she worked and her home, she'd begun to believe his strange tale—kind of hard not to when his eyes kept glowing violet whenever he looked at her. She only wished his mission had been to claim her. She wouldn't have minded becoming his mate.

"I am to mate with the human Amanda Beckwith. She has been chosen by the Oracle and my ancestors to be my mate."

"Who's this Oracle? Is she like a clan elder?"

Lex launched into an explanation. "The Oracle is the oldest being on our planet. She has always been and always will be. When the females of our planet were killed by a deadly virus, she, along with the spirits of our ancestors—"

Maya interrupted. "Wait a second. Did you say spirits?"

"Yes, all who die in the clan are buried in the mausoleums on one of the three moons, thus freeing their spirits to perform deeds. With the help of the Oracle, many are now tasked with finding suitable females for us as mates."

"That's barbaric," she exclaimed.

"What is?"

"Arranged marriages."

"It is our custom," he said, frowning at her. "We require females of other races to breed with and rebuild our population. Once they are selected by our ancestors, we are sent to retrieve them."

"You mean you kidnap them? Don't they get a choice?" Maya couldn't believe his chauvinistic attitude. Then again, it was kind of hot in a caveman type of way but also shocking for a woman who had grown up with the right to make her own choices. "And how do you think this Amanda will feel about that?"

"Why, she will accept the honor I extend her, of course."

Maya giggled. Lex frowned at her, obviously not seeing the humor, and she laughed even harder. "*Dios*, do you have a lot to learn about human women. I hate to break it to you, but while you are one hot alien, that doesn't mean this Amanda is going to drop everything and run off to be your wife. Women here have something called choices. You can't force us to do anything."

"Are you saying she would refuse me?" The idea seemed to perplex him. "No one mentioned this to me. My mission says I am to find my mate and claim her. There was never any mention that she might not wish to do so. Would you refuse?"

"Possible. Depends." His question flustered Maya and brought, once again, to mind vivid images of her kissing him while he ground his heavy body against hers. Maya flushed and dug her nails into her palm to control her raging hormones.

"It matters not anyhow," said Lex dejectedly. "My mission has failed. With my ship communicator not working, I have no way of locating my intended."

"Are you always so pessimistic?" she said. "We

have something called the Internet and phone directories. Chances are we can still find your lucky winner." And with those words, Maya wanted to shoot herself. *Estupido. Why would I help him when a part of me wants him for myself?*

"You'd help me?" Lex sat up straighter.

"Yeah, I guess I will. First, though, I need some dry clothes then some sleep," she said, hiding a yawn behind a hand. "I worked all night. So let me grab a couple of hours' sleep, and I'll help you find this Amanda person."

"Thank you," he said, standing when she did. Her cheeks blossomed with color, and Lex had to fight an urge to cup her face and kiss her 'til that bloom spread all over her body. Taking a deep breath to dispel his thoughts, he caught an acrid whiff. Sniffing, he realized the smell came from him.

"Do you have cleansing facilities that I might dispel the aroma of that *pool?*" he asked with clear disgust. It still appalled him how they squandered water.

"Sure. Just go through that door," she said, pointing with a finger and stifling another yawn.

Lex, who had no modesty, began stripping as he walked, grinning at her squeak behind him. He could hope only that his intended reacted the same way at the sight of his body. And he hoped she'd be as buxom as Maya. *She certainly has a bosom I'd like to bury my face in.*

Stepping into the tiny room she'd designated for bodily cleansing, he looked around, momentarily at a loss. He saw a small basin with metallic knobs and a mirror seated above it, a hard white seat, which when lifted revealed a hole with liquid in the bottom, and finally a cubicle with more metal knobs.

As he peeked down at his sizable erection, it occurred to him he should take care of his turgid problem before he cleansed himself. He had to do something about the hardness of his member that hadn't really left since he'd regained consciousness with the lovely Maya straddling him, her lips pressed to his.

Bracing one foot on the odd white seat, he wrapped a hand around his cock and slid his hand back and forth along its rigid length. Closing his eyes, he wanted to picture his betrothed with her pale hair and blue eyes, but instead, Maya filled his mind with her wild, curly hair, her energy-filled brown eyes, and her full lips, lips that would look perfect wrapped around his shaft, sucking. Lex held back a groan as he pictured her on her knees, one hand on his prick guiding him in and out of the wet recess of her mouth. He cupped his balls with his other hand as he continued stroking himself, the thought of her cupping him and—dare he even imagine—licking his sac making him tremble and break out in a light sweat. And would he find his pleasure in her mouth or turn her around and bend her over, pushing her plump bottom into the air in the perfect position for him to plunge his cock in and fuck her? With teeth gritted to prevent his shout, he came, his semen shooting across the small room into the upright cubicle.

Spent, Lex shook his head. He should feel guilty finding his pleasure thinking of someone other than his intended, but knowing, once mated, he would never think or be with another female again, he figured he'd best get his lusts out of his system now.

He stepped into the tiled box, anxious to cleanse his sticky body, and fiddled with the metal knobs inside.

At the first freezing blast of water, he let out a very unmanly bellow.

[4]

MAYA DIDN'T EVEN THINK. SHE HEARD HIM YELL and bolted into her bathroom. Upon seeing him, she stopped dead—well, motion-wise, that is. Her body was anything but dead, flushing from the tips of her toes to the top of her head and soaking her panties, barely covered by the T-shirt she'd changed into.

The reason stood in front of her—six feet plus inches of naked, eminently lickable blue skin and muscles that had to be illegal.

Narrowed violet eyes glared at her. "Your bathing cubicle shoots water!" Spoken in clear accusation.

"It's how we wash ourselves," she said, stifling a giggle while trying to keep her eyes above his waist, but curiosity, like gravity, drew them down. *¡Dios mío, he's hung like a god!* Too fascinated by the sight of his large blue cock, she couldn't look away. Hell, she didn't even blush, but desire roared through her, and she licked her lips, wishing she could lick something else.

As if he read her mind—or his shaft did—it lifted in greeting, lengthening and widening in interesting ways.

She heard a soft growl before crushing blue arms wrapped around her and hot lips found hers in a fierce embrace. The kiss from earlier paled in comparison to this one. Molten heat poured through her body, making her limbs sag, but he held her up and molded her against his hard body, his throbbing shaft a pulsing length of steel against her abdomen. Maya moaned in his mouth, and she reached up to clutch at his muscled shoulders. He deepened the kiss, his tongue sliding across the slit of her lips. She parted them, and he immediately slipped his tongue into her mouth, seeking and caressing hers. Fire lit a path through her body. It made her nipples tighten and her pussy throb. She whimpered against his mouth as he ground his pelvis against her. He pressed her back against the bathroom wall and left her lips to trace a line of fire down her neck.

Maya vaguely understood this was wrong. She also knew she should stop this. He had come here for another. She didn't jump into bed with men— even alien ones—she didn't know. But oh, how she wanted to lose herself for a moment and fully taste the passion he unleashed in her. She wanted to taste his silky blue skin. She wanted to feel that marvellously large and curved cock inside of her, pumping. She . . .

Had the phone not rung shrilly and interrupted the most erotic moment of her life, she would have fucked him. Forget the reasons why she shouldn't. She would have let him pound into her willing flesh 'til she screamed with the ecstasy his kisses promised. But reality in the form of a ringing phone intruded, as did her self-respect, albeit a tad late.

She tore her mouth from his and pushed at him. With obvious reluctance, he let her go and stepped back. Weak-kneed, she staggered out of the room to answer the phone, and to her disappointment, he didn't stop her.

LEX, breathing heavily and painfully aroused—again—watched her answer a communication device. Had they not been interrupted, he would have taken her like a rutting beast against the wall. He still wanted to, and judging by her flushed cheeks and the nipples that jutted prominently through the cloth of her shirt, so did she.

Raking his hand through his hair, he turned

back to the cubicle and stepped back in. He needed to find his famous discipline and control. With no other choice, he swallowed his shock over the earthlings' use of water for cleansing and turned the metal knobs, this time expecting the frigid liquid that hit his fevered body. The coldness of the water cleansed his body and helped ease his tumultuous erection, but it did nothing for his turbulent thoughts.

How can I want Maya when I am promised to another? He needed to find his mate quickly before he did something foolish—*like take Maya as my mate instead.* A treacherous thought that did not appall him as it should have but, instead, filled him with a deep sense of rightness, and that, once again, enflamed his ardor. He tried to push Maya and her heavy-lidded, passionate face from his mind and replace it with the blonde Amanda, but his mind rebelled and, instead, made him picture Maya sprawled on her back, waiting for him, her curvy thighs spread wide revealing a welcoming, wet sex.

Lex groaned and hit the tiled wall with a fist. *What is this madness? Have I been infected with an earthly virus? I am here to find my mate.* But until he did, his snide mind reminded him that he was technically free to be with whomever he chose. Only once bonded were couples expected to remain monogamous. Treacherous thoughts such as these made him groan, for he saw through them. He wanted to give himself permission to taste the delectable Maya, and more than just her lips. He longed to bury his face between her plump thighs and lap at the nectar he had faintly smelt when she'd responded so feverishly in his arms.

Realizing his thoughts wouldn't stay away from the erotic, he stopped trying. Finding a hard white bar of something that reminded him of the scent of Maya's skin, he cleansed himself, lathering the strange white bar over his body and shuddering uncontrollably when he thought of Maya using the same chunk on her own silky skin. He worked himself quickly again, his hand pumping his cock with sure strokes until he spent himself on the tiles. Finally clean, in body if not mind, he exited the bathroom with one of her towels draped around his waist.

"Bye." Maya put down the communicator device and turned to him. Licking her lips, a move that made the towel twitch, she dropped her eyes and flushed. Her fingers fiddled nervously at the threads of a blanket draped over the couch. "That was my friend Gina. She says the military are combing the streets."

"For me?" he asked, suddenly all business.

"Maybe. They're not saying. But just in case, you need to lie low. My drapes are already drawn, and it won't cause suspicion because everyone knows I work nights. But you're going to have to wait 'til nightfall to go searching for your mate."

"Very well."

"Good night then." Maya moved past him, the musky scent of her arousal still evident, and he turned to watch her rounded ass, peeking from the edge of her shirt as she went to find her bed.

Lex gave the couch a quick glance, immediately perceived it as too short, and followed her. He wandered through a food preparation area into another room. Even in the gloom, he could sense her like a magnet that drew him. Dropping his towel, and tempting the moon spirits, he lay down on the bed beside her. With a squeak, she sat up.

"What are you doing?"

"Sleeping."

He could tell she wanted to argue—the tenseness of her body said it all—but instead, she sighed.

"Whatever. Just don't hog the bed." She turned onto her side and ignored him. Exhausted, she soon slept, but Lex lay for a long time beside her, unable to stop his hand from softly stroking her cheek and hair.

Ancestors, why could you not have chosen Maya as my mate? He'd have happily fulfilled his mission already —more than once.

"SIR, WE'VE FOUND SOMETHING."

General Beckworth strode across the concrete deck to the edge of the pool, where a scuba diver clung to the side and held up a tiny object.

"What is it?" he asked squatting down to squint at the blob the diver held out in a gloved hand.

"Possible electronic device, sir."

"Can we tell who designed it?" The real question—was it of human or alien origin?

"We'll have to get it back to the lab to take it apart, sir."

"Do it." Immediately the evidence was bagged, tagged, and taken away for a prompt analysis. The military, unlike other legal agencies, had the means and resources for immediate action in these types of matters.

The general surveyed the milling personnel who flocked all over the outdoor swimming area for the hotel the dogs had led them to. Inside, even more staff had the daunting task of questioning all the hotel's guests and employees, so far to no avail. No one had seen or heard anything—yet.

Wands measuring all kinds of atmospheric and physical traces were being waved in a beeping cacophony all over the place. But the general didn't need their data, or even the object found in the pool, to know another one of those female-stealing blue aliens had returned.

The general still well remembered the last incident. The woman-stealing bastard had almost taken off with his daughter's best friend. If Amanda hadn't arrived in time and disabled the brute, he would have absconded with the chit. And instead of thanking them, the little slut had called foul. She still refused to speak to his poor daughter Amanda to this day and claimed they'd cost her the only man she could love. Deluded girl. The medics and psychologists had been unable to pinpoint a reason for the girl's affections for the alien being, but the general knew—alien mind control. It was the only possibility that made sense. It made him glad they'd taken no risks with the one they'd captured. The scientists had creamed themselves in delight when he gave the go-ahead on the live dissection.

This newest appearance, though, of a blue ET disturbed him. Apparently the loss of the one they'd captured and disposed of a few years back hadn't been incentive enough to stop sending the women-stealing aliens. But he had a new plan, one that was sure to get their attention. This time, once they got the ET, they'd keep him alive, just not whole. Perhaps if they sent him back minus a few body parts, the blue bastards would keep their procreation problems away from the planet Earth. And if not, bring it on. Despite what the White House said, the general was ready for—make that eagerly awaited—an alien invasion.

[5]

MAYA WOKE TO HARDNESS—THROBBING, DECADENT,
moisture-pooling hardness.

¡Dios mío! She lay sprawled across the alien's
chest like some plump, slutty blanket, and instead
of jumping off like a good little girl, she snuggled
closer.

In her twenty-six years, she'd only rarely slept
with men. Her work hours made it hard to date,
and her plump size, while garnering male attention,
always seemed to be of the temporary kind. Maya
preferred the men in the books she read, strong
men who took a woman and cherished her forever.
Would Lex be that type of man? From what she'd
experienced, he'd be a giving lover, a thought that
made her flush. Either way, it didn't matter. He
hadn't come to Earth for her.

Sighing, she made to move away, but thick arms

wrapped around her like steel cord, and a husky voice said, "Stay."

Her heart fluttered, and the throbbing between her legs intensified, naughtily so. "I shouldn't." But oh how she wanted to, and honestly, she couldn't really think of a reason not to. Screw her heart. Screw the mate he'd come for. Her body wanted him—now.

"Neither should I, but I'd say we both need this."

She wanted to ask what they needed, but she found herself rolled onto her back, his heavy weight settling between her legs. She gasped when he pressed his evident erection against the damp crotch of her panties, making her pussy clench in arousal. His eyes, alight with what she had begun realizing was desire, gazed into hers intently. Maya ran her tongue over her lips. He watched her avidly then swooped to claim her moistened lips. Frantically, they meshed lips and tongues, panting into each other. But they both wanted more.

Sure hands stripped her shirt from her before she could protest, and when his lips latched around her already erect nipple, she opened her mouth, only to moan. Swirling his tongue around the tip, he inhaled it into his mouth, sucking her soft flesh. Maya shuddered with longing, and liquid pooled between her thighs. She clutched at his short hair as he switched his mouth to her other breast, his molten touch making her shiver all over. Strong hands gripped her tits and pushed them together, a move that brought her nipples side by side, and he used this new position to quickly flick his tongue and mouth from one nub to the other.

"More," she panted, the pulsing between her legs like a frantic heartbeat.

Shifting his body to the side, his long fingers found the edge of her damp panties and pulled them down. The cooler air of the room tickled against her moist nether lips, and she trembled when she felt his fingers stroke her lightly down there. Parting her, he slid a finger in, groaning himself when she tightened her muscles around his digit. As he trailed a line of fire down her belly with his mouth and tongue to the dark curls above her pussy, she quivered in anticipation.

Gone were all thoughts of right and wrong. She couldn't stop him now, and she didn't want to. The pleasure built in her, more overpowering than she'd ever experienced, and she moaned eagerly as she arched her body, impatient for his touch.

Spreading her thighs wide, he pushed her legs up and back and exposed her to his view. She squirmed, blushing at the intimate look he bestowed on her sex.

"So beautiful," he whispered, his eyes meeting hers. She gave a shudder at the glow that emanated from them, a smoky, hot gaze that made her tremble. He smiled at her wickedly before tilting his head and licking her.

Maya cried out. The hot laving of his tongue against her clit spread rapture throughout her whole body. She thrashed and bucked as he licked her thoroughly then sucked her.

"Por favor," she panted as he probed her deeply with his tongue. "Let me taste you too."

He paused in his ministrations to look at her with hooded, smoldering eyes. "Truly?"

She just nodded. He seemed surprised, but she really wanted to taste him. He moved to lay on his back, his cock jutting proudly. "Bring me your sex," he ordered, and she eagerly obeyed.

Dripping with desire, Maya positioned herself over him. His arms wrapped around her thighs, and he feasted on her again, his hot mouth wringing soft cries from her. Distracted by his actions, it took the poking of his shaft on her chin to remind Maya of what she intended to do.

She ran her tongue over the swollen blue head that bobbed in front of her, and she felt more than heard his muffled groan against her nether lips. She ran her wet tongue down the long length of his cock and then back up again. A drop of moisture appeared at the tip, and she swirled her tongue over it, tasting him on her tongue, a sweet flavor unlike any she'd tasted before. Eager for more, she took him into her mouth, a move that made him buck. It seemed her blue alien wasn't as in control as he pretended.

Their sixty-nine position was decadent, their oral play highly arousing. She bobbed her head faster and faster, a speed he reciprocated on her pussy. But it was the addition of his long fingers inside of her, stroking her G-spot as he continued his oral ministrations, that finally made the mounting pleasure in her explode. She screamed, a sound muffled by the thick rod in her mouth, as she orgasmed hard around his fingers. His body went rigid under her, and bellowing her name, Lex came in her mouth, his hot juice sweeter than any cum she'd tasted in the past. She swallowed it all, suctioning his cock 'til she heard him hoarsely say, "Enough. You will kill me with pleasure, earthling."

Trembling still with aftershocks, Maya smiled. *What do you know? Aliens do it better.* And even though she'd just come hard, Maya felt her blood quickening again as an erotic visual of him plunging his cock into her still-throbbing pussy ran through her mind.

As if Lex read her dirty thoughts, his shaft twitched, and he groaned.

Nice to see I have the same effect on him, she thought with a satisfied inner smile.

But then she reminded herself he wasn't hers to keep, and with a scowl, she rolled off of him.

LEX WATCHED with hooded eyes as Maya covered her delectable curves, her face expressionless, even as her slamming of drawers indicated ire.

Didn't she enjoy my touch? Actually, he knew she had. The taste of her—ambrosia, for sure—still lingered on his tongue. Why her displeasure then?

Fabric came flying at him and hit him in the face, along with a terse, "Get dressed."

Confused by the earthling's reaction, and even more by his—*I want her back in bed, naked*—he dressed in the odd clothing she'd given him. The shirt, with short sleeves, stretched tight across his shoulders and featured a faded picture of a rainbow. A pair of short pants that left his legs bare completed the makeshift outfit, and thus attired, he went looking for her out in her main living area.

He found her in the food preparation area banging around, and he approached tentatively and slowly like one would with a ready-to-bolt Jelaxian mount.

"May I inquire as to your apparent anger?"

Flashing dark eyes faced him. "You."

"Me?"

"I don't fall into bed with strangers. Actually, I don't bring them home either." *Slam.* She tossed raw ingredients into a round, shallow bowl that sported a handle.

Lex muddled through her words, not understanding completely but able to guess. "You are angry that we found pleasure with each other? Does your society frown upon sexual intercourse between unattached adults?"

Her mouth dropped open, and she shook her head. "No, sex isn't the problem."

"Then I do not understand. Did I not perform adequately?"

Maya blushed. "You know you did. But it can't happen again. You came here for your mate, remember? I don't think she'd like finding out that you banged me while you searched for her. I know I wouldn't." She said the last under her breath, but Lex heard her, and despite all his justifications, he knew she was right.

Sighing, he ran a hand through his short hair. "I apologize for my actions. You are correct, and I have no excuse for my lack of control. I will endeavor to act respectfully from here on in out of consideration for my future mate."

Lex could have sworn he saw a flash of pain in her eyes, but it left as quickly as it came, and with a stiff nod, Maya finished whatever she did in her food preparation area and handed him a plate with steaming food.

They ate in silence, Lex too fascinated by the concept of food cooked and created from raw ingredients and enthralled by the taste to do any more than eat. On his planet, only the finest restaurants and naturalists cooked in that method. Everyone else used a food replicator from the culinary series. The newest one, the Culinary 6000, boasted over one million dishes.

At the completion of their meal, Maya washed the dishes using—*wince*—water. Lex still had a hard time adapting himself to the way these earthlings used and treated water so casually. He also learned another lesson. Dishes that were washed must be dried, a job she relegated to him by flinging a worn towel at his face.

The chore quickly done, Maya moved back to the living room area and opened an odd rectangular contraption. The screen on it lit up, and she tapped a series of commands.

Interested in this piece of technology, Lex sat beside her on the couch, only too aware of her body next to his. A part of him wanted to grab her up into his arms, take her back to her bedroom, and join his body to hers in a way that would leave them both sated, but her words from earlier echoed in his mind.

I am here for another. I must concentrate on my mission and not allow Maya and her delicious body to distract me. Now if only his rock-hard cock would listen.

"Amanda Beckworth," Maya muttered. "Where are you?" She typed furiously and, with an "Aha!", pulled up a screen with the same picture the computer on his ship had found.

The non-smiling face of his intended stared at them from the screen, and Lex tried to find the sense of connection—and lust—that Maya provoked in him. Nothing, not even vague interest, stirred him.

"She's pretty," said Maya, sounding dejected.

"She's too pale," said Lex, without even thinking of curbing his tongue.

Maya looked startled at his statement, but looking at the pale white skin of the mate his ancestors had chosen, Lex couldn't help wishing that Amanda's skin was a soft tan color like Maya's, a color that reminded him of a decadent treat called caramel that Kor's human mate, Diana, had introduced him to. Caramel Maya—Lex hardened painfully as he remembered her sweetness, and oh, how he longed for another taste.

Maya kept typing away and let out an exclamation, unaware of his erotic thoughts. "*Mierdo*!"

"What?" said Lex, looking at her screen but unable to read the gibberish characters.

"Don't your ancestors like you?"

Lex was beginning to wonder the same thing. "Why? Is there a problem?"

"They selected none other than a military liaison for your mate, the daughter of a general, no less."

"That is not a good thing?" he said, not fully grasping the issue.

"If the military is after you, then no, that's not good. If she decides to reject your suit, she could turn you in. Lucky for you, she lives off base."

"You think she might refuse?" Lex couldn't help feeling elation at the thought of avoiding the trap—yes, that was how it felt, he realized—that his ancestors had set. Perhaps they had erred, a blasphemous idea, yet one that he clutched at.

"She might not be too eager to leave her life behind to go become some dutiful housewife."

"Would you?" The question popped out unbidden, but now voiced, he leaned forward and watched her, waiting for an answer.

"I would love an excuse to leave this place. I don't suppose you've got a brother or a buddy who's also looking for a mate?"

Her words said jokingly enveloped him in a rage whose cause he couldn't understand. Why would the thought of her mating with another bother him? But the urge to hit something—say the male who dared touch her—nearly made him boil over. And for the first time, he truly understood her words from earlier. *Is this how she feels when she thinks of me mating with another? This . . . this jealousy that I never knew could apply to one of the opposite sex?* No wonder she'd seemed annoyed.

Closing her handheld computer, Maya stood up

and headed to her sleeping quarters. "I'm going to get dressed and run some errands. I want to see if I can find you some clothes that fit better, and I'll take a drive around the neighborhood where your Amanda lives."

Lex remained on the couch lost in his thoughts. *But I don't want Amanda. The question is, do I have the courage to reject tradition and the wishes of my ancestors?*

Could he be so selfish as to put his foolish desires ahead of those of his race and their need to rebuild their population?

Lex sighed, not liking the answer.

6

THE STREETS CRAWLED WITH MILITARY JEEPS AND personnel. Maya, entering the thrift shop where she did most of her shopping, greeted the owner, whom she knew well.

"What's up with the soldiers?" she asked, glancing out the front window.

"Aliens," said a gleeful Marco. "The military isn't saying, of course, but my cousin whose sister is married to the brother of the assistant to the base commander says they tracked the alien to town."

Maya didn't try to follow the convoluted family connection the news came from, but the chill from his words, though, made her ask, "Do they know where he is?"

"Nah, the dogs lost his trail apparently. They haven't started a door-to-door search, but it's coming."

"Would you turn an alien over if you found one?" Maya asked casually as she browsed through the bins.

"Never. Knowing what the military would probably do, that would just be asking for an intergalactic war."

Maya smiled. She remembered many a night by the glowing embers of a campfire listening to Marco and her parents discussing the military and their probably violent reaction to space invaders. She wished her parents could have lived to meet a real, live alien. *I hope wherever your spirits are that you can see him. You were right. There is life out there.*

Maya finished her shopping quickly, ignoring Marco's raised brows at her choice of dark male clothing. But he rang up her purchases without question, and Maya drove from there, as promised, over to the neighborhood where the unknown Amanda—whom she already hated wholeheartedly —lived.

The streets of this quiet suburban neighborhood appeared clear of the military presence that prevailed in town. But once she saw Amanda's house, it became readily evident that Lex would be insane to try to confront her on her home turf, for not only was her yard gated with a high fence a Beware Dog signed had also been posted. Affairs didn't improve when she noticed a military Jeep in one of the neighboring driveways.

But the choice would be ultimately up to Lex. Which reminded her, she had yet to ask him how, and when, he'd be departing—*grrr*—with his bride.

Maya's hands clenched her steering wheel tightly. She hated that, after such a short time, she'd fallen so hard and quickly for an alien who didn't want her. Well, not forever anyway. He'd proven quite passionately that he wanted her body. Maya squirmed in her seat. *Was I hasty in telling him no more naughty stuff? I mean, it's not like he's actually dating or hooked up with this woman yet. She doesn't even know he exists, so is it really cheating?* Maya hated that her mind kept justifying and looking for excuses to seduce him. She already had an idea her heart would hurt when he did finally snag his mate and leave.

And she didn't like it one bit.

———

Maya had left hours ago, and Lex began worrying. What if the enemies who'd chased him had captured her? She could be in danger. Hurt. Or walking through the door with a grim look.

Quick strides brought him to her side, where he enveloped her in a crushing hug before he shook her.

"What took you so long? I was worried about you. Are you injured?"

Looking bemused, Maya just gazed up at him, the longing clear in her eyes.

Lex gave in without a fight and raised her higher for a kiss. She returned his embrace for a moment before pushing away.

"Hi," she said breathlessly. "As you can see, I'm fine, so you can put me down now."

Lex wanted to protest but clenched his jaw instead as he let her feet touch the floor. Maya avoided his eyes and moved past him into the living area. Crinkling sounded, and once again, flying material hit him. Apparently she had a penchant for throwing things.

He perused the clothing she'd brought him, dark pants of a strange material, a dark shirt, and a scrap of material for the groin similar to what she'd worn.

"Thank you."

"No problem. You did stay out of sight, right? The military is crawling all over downtown. They're not really saying what they're looking for, but the rumor mill has been busy. The one I liked most was the one saying you were an eight-foot green lizard man here to devour our virgins."

Lex chuckled. "You jest?"

Maya smiled and shook her head, her brown curls bouncing. "It's better than the one that says you're actually a cyborg set to blow up during the balloon festival."

What strange ideas these humans had. "And my mate?" Lex had to force the words out, and he could have kicked himself when he saw the slight wince on her face.

"Her place is pretty tight. At least one dog, maybe more, and she's got at least one military neighbor, but I'd guess with the base being so close, there's probably more. I wouldn't recommend hitting her place 'til real late. If she screams when she sees you, there's no telling what will happen."

Lex, at this point, would have preferred to never encounter this Amanda person, but the needs of his planet had to come before his own.

"So what would you suggest we do?" he asked, knowing he still needed Maya's help, this strange world being more than he could handle on his own.

"Nothing right now. I've got to get to work before they fire my ass."

Work? Lex puzzled over this. He'd noticed Maya lived on her own without male family members to care for her, but the idea that they also made their women work shocked him. The females on his planet held some positions, but the majority preferred the role of mate and mother.

Maya emerged wearing the same outfit as the previous day, a white blouse and skirt. Her hair had been pulled back tightly and fastened to her head.

"When will you return?"

She kept avoiding his eyes and sighed when she

replied. "I'll try and cut out early. Fake a tummy illness or something. We'll go and visit your fiancée once I get home."

And with those words, she left, but her presence remained and refused leave his mind. He tried lying down on her bed, but her scent clung to the sheets, and before he knew it, he had his cock in his hand, stroking it. He slid his hand up and down his dick, harder than steel already, remembering the way her scalding, wet mouth had suctioned him. He'd only wished he could have seen her, watched those luscious lips sliding back and forth. He would have laced his fingers in her hair and guided her in a rhythm. Lex's breathing hitched as he pumped himself faster, the fantasy playing out in his mind too erotic to resist. He remembered the way she'd swallowed his semen, draining him and enjoying it. Lex reached for something to shoot his cum into, and his fingers found the scrap of material that had covered her cunt. He brought it to his face and sniffed. The musky scent of her arousal still perfumed them. *By all the moons, she tasted so sweet.* He wrapped the fabric around his cock and continued stroking, now picturing her on her back again with her beautiful pink sex exposed, her lips glistening and her clit swollen. He thought of sliding his cock into that moist haven, and with a shout, he came hard into the cloth.

Lex couldn't believe he'd come again. What

earthling sickness was he afflicted with that, even when she was not there, he could not stop thinking of her? Wanting her?

Lex groaned. *Ancestors, help me.*

But no one answered, and she continued to fill his thoughts—and his cock.

7

Maya walked into absolute chaos. Military personnel swarmed all over the hotel, and her stomach tightened in fear. Somehow they'd figured out Lex had been here. She made her way to the employee locker room, where staff buzzed.

". . . doing a room-by-room search."

". . . saw them with a Geiger counter . . ."

The words flowed over her, and Maya pasted a smile of interest on her face, all the while thanking the fact that she'd shown up for work. Calling in sick today would have instantly put her in the spotlight.

But she wasn't out of the woods yet.

Andre, the night manager, walked in and clapped his hands, quieting the clamor. "You may have noticed that the military are here. They are seeking someone who they believe was last seen at our hotel."

Murmurs sounded, but Andre clapped his hands hard, and the room silenced again. "All who were on duty last night are wanted for individual questioning. Your cooperation is expected."

And with that, the cacophony started up again, and Maya rubbed sweating palms on her linen skirt. *¡Dios mío! I'd better lie convincingly, or Lex will have worse problems than trying to meet a possibly reluctant mate.* Visions of scalpels and various supposed alien autopsies her parents had studied flashed in her mind, and Maya winced.

I won't let them catch him.

She found waiting hard, even more so considering everyone just wanted to talk about one thing —the alien. The only problem with that? None of them had the slightest clue what they were talking about. Maya tried to act normal. She listened, nodded, or exclaimed in the right spots. She crossed herself several times, but still she was almost glad when her time arrived and they called her name. She walked behind the gun-toting soldier into the hotel suite the military had taken over then almost stumbled when she saw who waited to question her.

"I'm Lieutenant Beckworth," said the blonde, who looked even cuter and perkier in person.

Maya, feeling big and ungainly in front of this

slim, graceful woman, slumped into the chair set in the middle of the room.

Shuffling some notes with smooth hands that had obviously never worn rubber gloves for eight hours straight, Lieutenant Beckworth surveyed Maya with unfriendly blue eyes. "You are Maya Romero?"

"Sí, señorita."

"You are to address me as lieutenant or ma'am."

Gritting her teeth, Maya tried to not let the rebuke sting. It wasn't the woman's fault Maya took an instant dislike to her.

Maya answered the basic questions posed of her —date of birth, place of residence, occupation, and then they got to the crux of the meeting.

"You were on duty until five a.m. according to the time card?"

Maya just nodded.

"Did you see anyone or anything out of the ordinary?"

Hmm, like a big blue alien? "No, ma'am."

"Do you drive?"

Maya nodded, trying to avoid speaking as much as possible, not wanting to expose her nervousness to this sharp-eyed questioner. *And to think Lex wants to mate with her. Ai, she looks more like the type to wear his cojones around her neck as a prize. I don't see her going willingly with him, or any man. Dios, but she's a cold one.*

"You park your car on the other side of the swimming pool area, do you not?"

"Sí." A bead of sweat rolled down Maya's spine.

Cool blue eyes stared into hers, and it took all of Maya's willpower not to squirm under that scrutiny. "Did you take your usual shortcut through the gate yesterday?"

How did she know? Maya debated lying, but this woman obviously had information. Maya needed to tread very carefully.

"Sí, I did, señorita, I mean Lieutenant. But it was very dark outside. I did not see anything."

Pale, perfectly manicured fingers tapped against the sheaf of paper in her lap. "Did you hear anything?"

Maya smiled eagerly, and the lieutenant leaned forward. "Yes. I heard dogs. They were barking a lot."

Lex's intended mate questioned her for several minutes more, but Maya stuck to her story. Finally the interview came to an end, and Maya, on impulse, asked a question of her own. "I hear you're looking for an alien. A big lizard one," she threw in for good measure. "What will you do if you find him?" asked Maya.

Lieutenant Beckworth smiled, a tight-lipped smile that didn't reach her eyes, and that chilled Maya to the core. "Nobody ever said anything about an alien, but if such a thing were found, it would be apprehended and kept in government custody."

"Even if they came in peace?"

"Beings who come in peace don't hide like criminals. Now if you don't mind, I don't have time to gossip about baseless rumors. Please tell the officer outside to escort your next co-worker in."

Maya scooted out before her tongue got her in trouble. Mind, it was nothing compared to the trouble Lex would have. Somehow Maya didn't get the impression Lieutenant Beckworth would be agreeable to becoming Lex's mate. But if she told Lex that, would he believe her or accuse her of being jealous and trying to sabotage something he obviously wanted?

Maya still didn't know what to do when Andre told her to take the rest of the night and next few days off. The military had kicked out all the guests after rigorously questioning them, and there was no telling when they'd decamp.

That suited Maya fine. She had one big blue alien to help.

But it seemed like forces were working against her, for a mile and a half or so from her house, her car, that rusted piece of *mierdo*, died with a choke and a rattle.

Maya leaned her forehead on the steering wheel and cursed colorfully in Spanish for a few minutes. Of all the times for her car to die, this had to be the worst. However, sitting here and moaning over it would get her nowhere. Sighing, she grabbed her bag, and leaving the keys in the ignition in the hopes someone would steal the damn thing, she began walking by the faint illumination of the small houses that lined the road.

When the first thug in ripped jeans stepped out in front of her, Maya wasn't worried. She had a can of mace clutched in the hand that hid in her purse. But the rancid, unwashed smell signalling the presence of the second guy behind him... well, that wasn't so good.

Where is a hero when you need one?

LEX WAS BORED out of his mind. He'd finally stopped masturbating—not an easy task. Through trial and error, he'd figured out how to turn on the vid screen, but the odd programming confused him. Who was this Seinfeld, and why did everyone find him so amusing?

He paced the confines of Maya's home waiting for her to come back, and it was while he walked back and forth that the uneasiness set in, a niggling feeling that something was amiss. Lex tried to ignore it—leaving the safety of her home would be unwise—but the lingering sense of wrongness—*Maya is in danger!*—grew. Unable to take it anymore, Lex cursed and looked for something to disguise himself. He found, buried in a closet, a hat with a brim on one side. Placing the strange hat on his head and pulling the narrow brim low over his eyes, he left the confines of her house.

Thick darkness blanketed the road and surrounding houses. Lex thanked the clouds that covered the moon, only a night away from its fullness and the end to his mission one way or another. He scanned the darkness, unsure of which way to go.

A faint cry sounded, and Lex took off running. He didn't question his instinct, nor did he care who saw him. Maya faced danger. She needed him, and he would not fail her.

His long-legged stride soon brought him in sight of a struggling trio, the gleaming white of Maya's clothing a beacon in the darkness.

Bellowing in rage when he saw her struck and pushed to her knees, he added a burst of speed and, with a soaring leap, tackled the assailant who dared touch Maya.

They hit the ground hard, but Lex barely noticed the impact, his fist already drawing back and then connecting with a satisfying crunch. The body under him went limp. Lex jumped up, the blood rushing through his body as he breathed heavily through his nose and regarded the other attacker, who had foolishly remained and balanced a puny excuse for a knife in one hand.

Lex grinned, not a nice smile for sure, and he saw the idiot with the knife freeze for a moment then, even more stupidly, advance. Lex beckoned him on, the rage coursing through him needing an outlet.

Maya gasped behind him, but Lex was busy. His hands moved lightning fast as he blocked and evaded the knife-wielding miscreant. Lex had been taught by the best, and with a grab of the foul-smelling human's arm and a twist, he had him on his knees. The sound of a knife clattering became the only sound other than their harsh breathing.

Movement beside him made him turn his head, and he saw Maya come to stand next to him. She placed a hand on his arm. "Are you okay?" she asked, concern in her brown eyes.

"Me?" Lex twisted the arm of the thug he still held and made him cry out. "Are you? I saw these villains attack you. Shall I kill them for you?"

Maya's eyes widened. "Uh, no. That won't be necessary. Thank you, Lex."

Her soft words did strange things to him, but one need rose above the rest. Letting go of the downed human, he swept Maya into his arms and, with a long stride, carried her back to her house.

Her laughter sounded. "I can walk, Lex."

"Quiet, woman," he growled. Lex wasn't

working on logic anymore but pure emotion. He didn't understand what he felt but knew he needed to hold her close.

Even when they reached her house, he didn't put her down. He kicked the door closed with his foot and kissed her, hard.

Despite that morning's declaration of never touching him again, she responded eagerly and frantically to his embrace. Her wet, sinuous tongue met his in a fiery clash that had him fit to burst in his pants. Turning her and pressing her back up against the wall, he guided her legs around his waist. He continued to plunder her mouth, even as he tugged up her shirt and slid his hands under it to stroke her soft skin.

The skirt she wore hitched around her waist, and her molten core, covered by the barest scrap of material, pulsed against him. Lex rubbed his covered erection against it, and she moaned in his mouth.

"Tell me what you want," he said in a husky voice.

"You. I want you inside me. *Por favor.*"

Her "please" at the end almost tore away what was left of his control. Using one hand, he tore the impeding fabric from her crotch and pressed his hand against the moistness of her desire. She mewled in his arms, her fingers clutching tightly at his shoulders. He slid his fingers inside her wetness and stroked her, finding that sensitive spot and rubbing it. She keened and wiggled in his grip as her pleasure built.

"Don't stop," she gasped. But he did, pulling his fingers out of her moist sex. She wailed and pressed herself against him, her passion a thing of beauty to behold.

Fumbling with the button to the pants he wore, he freed his erection, its hard length popping out and slapping against her cunt.

Maya cried out and gyrated her hips. He wrapped an arm around her waist securely and used his other hand to guide himself into her.

He almost came at the contact. Wet, tight, and oh so hot, her channel wrapped around his shaft snugly. By the silvery moons, she fit him perfectly. Placing both hands just under her buttocks, he moved her back and forth on his cock. She whimpered, her head thrown back as she undulated against him in wild abandon. He claimed her lips, his hips pistoning faster, a speed she welcomed with clenching muscles.

When she cried out his name and her pussy convulsed around his rod, Lex could hold on no longer. He poured himself into her, digging his fingers into her plump ass cheeks.

Spent, he stumbled, still holding her, to the couch, where he collapsed with her on his lap. She snuggled into his chest, and Lex stroked her hair.

Sadness tinged the moment, for no matter how wonderful and shattering the moment they'd just shared, Lex still had to do his damned duty.

"I wish they'd chosen you for my mate," he whispered against her hair, the wet tears that soaked his shirt making him angry at the tradition that not so long ago he had held so dear.

How could the Oracle have chosen so wrong? And why can I not, for once in my life, forget protocol and follow what I know is right?

[8]

Maya couldn't help the tears—stupid girly emotions. However, she just didn't understand. If he wanted her, then why couldn't he have her? "Aren't you allowed a say in who you choose to spend your life with?"

He continued to stroke her hair and sighed. "I guess it might seem strange to a society that doesn't deal in arranged bondings. But there is a reason for the way we do things. Would you care for a history lesson so that you can better understand?"

"*Por favor*," she said, needing a reason as to why that, even with the strong connection between them, he could not buck tradition.

"The planet I come from is called Xaanda. It is larger than your planet, with two suns and three moons. We've been space-farers for quite some time now, and our explorations brought us in contact with a planet of beings who thought to conquer us. They released a deadly virus on our world, one that killed almost all of our females, and many of those that survived ended up barren. Our numbers dwindled drastically, especially after we took our revenge, our race heading toward sure extinction, for we did not have enough women left to mate with, not to mention the violence and fighting that went on over who would breed with the survivors."

Maya listened in horrified fascination. The concept of killing on that kind of scale shocked her, and yet, look at Lex. He had warrior written over every inch of him.

Lex continued. "The Oracle, the wisest being in the universe, or so we believe, made a proclamation. She claimed the spirits of our departed clan members had offered to help us rebuild our society by going forth into the galaxy and finding us suitable alien mates. The mates they chose would be a perfect match in temperament and physical bearing to ensure successful mating and, in turn, procreation of our species."

"But how could they know if you'd love who they chose?" she interrupted.

"Love?" Lex sounded puzzled. "I've heard of this term, which translates to a very strong affection for one person. But in my world, affection has nothing to do with bonding. Males and females mate so as to reproduce and provide our society with healthy Xamians."

"Then you don't know what you're missing out on," she mumbled. Louder she said, "So, you let some long-dead ghost decide who you should spend your life with?"

"Yes."

"And what if you hate that person, or they hate you?"

Lex didn't answer immediately. "I don't know. I've never heard of it happening before. I know, occasionally, an alien chosen for bonding will fight against her destiny, but in the end, once the first child is born, they all seem to come around."

He spoke of marrying someone so clinically, coldly. It appalled her that they entrusted their future and happiness to someone else's, make that a ghost's, suggestion. Maya didn't like it. Of course, that could have to do with the fact that they hadn't chosen her. She loved Lex and . . .

¡Dios mío! When had that happened? It made no sense. He didn't want her. She barely knew him, but in spite of that, Maya couldn't imagine a life without him. And yet, she was about to help him get the other woman.

"So, even though you are not sure of their choice, you will obey?"

He turned her on his lap to face him, his fingers stroking the tears that ran down her cheeks. Lightly he kissed her. "It's my people, Maya. What I feel with you . . . I can't describe how it feels, but my duty must come first. I am so sorry. If I had any other choice—"

Maya couldn't listen anymore, her heart cracking. "I need a shower."

She left him sitting looking dejected and shut herself in the bathroom, the tears falling unchecked. The hot water didn't erase her unhappiness.

How can I ask him to betray his people? To forgo his honor? He's trying to be noble, a trait you never see anymore. I need to respect that, even if I don't like it.

The thought of what she had to do next didn't make her happy. But there was one thing she could do for herself before she handed the alien she loved on a platter to another woman.

Walking back out into the living room, where Lex still sat, she made a small sound. When he turned to look, she dropped her towel and said, "I know you have to do your duty by your people, but please, make love to me one more time."

AT HER WORDS, Lex lost his ability to breathe. If Lex could have had his way, he'd have worshipped Maya's body for the rest of his life. And much as he feared it would hurt him to remember later, he couldn't deny her last request, not when he wanted it too.

She looked like an absolute goddess standing there, naked, curvy, and, for the moment, his. He stripped out of his clothes, glad he'd washed himself in her food preparing area while she cleansed herself in the cubicle. He swept her into his arms, her soft nude form enflaming his lust as he carried her into her sleeping quarters. Laying her down on the bed, he covered her lush body with his. Scorching kisses led to roaming hands. He cupped and squeezed the fullness of her breasts, enjoying her pants of pleasure as he teased her nipples with his lips and teeth.

"Suck them," she begged when he blew on them, teasing her.

He did as she pleaded and sucked on her tender flesh as she writhed under him. Even as he feasted on her hard berries, he slid his hand down and found the apex of her thighs. He parted her slick folds and delved between. A low grunt escaped him when her juices coated his probing digits. *She's so wet for me.* He slid two fingers in and pumped her as he nibbled on her nipple. She ripped at his hair, keening.

Her reaction to his touch was both wild and gratifying. Lex suddenly found himself parched for a taste of her. He slid down her body, trailing soft kisses over her rounded belly. He nuzzled her silky curls, teasing her. He loved the way she bucked and arched for him. He bypassed her molten core and nibbled her tanned thighs. The tantalizing scent of her arousal surrounded him like an erotic perfume.

"Lick me," she whimpered.

Unable to resist any longer, he latched his mouth onto her sex. And oh, the scream she let out as she came instantly for him, her muscles spasming as he stroked her clit with his tongue while fucking her with his fingers. He kept working her even as she came, her nectar gushing sweetly into his mouth. He built her up again using his tongue and pumping fingers. When he felt her body poised on the verge of another orgasm, he knelt between her legs and grabbed her thighs, pushing them up high.

"Look at me," he ordered gruffly.

Maya opened her passion-glazed eyes, and Lex groaned at the emotion he saw blazing in her face. Holding her gaze, he slid into her tight sheath and paused to enjoy the pleasure of being held so snugly inside her. She moaned and bit her lip as he moved slowly in her, pushing his length to the hilt inside her and then swirling it, a motion that made her cry out each time, and through it all, her eyes never left his.

Holding her legs up, he plowed into her velvety wetness, his cock thicker and harder than he'd ever imagined. He filled her up, loving how she took every inch, her body clenching sweetly around him.

Faster he moved, his gaze locked to hers, and so he saw when the rapture hit her and she screamed, "*¡Dios mío*, Lex!"

Lost in the bliss, she finally closed her eyes as her pussy quivered in waves that wouldn't stop. Lex couldn't hold it any longer. A last mighty thrust inside her and he came, his whole body shuddering with the intensity. He collapsed on top of her, and her arms came up to curl around him. And his heart, an organ he'd never thought of or felt before, tore in half when she said, "I love you."

9

THEY MADE LOVE THE REST OF THE NIGHT, NOT speaking of what had to be done. Instead, they joined their bodies, time and again, as if trying to make up for a lifetime of lovemaking they would never have.

When the golden fingers of dawn crept through the cracks in the blind, they fell into an exhausted slumber. But when they woke sometime late in the afternoon, they needed to face reality.

"How long do we have before your ship comes back to get you?" she asked as she cooked them some food.

"Tonight, when the full moon rises, I need to be in the field of gypsum."

Maya closed her eyes and swayed. *So soon. But I wanted more time.* Yet, one more day, or even two, would never be enough. She wanted what she couldn't have. She wanted him forever. And it didn't help that she knew he wanted it too.

If only she were psychic like her great-aunt— may she rest in peace. She'd have called up someone's ancestors and made them change their choice. Which begged the question, what did you threaten ghosts with?

Composing herself while devising means of torturing meddlesome spirits, she kept frying the chicken that would stuff the tortillas she was also making fresh for dinner. This task kept her occupied for a few minutes and brought to mind something he'd said. "How do you know it's the full moon tonight?"

"I'm a moon warrior," he said then dropped a kiss on her exposed nape, startling her and igniting, to her surprise, that fire in her loins again. "We always know what phase the moon is in."

Maya scooted from his distracting embrace and plated the food before it burned. Sitting down to eat, she resumed her previous train of thought. "I hadn't realized we had so little time. I'm sorry."

"For what? It's not your fault I haven't completed my mission. If I cannot claim Amanda before the moon rises, then I will return to my world and admit I failed."

"What will happen to you?" Maya clamped down on the elation that threatened to bubble over at the thought of him not claiming that *puta*. How could she get excited when his failure could mean punishment by his people? Would they kill him? Hurt him? Exile him? Maya knew she couldn't allow that to happen. But how could she ensure he succeeded?

LEX ADMITTED, even if only to himself, that he wanted to fail. He didn't want to mate with this Amanda. In fact, he hoped he couldn't find her or that she protested enough that he could return empty-handed and claim, without lying, that he'd failed to complete his mating mission. Then he'd beg, if he had to, for the option of taking Maya as his mate instead. Tradition be damned. He'd fallen for the earthling emotion of love. What else explained this overpowering desire of his to claim her as his forever more?

But he said nothing of this to Maya, lest he raise false hope, so he only half listened when she mused aloud different ploys for approaching Amanda Beckworth.

"¡*Dios mío*, I have it!" she exclaimed suddenly. "The balloon festival."

"And how will balloons help?" asked Lex, curious at how her mind worked.

"Everyone goes to the festival."

"And if she doesn't?" He'd go home empty-handed—perfect.

"Don't worry. She'll be there," said Maya vehemently.

Lex wanted to tell her not to bother, but while she busily plotted, he thought of what he would say to the Oracle once he returned without his chosen mate. A scary thought, indeed, for it had never happened before.

The hour grew late, and Maya left the room to freshen up and dress. Lex's gut clenched as the hour to leave Earth—make that leave Maya—approached. Just the knowledge that in a few hours he'd be several light-years away made his gut clench. He didn't like the thought of leaving her alone without his protection. He had to find a way to convince the Oracle to change his mission—to give him the mate he wanted.

Maya appeared as he fought despair, and like a ray of sunshine, she drove all thought from his head. She wore a lovely gown that hit just below her knee in a bright red that showcased her curvy figure and shot a bolt of pure lust through him. He had to have her one more time. His glowing eyes must have given away his intent, for she squeaked, "Lex, we don't have time for this."

"Yes, we do," he growled, grabbing her hands and holding them above her head. Her eyes glazed over, even as she protested.

He pulled up the loose skirt of her gown and tugged down her panties—that stupid piece of material kept getting in the way of his questing fingers. When he bonded with her upon his return, he'd burn every pair she owned. He slid his hands between her thighs and found her wet and ready. Turning her, he bent her over the back of the couch and raised her skirt up high, exposing her rounded, caramel cheeks. He released his cock from the confines of his slacks, and it sprang forth, eager and seeking. Positioning himself between Maya's legs, he rubbed the swollen head of his rod against her slit. She moaned and shook her ass at him, a tempting invitation he couldn't resist. Poising his rod at the entrance to her sex, he grabbed a hold of her buttocks and thrust into her. He grunted at the slick, hot feel of her cunt and dug his fingers into her ass, spreading her to better watch his shaft pumping in and out of her welcoming pussy—a beautifully erotic sight that threatened to make him spill too quickly.

"Harder," she panted, pushing back against him in an effort to take him deeper.

Lex complied, slamming himself into her, the tip of his rod rubbing the sweet spot inside and making her keen. He increased his pace as if somehow, if he fucked her hard enough, he'd brand her and make her his. *I don't care what the Oracle or my ancestors say. She is mine!*

Bellowing, he creamed her, his juices milked by her convulsing cunt as she came with him. He stood there for a moment buried inside of her, their two bodies shuddering with aftershocks. He didn't want to leave.

Maya squirmed out from under him.

"Just give me a second to wash up, and I'll call a cab to take us to the festival."

While she cleansed herself, Lex came up with a plan, one he didn't intend to relay to Maya. Essentially, once they got to this festival, he'd give her the slip. He wouldn't even try to find Amanda. He'd just move off into the darkness and make his way to the gypsum fields. He'd memorized the maps she'd shown him, and along with a compass she'd found for him, he felt confident he could find his way. The festival, after all, was very close to the fields already.

His new mission—find his ship, return home, and convince them they'd made a mistake and insist they let him have Maya. If they said yes, great. If they didn't, then he'd come back for her anyways. And when he did, he'd never leave her again. There were many places in the galaxy that they could go and live together. He might have to forsake his duty and honor to his people, but at least he'd have Maya.

A perfect plan, he thought, but he hadn't counted on Maya.

10

Maya hated that she'd kind of lied to Lex. When she'd gone to the bedroom to dress, she'd done one other thing—a sneaky thing. She'd called Lieutenant Beckworth, a conversation that left her with an icy feeling of dread.

She'd whispered as she dialed the hotel and asked the stranger who answered to pass her to the lieutenant. She'd almost hung up when Amanda came on the line with a brusque, "Who is this?"

But telling herself she had to do this for Lex, she replied, "It's Maya Romero."

"The maid." Lieutenant Beckworth's tone took on a softer tone. "You have something to tell me?"

The fact that she'd remembered her had taken Maya aback. Swallowing her misgivings, she'd forged ahead. "I have information on the blue one."

An exclamation of surprise sounded but was quickly muffled. Speaking with barely restrained excitement, Amanda said, "Really? Tell me more."

"No, it's—it's not safe here."

"Why don't you come to the hotel then?"

"No, I don't want to be seen talking with you. Meet me at the festival, by the cotton candy stand. And come alone, *por favor*. I only feel comfortable talking to you."

"Of course, Maya. Anything you say. I'll meet you there in an hour," said Amanda in a sweet tone that did nothing to reassure Maya.

She hung up shaking. *Forgive me, Lex. I can see in your eyes that you would betray your people for me. But I won't be responsible for the loss of your honor.*

She just hoped that the secret rendezvous she'd planned for Lex turned out all right. Or had she just gift-wrapped and handed him to the military? What a negative thought, one that she shouldn't even be thinking. She wouldn't let his people exile him, or worse. So taking a deep breath, she'd joined Lex in the living room, only to regret the phone call when he'd made such desperate love to her.

They held hands in the cab all the way to the festival, not speaking a word. She'd found him an old hooded sweatshirt and some shades to help disguise him. The darkness and strobing lights of the games and booths would also help. But just in case . . .

"If someone notices you have blue skin," she told him as they left the safety of the cab, "tell them you're part of the Blue Man Group."

Lex squeezed her hand in reply. They waded through the throngs of people, the cacophony even at this time of night unbelievable. Spotting the cotton candy stand, she craned, looking for anybody who looked military in bearing. The coast seemed clear. Pulling her hand free of his, with a plummeting stomach, she prepared to leave him so he could be with the woman his people had fated for him.

She had a hard time controlling the tears that threatened, so she spoke quickly. "Why don't we split up? You go that way," she said pointing toward the rendezvous point, "and I'll check this way."

She could see the question in his eyes, but she turned and darted through the crowd before he could speak, unable to stay by him any longer as the tears fell unchecked from her eyes.

I love you, Lex. Forgive me, and be happy.

WHEN MAYA ABRUPTLY LEFT HIM, her eyes shiny with tears, Lex had almost gone after her. The same emotional ripping he suffered at their forced separation affected her just as strongly. But at least she'd given him the opening he needed. It was better this way. Now he could just slip away without the painful good-bye he'd feared and without making her promises he couldn't be sure of keeping.

I will come back for you, Maya. I promise.

Lex flowed through the crowd in the direction she'd pointed him in, which coincided with where he was heading anyways. As he came up to a brightly lit stand offering fluffy pastel-colored clouds on a stick, all the air left him in a whoosh as he came face-to-face with none other than his intended mate.

Oh, Maya, what have you done? He knew this had to be her doing, her way of making sure he completed his mission, a mission that he knew, looking down on the petite blonde, he'd have never gone through with, even had he never met Maya. There was no mistaking the look of loathing in the eyes of Amanda Beckworth, nor the disdainful curl of her lip. Nor was there mistaking his instant dislike of the woman his ancestors thought would be perfect for him.

"Well, well, if it isn't the alien himself. We've been looking for you."

Her words confused him until he saw the men in uniforms pushing their way through the crowd to them. Lex began scanning the area around them and barely registered Amanda's next words.

"I'm going to make sure you and the Latina

you've infected are locked away, unable to hurt or convert any other humans."

Lex froze at her words. Was she implying that Maya was in danger? He'd no sooner thought that than he heard Maya's scream.

"Run, Lex!" she cried. "It's a trap."

Not without her, he wasn't. Rage that these humans would mistreat his woman coursed through his body. Shoving Amanda to the side, and not feeling an ounce of regret, for she stood in his way, he charged through the crowd toward the commotion he could see over the tops of the shorter humans' heads.

A snarl emerged when he saw Maya struggling between two soldiers, cursing at them colorfully in Spanish instead of fainting like a normal woman. When one of them backhanded her, Lex lost it completely. The knives he'd brought as a "just in case" came swirling out. Around him people screamed and stampeded away. The soldiers' eyes went wide as saucers as he came at them, blades flashing. Letting go of Maya, they grabbed for their firearms. Too slow.

Lex, in a whirling dance he'd learned as soon as he could walk, incapacitated them with sharp knocks to the backs of their heads. He didn't kill them out of courtesy to Maya, who might not like to see the blood of her fellow earthlings spilled, no matter their violent intent. Their unconscious bodies slumped to the ground just as Maya grabbed him by the arm and tugged at him.

"We've got to go."

"Are you okay?" he asked, following her through the thinning crowd.

"Yes," she panted. "Quick. You've got to get out of here."

Now there was an understatement. Uniformed personnel came pouring from all around, their guns cocked and aimed at them, but not firing—yet.

AMANDA WATCHED GLEEFULLY as the blue alien tried to run with his mind-controlled human slave. They wouldn't go far. The place was surrounded. Her father, the general, would be so proud. Disgusting alien creature. She still couldn't understand why her former best friend and now this simpleminded Latina fell for them. It had to be an alien virus or psychic power of some type. What else could explain their behavior? She certainly felt nothing except disgust for the ET.

Impatient at having to wait, she wished the damned civilians would get out of the way faster. She couldn't give the order for her detachment to shoot the tranqs they were armed with 'til they had a clear shot. Too many witnesses and flashing cameras.

But she wasn't worried. There was nowhere for them to go. Not unless he suddenly sprouted wings. And that was when the universe decided to work against her.

11

Panic fluttered in Maya's chest as she saw the trap closing around them, the ranks of soldiers forming an impenetrable wall. *This is all my fault. I should have known that puta could not be trusted.* She'd made a stupid decision, all in the name of doing what was right, and now she needed to fix it.

Mami and Papi, if you are watching and listening, help me find a way to save him.

She and Lex continued running toward the edge of the festival grounds, where she hoped the row of troops would be thinner, and that was when she saw it, the answer to her prayers. One huge inflated balloon with a basket was tethered and their ticket out of danger. The sign beside it said, "Take your sweetheart for a night flight and show her the stars like she's never seen before." Maya almost laughed, but instead, she dragged Lex toward the balloon.

"The balloon," she panted. "Get into the basket, and cut the ropes."

The crowd had gotten thinner here, and Maya could see the soldiers stopping to take aim.

"Duck," she screamed.

Lex, instead, in a move too quick to see, flashed a silver blade, and with a pinging sound, the missile shot at him went to the side.

Dios, he's like a superhero.

Reaching the balloon, Lex grabbed her and threw her in, jumping in after her. Quickly, he cut all the tether ropes, and the balloon began to rise. Maya stood by the burner and gnawed her lip, trying to remember how to increase the flame. They needed to rise faster. She fiddled with the knobs and stumbled on one that made the flame shoot higher, and with a lurch, they rose faster, but not fast enough.

She could hear the cracking sounds and the whistles as the soldiers fired at them and poked holes in the fabric of their balloon. Even worse, they were drifting, and she had no idea how to steer.

"I'm sorry," she whispered, despair over the impossibility of their situation crashing over her.

Lex, the *idiota*, just grinned at her with gleaming teeth. "Until we are dead, there is always a chance."

Maya wished she shared his optimism.

───────

LEX SAW Maya had reached the end of her endurance, but he, on the other hand, had hope for both of them. The balloon actually worked similarly to the ones he'd used before on a planet that used ballooning as their main source of transportation. He took over the burner, keeping the flame burning high and hot to compensate for the leaking of the hot gases through the tears. They left the sound and lights of the soldiers and festival behind, the shining light of the full moon their only beacon. The wind blew gently and, luckily, in the direction they needed to go.

Maya slipped her arms around him and pressed her face into his back. He wanted to tell her everything would be all right, but they hadn't quite made it out of danger yet, even if, according to his compass, they should be floating over the gypsum fields. A good thing, for the balloon was definitely losing altitude. Now, if only he could find his ship before the military for this planet did.

"Brace yourself," he warned, turning to tuck Maya into his chest so as to protect her from impact when the woven basket hit the ground and skidded in the crystals. Several bumps later, the balloon came to rest, the silken fabric of the balloon collapsing.

He swung Maya over the side then leapt out after her and grabbed her hand. Running would do them no good now. So, tugging her a small distance from the balloon, he stopped and cradled her in his arms, lowering his head for a kiss.

She melted against him, her lips parting under his, but that lasted only a second. "*Dios*, are you crazy? We don't have time for this. You need to find your ship."

"My ship will find me." He hoped. She shivered in his arms as the sounds of baying dogs sounded in the distance, and he hugged her tighter. The moon shone brightly on them, and Lex wondered where in the silvery moons the stupid AI was with his ship.

He'd no sooner thought that than the welcome sound of his craft's engines sounded. Bright lights suddenly came on above them, and a hot wind whipped around them as the spaceship came in for a landing.

Lex smiled at the look of shock on Maya's face. *If she likes that, wait 'til she sees what else my planet, make that the whole galaxy, has to offer.* For she was coming with him. He had no intention of leaving her behind. His orders be damned. Maya was his mate, and he was taking her home.

The hatch opened, and the ramp extended. Lex began walking, but Maya dragged behind and pulled her hand from his. He turned to see her standing with her arms hugging herself.

"Aren't you coming?" he asked, his brow creasing.

"But I'm not your mate," she said, ducking her face.

"I don't care."

His words shocked her, and she looked at him with shining eyes. "But your orders . . . your ancestors. I'm not the one they want you to have."

"Not the one!" Lex almost shouted at her. He strode back to her and grabbed her in his arms and claimed her lips fiercely. "You are coming because I want you with me." Lowering his head, he kissed her again, a sweet embrace that he hoped relayed exactly how he felt.

But when he raised his head, her face remained determined.

"You don't want to come with me?" he asked in a voice tinged with disbelief.

Tears flooded her gaze. "Of course I do, *idiota*, but if you come back with the wrong mate, what will happen to you? I will not be the reason you are punished."

Silly woman. Did she not yet realize that not being with her was the worst punishment anyone could mete out?

Bobbing lights appeared in the distance, along with the sound of baying dogs and growling motors. He'd run out of time to convince and get her to come of her free will. So taking a page from his ancient ancestors, he ignored her protests and, hoisting her up, flung her over his shoulder and jogged to his ship.

She bounced and jiggled as he ran, and he could hear her swearing up a storm behind him as she pummeled him half-heartedly.

"Lex! I will not let you ruin your life for me."

He gave her a smack on her tempting bottom, which made her squeak. "Quiet, woman. I don't care what my orders were. I will have no other, so they'd better accept my choice because I am not changing my mind."

She quieted after that, and when he put her down finally in the cleansing chamber that would decontaminate them, she just looked at him with wide eyes.

"Computer," said Lex, "get us out of here."

"Right away, Captain, and may I say congratulations on completing your mission."

Lex didn't correct the computer. As far as he was concerned, his mission was a complete success. He'd found his mate, and as soon as they both got naked, he intended to make it official.

12

MAYA STOOD FROZEN, AFRAID IF SHE MOVED OR spoke the dream might shatter. Lex wanted her. Not just that, he was taking her into space. She wished she could say she felt bad that he'd failed his people, but a selfish part of her was cheering madly. He'd chosen her!

And now he was getting naked. *¡Dios mío!*

"Take off your clothes, Maya," he said, his blue, muscled body approaching, led by his erect cock.

"But . . ."

"Get naked for me."

His eyes glowed with desire, and Maya shivered. With shaking hands, she tried to undress. Lex let out an impatient sound and, using his strong hands, ripped her dress in half and, in seconds, had her panties gone. Naked before him, coiling heat coursing through her, she licked her lips in anticipation.

He groaned. "Hold that thought. First, we need to do something."

"What?" she asked. They were both naked. What could they possibly need to do first?

"Maya, will you bond with me?"

"I-I will." Screw his mission. He'd made his choice clear. She could do no less, and no matter what happened, at least they'd be together.

"We need to kneel," Lex said, dropping to the floor in front of her. She followed suit, and when he put his hands up, palms facing her, she aped him and placed her hands against his much larger ones. A tingle shot through her, almost like an electrical current.

"Repeat after me," said Lex, his eyes solemn. "My life, my soul, I pledge to thee."

Her throat tight with tears of joy, Maya spoke in a whisper. "My life, my soul, I pledge to thee."

"Forever joined for eternity."

As soon as Maya repeated the words, staring into Lex's beautiful eyes, a jolt hit her. She heard a loud crack, and energy thrummed throughout her being and into Lex and back again, like a completed circuit that joined their souls forever more as one. Maya had the sense of coming home, and the closeness, not to mention love she could feel, overwhelmed her. And made her hornier than she'd ever been.

As if of one mind, they dove onto each other. Hungry lips met and opened wide to allow their tongues to clash. Maya's feverish body met the even hotter skin of her husband, her mate. She groaned at the fiery feel of his cock throbbing against her lower belly. She arched against him, rubbing her hardened nipples onto his chest. Long fingers found her wet slit and toyed with her, using her own juices to moisten her clit for playing. Back and forth, he stroked her as Maya panted into his mouth. She needed him in her now. She pushed him back, and when he didn't immediately comply, she growled, "Lie down."

Immediately, he lay on his back, the two of them past the point of caring that there were probably better places than the floor for coupling. She straddled him, poising her moist pussy just over the head of his cock, teasing him.

"Tell me what you want?" she asked huskily, inserting just the tip of his shaft into her sex. Finally her turn to tease him.

"You, forever."

Lust and love shot through her at his words, and she dropped herself onto him, impaling his whole length with a scream of ecstasy that he echoed. Slowly, she moved on him, rocking back and forth, applying friction to her clit, even as his rigid head pressed against her G-spot inside. His hands clasped her hips, and he helped her as her pleasure built inside her like a tidal wave, higher and higher. He ground her hard against him, and faster. Then he grunted out the words she never thought she'd hear.

"I love you, Maya."

With a keening cry, Maya came, the wave of her orgasm crashing over her in shuddering waves that made her quiver. Bellowing her name, Lex came as well, his hot seed filling her and consummating their alien marriage.

She collapsed on him, breathing hard, but she still managed to say, "You love me?"

Lex chuckled, his chest vibrating under her cheek. "Yes, even though on my world we do not have a word for love. My friend Kor tried to explain it once to me, and I thought he was crazy. Yet, these feelings I have for you, I know not what else they could be. It's as if my whole world revolves around you. I want to keep you happy and safe forever."

"Oh, Lex." Maya's eyes flooded with tears, the beauty of his words moving her. "I love you too!"

She would have said more, but a strange sensation began crawling up her body, and she jumped up, looking to see what the hell it was.

MAYA HOPPED ABOUT, her heavy breasts bouncing,

and Lex grinned as he lay on his back with his hands behind his head. Much as he was enjoying the show, he figured he should explain.

"The AI unit has activated the decontamination and cleansing process."

"What? But . . ." Maya blushed. "It feels . . . naughty."

Lex smiled wider. "Yes, it does." He got to his knees and shuffled over to her as she stood there, her body flushed with arousal. He buried his face in the softness of her belly, but he could smell her need. He stood and pushed her back against the chamber wall, his lips meeting hers in a sweet kiss. He nudged her thighs apart with a foot, and he knew it when she felt the microscopic cleansing on her sex, for her lips parted on a sigh.

Both their bodies clean again, Lex swept her into his arms. He had a comfortable bed he wanted to introduce her to. As he carried them—both naked—to his quarters, she teased him, nibbling on the skin of his neck, enflaming his passions and tempting him to forgo the bed and take her then and there against the wall.

But he restrained himself and dropped her onto a pillowy mattress, where the vixen smiled at him with heavily lidded eyes. She crooked a finger at him and spread her legs, pulling her knees up, exposing herself to him. Lex almost came right then, especially when she licked a finger and touched herself. It was then that he noticed it. Around her wrist, like a piece of ghostly jewelry, she wore the gray spirit band of a mated one. His ancestors must have approved the match. Lex wanted to laugh with sheer joy. Perhaps things would turn out right after all.

He dove onto the bed between Maya's thighs to get an up-close look at her stroking herself, a sight he would surely never tire of.

"Um, I hate to interrupt," said the AI unit, "but the Oracle is on the vid comm waiting to speak to you."

Maya scrambled for the bedcovers while Lex cursed silently at the horrible timing. "You don't need to cover yourself. We are alone on the ship."

"But the voice?"

"Just the computer. I'm sorry. I need to take this vid comm call."

"Will everything be all right?" she asked, worry in her eyes.

"Everything will be fine. Don't finish without me, though," he said ruefully, looking at her flushed face and tousled hair.

Maya smiled seductively and flung the covers off. Eyes riveted to the show she put on with her finger, he dressed quickly in a pair of slacks and a loose shirt. The quicker he spoke to the Oracle, the quicker he'd be back in bed. He gave Maya a light kiss that turned into a scorching one with tongue. The AI interrupted by clearing its imaginary throat, and with a rueful smile to Maya, Lex made his way to the command center to face the Oracle, the one being who had the power to bless or curse his changed choice in mates.

The petite Oracle's veiled face filled the large screen in the command center, and Lex dropped his chin under her gaze, staring at his bare blue feet. Few ever got to speak to or see the Oracle. This didn't bode well.

"Lex'indrios Vel Romannu, did you complete your mission?" said a voice that had started and stopped wars.

"I'm afraid I failed in the mission you sent me on," said Lex, cursing the moment that had come too soon. He'd hoped to have time to prepare his speech detailing the reasons why he'd disobeyed orders.

"Did you collect your mate, Maya?"

"No, I—" Lex looked up in astonishment at the screen. "Wait a second. Did you say Maya?"

The Oracle inclined her head. "Indeed. Maya Romero, your mate. You did do the binding cere-mony, did you not?"

"Yes, but how? I thought . . ." Lex trailed off, flustered.

"Maya was always the one meant for you."

"But why tell me it was Amanda then?" he said,

suddenly angry at all the unnecessary angst he'd gone through.

"Your ancestors and I felt it important that you want Maya for herself and not because you were told she was yours. I've been doing a lot of talking with an earthling mate named Diana here. You should know her. She's Kor's wife. And she said the whole mating process would be easier to accept if both sides felt they were part of the choice. Did you choose Maya? And in return, she, you?"

"Yes, but do you realize the anguish you put us both through?"

"A little hardship makes the feelings only stronger. Congratulations on your mating."

The vid screen went blank, and Lex sat there stunned. *I was always meant to be with Maya.* He knew he should feel angry at the trick that had been played on him, but at the feel of her soft hands on his neck massaging him, and a plump bottom settling on his lap, all he could think was, *Thank the silvery moons she is mine.*

Maya had thrown on a robe before joining him, but he still had easy access to her body, and he used that to his advantage, stroking her soft flesh.

"Lex," she panted, "wait a second. Did I hear the Oracle right? Was I supposed to be your mate all along?"

"Yes," he growled

"Oh," she exclaimed, a sound she repeated

when he pulled up the loose skirt to probe her with a finger and found her wet already. Lex decided to indulge in a fantasy of his.

"Strip," he ordered.

Maya stood and, curving her lips in a sensual smile that sent all his blood rushing to one spot, unfastened her robe and let it slide to the floor. Lex stood and divested his own body of its garments. Freed from his pants, Lex's cock twitched at the sight of her nude, caramel hued body.

He pulled her toward him and cupped her buttocks, lifting her. "Wrap your legs around me." But he needn't have spoken, for, as if she read his mind, she guided his shaft into her sex with a sigh and hugged her legs around him like a vise. Lex groaned at the feel of her silken sheath, but he still didn't quite have her where he wanted her. He walked 'til he had her back leaning on the vid screen that now showed the galaxy they traveled through in all its cosmic glory. Then he fucked her on this vertical bed of stars, his rod plunging into her as her fingers clutched tightly at his shoulders.

When he finally came deep inside her black hole, he closed his eyes and saw the universe explode, a phenomenon he could only find in her loving arms.

EPILOGUE

Maya quivered in anticipation as she set foot on her first alien planet, not the world she'd be living on yet but one Lex insisted she see. It had waving pink grass that tickled her ankles in a sensuous way. The trees in the distance appeared to be purple, and a babbling brook flowed with the colors of a rainbow, a pastel perfect planet made for pleasure.

Twirling around, she caught sight of Lex—her very own alien husband and lover. Smiling at him, she sent out a mental message to her departed parents. *I wish you could have lived to see this, Mami and Papi, and to know you were right. There is other life out there, and it turns out, when it comes to love, we're not so different after all.*

ALIEN MATE 3

[1]

"Congratulations. By decree of the Oracle, I am here to announce that your accomplishments on behalf of your clan and our world have won you the highest honor. You are to be mated."

Stunned, Reg gaped at the message bearer. Panic took root in his stomach and made him feel slightly ill at this unexpected and unwanted turn of events. He wanted to rail against the injustice. Plead for mercy. Then sanity prevailed along with a deep-seated need for self-preservation.

"Never. Not happening. I'd rather get sucked into a black hole." To punctuate his stubborn words, Reg crossed his arms and glared at messenger of bad news on the view screen.

The light blue face of the Oracle's attendant creased in puzzlement. "You are refusing the prestige of being chosen worthy enough to claim a mate?"

"That is correct. I have no interest in shackling myself to a female." By his ancestors, he'd rather die first. Mating would mean no more space exploration and discovery. No more adventures. Binding himself to a female and, in turn, planetside was an abhorrent thought he refused to entertain.

"But—but—" The attendant seemed at a loss for words. "Your ancestors are already seeking your perfect match. No one ever says no. This is supposed to be your reward for all your hard work."

"I am saying no, and if you want to reward me, give me a raise. Now, if that is all, may I return to my current mission?"

Flustered, the servant to the Oracle had opened her mouth, probably to argue again, when suddenly, she disappeared. In her place, the veiled form of the Oracle herself, the spiritual leader for his people—a diminutive female who ruled the various clans with a titanium fist—appeared.

"First class warrior Reg'iantros Vel Veratu, have I heard correctly? Do you refuse the gift we bestow upon you?"

Reg was now the one caught off balance, face to face with the woman who had started and stopped wars. He ducked his head in respect, not daring to look her in the eye, or the veiled area he assumed hid her eyes. "Sorry, Oracle, but the idea of settling down is repugnant to me. I appreciate the gift you would bless me with, but I would prefer to continue as I am."

"I see." Two simple words that held a wealth of meaning—one he didn't understand. The covered head of the Oracle tilted to one side, and when she spoke again, Reg thought he heard mirth in her tone, impossible of course. The Oracle never joked, or so he assumed. "Very well then, we will pass the prestige on to another. Now, before you resume your mission, though, we require you to perform a small task. Nothing too taxing. We need you to divert from your current course and head, instead, to the orbit around the planet known as Earth. The ancestral spirits are asking that we rescue an earthling who is about to be killed by a stray asteroid. The ancestors claim she is excellent Xamian mate material and is to be protected until such time as a lucky male is chosen for her."

Poor sap. Now that he'd slipped the noose of matrimony, Reg felt sorry for others caught in the trap. As to the mission, it seemed simple enough, if odd. "Why do her people not save her themselves?"

"They find themselves in a quandary, as the female in question is in a vessel orbiting their planet and they cannot reach her before the asteroid hits and destroys the habitat in which she currently resides."

"How can they have achieved space travel and

not mastered rudimentary space protection?" asked Reg baffled.

"They've evolved differently than our own people, no matter our physical similarities. Now, will you rescue the woman?"

"Sure, just send me the coordinates." Any excuse to stay in space longer was welcome. Besides, he was curious about the earthling. He'd seen a few from afar on his home planet on his few visits, and they'd appeared exotic to him with their pale, almost pink skin.

"Excellent." The Oracle seemed well pleased with herself, and once again, Reg could have sworn he heard laughter in her voice when she signed off saying, "Good luck with your new mission."

Reg didn't need luck. As a first-class space warrior, he never failed in his duty, and his skills were without compare. Rescuing a female in distress would be simple.

But as he redirected his vessel to the earthling's location, he couldn't shake a sense of foreboding. *Why do I feel like my life is about to change? And worse, why does it seem like I can still hear the Oracle laughing in my mind?*

[2]

"OH FUDGE. I'M GOING TO DIE." EVEN UPSET AS she was, Penelope couldn't swear with real words, her upbringing, with a strong emphasis on manners, too strongly instilled. Her lack of strong vocabulary had made her an object of ridicule among her peers in the space program she'd signed up for, but she'd borne their jokes with gritted teeth and stayed true to herself.

Her breath came fast and hard as panic clawed at her. She dropped her face into her hands, too shocked to cry at the news NASA had just relayed. Sure, when she'd undertaken this quest, she'd understood there were risks and filled out the proper forms, including a will—not that she had much to give or anybody to give it to. *I wonder what they'll do with my collection of glass cats.* What a stupid thing to think of at a time like this. Who cared? She was about to die.

NASA's life-changing words played over and over in her head like some sick joke.

"*...regret to inform you that a small asteroid is headed on a collision course with your pod. Impact is unavoidable and will occur in less than fifteen minutes. We regret that computer simulations give you no chance at survival. Sorry. We've already downloaded all your latest observations so that your work is not lost. Would you care to relay any last words to family and friends?*"

Instead of replying, she'd switched off the communicator. Somehow, she didn't think the crew at Cape Canaveral would appreciate hysterical screaming. Penelope pressed her face up against the porthole window and squinted at the darkness, wondering if she'd even see the small rock coming to blow her into galactic bits. *I wonder if my remains will fall to the ground in a bloody Penelope rain, or will I orbit earth forever in frozen chunks?* Gross thoughts, but she couldn't help the macabre humor. It was that or give in to the hysteria bubbling inside.

And to think I was so proud I'd beaten out everyone else for this job. Hundreds had jumped at the chance to be sent into space to live for one year in a pod alone with only the stars and NASA staff on the intercom for company. They wanted to conduct a study on the effects of space on a person both mentally and physically. And Penelope had won. In a rapid blur, and before she could realize what it really meant, she'd found herself examined, inoculated, and given a crash course on space pod living and repair. Then, wham, she'd found herself weightless in space.

Reality, of course, differed from the simulations. For one, it was much harder to pee without gravity than she'd expected. There had been a few incidents before she re-learned to use the potty without having to clean up floating drops of urine—so gross. And the food, freeze-dried rations, were so unappetizing she would have ended up a skeleton had she been able to exercise without bouncing off the pod's instrument panels.

However, small irritants aside, to her surprise, she discovered she enjoyed the quiet peace of space. Her living quarters were small, most of the habitat space taken up with environmental needs such as air and temperature control, but she survived in her cramped home. She used her time to read and took notes on the experience. She'd written a hundred pages for her thesis already. When she found herself getting lonely, she cheered herself by imagining her name and picture on the front page of all the major science magazines. This was to be a crowning achievement for her and a dream come true. What a nightmare instead.

She'd definitely make the news now though, probably with headlines of "Asteroid Kills Geek

Girl." Pity she wouldn't live long enough to enjoy her fame. Penelope stamped the floor in frustration, and the impact shot her up to bump her head on the ceiling of the pod as she forgot the gravity situation. The light whack didn't actually hurt, but she rubbed her head anyway as tears brimmed. *It's not fair! I don't want to die.*

Agnostic, she didn't believe in a god or religion, but she dropped to her knees—kind of, if you counted bent knees while floating in a gravity-free zone kneeling—and suddenly converted. With her eyes clamped shut and her hands clasped together, she prayed fervently.

"Please God, Yahweh, Aslan, Buddha, or whatever name you prefer, it's me, Penelope. I know we've never talked before probably because, according to science, you don't exist. But if, by chance, research is wrong and you are actually real, I don't suppose you'd find it in your heart, if you have a heart that is, to save me, somehow. I'd be ever so grateful."

"I am here to answer your prayer, earthling. Consider yourself saved."

At the sound of the deep voice behind her and the hand that touched her shoulder, Penelope screamed and, in a very illogical move, especially for her, passed out.

REG STARED at the female in the silvery jumpsuit floating facedown in the barbaric craft and wondered why she'd reacted so strangely.

He spoke aloud, switching back to his mother tongue instead of the crude language earthlings used. "Ralph, is the Earthling ill?"

Alpha 400, the newest AI model for his space-craft—intelligent and imbued of enough person-ality to demand a name—replied via ear transmitter. "I believe you frightened her."

"But I heard her request to be saved. Why would she be scared when I have arrived to grant her wish?"

"My records indicate that females of all species tend to react in unexpected ways, even when given what they've demanded. Now, if I might suggest, you should gather her that we might teleport off her vessel. The asteroid is due to impact in less than five hundred lunar millicycles."

Reg leaned down and turned the female over onto her back. He sucked in a breath. *What a lovely creature.* Her skin was the white of the snows on Lentarra Five. Her hair the rich red of the fires on Altykia. Her full mouth was slightly parted and soft-looking, tempting him for a moment to kiss her awake.

With a mental slap, he reminded himself she wasn't a space doxy in some galactic brothel—if she were, she'd probably demand a high price. Bringing his mind back to the situation at hand, he slid an arm under her head and gave her a light tap on the cheek. Her delicate lashes fluttered, and she opened her eyes. Instead of screaming, she smiled dreamily at him.

"What do you know, there is a heaven. How extraordinary, but I have to say I didn't expect angels to be blue."

"I am not an angel, whatever that creature might be. I am a Xamian warrior here to rescue you."

"A Xamian what?" Her green eyes widened. "Oh sweet baby corn, you're an alien." She flailed in an attempt to right herself in the gravity-free space. "You've come to abduct me. How grand!"

"Rescue," he corrected. "Now hold on tight. We're going to transport back to my vessel before this one disintegrates."

The female flung her arms around his neck, and Reg wrapped his own arms around her slight frame, not understanding the instant interest his cock took in this female. Pretty face or not, her frame was slimmer than he usually preferred, but his shaft, turgid in his own jumpsuit, didn't seem bothered by it.

"Ralph, we're ready."

A heartbeat later, he found himself back in the decontamination chamber of his ship. He unwound the female's arms from around his neck —reluctantly.

She looked around with bright-eyed curiosity, thankfully not yelling like she had earlier. Reg, in the more natural light of his ship, found her even more enchanting, her exotic coloring making her appear as a fragile bloom, one he longed to pluck. He said nothing as she explored, waiting for her to speak, but when she finally did, he almost choked.

"Now that you've abducted me, does this mean you're going to strip me naked and probe me?"

[3]

THE ALIEN WHO'D KIDNAPPED HER—OR RESCUED her like a knight in a tinfoil jumpsuit—began to choke. Startled that her blue captor might die before she'd asked him some questions—and studied him—she thumped him on the back, hard.

"Are you okay? Is it the atmosphere? Do you need some mouth to mouth?"

The hacking cough turned into a wheeze then rumbles, which suspiciously sounded like laughter. Moving to stand in front of him, she looked up—and up some more—into his face and saw that yes, indeed, he was chuckling.

Penelope, who preferred Penny, stuck her hands on her hips and glared at him. Not that it had any effect. The blue hunk continued to laugh. And the more he guffawed away, the longer she had to study him, and as male specimens went—wow!

Not very scientific, she knew, but never before had she encountered a male who stirred her libido's interest like this alien. He towered over her, a veritable giant, and even though his silvery jumpsuit covered him, it did nothing to hide the thick, bulging muscles that strained the material. Broad of chest, tapered in the waist, thick in the thighs and bulging in a place that made her blush, he was the epitome of maleness. She wondered if his kind perhaps emitted a pheromone to attract females, for she could find no other explanation for the coiling warmth in her sex, the tightening of her nipples, and the wild urge she fought to jump on him and suck on his blueberry lips.

For the sake of science, of course. How she wished she'd thought to grab her notebook so she could document her findings so far on her first extra-terrestrial meeting.

Finally, the ET calmed his mirth and, with a twinkle in eyes that she would have sworn glowed said, "Female Earthling, that was vastly entertaining. But I fear, pleasurable as probing you might be, that was not my purpose in rescuing you."

"Why kidnap me then?" Penny's cheeks reddened with his rejection, polite as it had been. How foolish of her to think for even a second he'd be interested in a geek like her. Her time in space might have corrected her minor chubby issue, but it still didn't mean she'd suddenly become attractive to the opposite sex. Glasses or not—eye surgery having corrected her vision issues before her trip—with her pale skin, fire-engine-red hair, and unremarkable features, her geeky exterior packaging just didn't scream "Ravish me." A fact she lamented as butterflies danced in her tummy.

"I didn't abduct you. I saved you from this." He swept his hand outwards, and a portion of the wall suddenly lit up with a movie, make that a live video, of what she recognized as her habitat in orbit around Earth— more recently known since NASA's message to her as Penelope's Final Folly. As she watched it tumbling around, a boulder came out of the blackness of space and hit it. With a lovely explosion that sent minor shockwaves through the alien vessel, her home for the last eight months disintegrated into space junk. *And if my blue hero had arrived a few minutes later...* She swallowed back tears of relief, thankful she'd escaped the violent death.

The screen switched off with her still staring, and she startled when he touched her lightly on the shoulder.

"Are you all right, Earthling?"

"My name is Penelope Stanton, but my friends call me Penny." The words came out automatically as she struggled to regain her composure. *I didn't die, so I need to stop blubbering like a ninny and start paying attention to the most amazing thing to happen to me ever.*

"Greetings, Penny. My name is Reg'iantros Vel

Veratu, but you may call me **Reg**," he said with a brilliantly white smile. She was relieved to see his shiny choppers didn't include razor-sharp points or extended canines. *Fingers crossed, this means he didn't snatch me for dinner.*

"I can't believe I'm meeting a real alien," she exclaimed, her fear fading as excitement over this monumental find enveloped her. "I want to know everything about you. Do you live in this galaxy? Do you come here often? Are you alone on this ship? How big is it? Do—"

The more she spoke, the more his violet eyes widened, and he even took a step back from her. Surely it wasn't fear that creased his brow?

"You are certainly inquisitive. Unfortunately, I don't really have time to answer all your questions. I have another mission I must now attend to. If you will give me a location to deposit you on your home planet, I will send you there and be on my way."

He's trying to get rid of me. Penny thought fast. If she went back to Earth without proof, no one would believe her, even if she suddenly appeared out of nowhere. Knowing the jealous nature of the academics, they'd declare the entire habitat-in-space project a hoax. No, she had a much better idea, which her curiosity—and not her aroused libido— encouraged her to voice. "I can't go back to Earth now."

He frowned in incomprehension. "Why ever not? It is your home."

"But how would I explain my escaping the pod? In case you hadn't noticed, they left me to die. By now they would have seen the habitat explode and news of my death will already be making the news."

"Then we must get you back quickly that you might dispel the falseness of these reports."

"And how do I explain how I got away? We don't have teleporters on Earth. And if I tell them an alien saved me, they'll lock me up in a loony bin. I'd much rather go with you. I mean you did, after all, kidnap me."

"I did not kidnap you." He almost yelled his reply.

Penny hid a smile and made a mental note —*Alien subject has emotions.* "Fine then, you rescued me. But now you have to take responsibility. I can't go back home. It would be academic death for me, as I'd probably be accused of faking the whole living-in-space thing. And even if the folks back home did believe me, they'd probably lock me away forever in some lab to quarantine the planet from alien diseases. Heck, they might even dissect me. So, since my current dilemma is kind of your fault, I think it only fair that you take me with you."

"Take you with me?" He looked at her with glazed eyes.

Penny nodded. "Yes."

"But why? No, wait. Don't answer that." Reg rubbed a hand over his face, and his shoulders slumped in defeat. "I will need to inform the Oracle that her simple rescue mission is coming with me."

"Who's the Oracle? And what do you mean rescue mission? Are you saying you didn't kidnap me on a whim? What interest does your Oracle have in me? Is this some kind of alien plot?"

Reeling from the onslaught of questions aimed his way, because apparently she couldn't halt in her excitement and nervousness, his gaze darted around as if searching for escape. He'd soon learn Penny possessed the traits of a canine breed. Once she got her teeth into something, she didn't stop until her curiosity was satisfied.

"So where do you live? Is everyone blue like you?"

He didn't reply. Instead, he turned and removed something from a drawer, which slid open from the wall. With a quick turn, he came striding toward her, and she suddenly gulped. He was awfully big, and he looked rather frazzled with all the questions. She shut her mouth—possibly a tad too late judging by his countenance. Her sealed lips didn't last long when she saw he held something odd-looking in his hand.

"What's that?"

"Peace and quiet," he replied, poking her in the arm with some kind of Star Trekky needle. A pinch later, and she found her eyes closing without volition and only briefly registered big arms catching her as she slumped down.

I wonder if he's gonna probe me n— Thought vanished into the blackness of unconsciousness.

REG LOOKED DOWN AT THE UNCONSCIOUS FEMALE—
Penny—and cursed his luck—and raging erection.

"Ralph, what am I supposed to do with her? I
can't keep her on board. She'll drive me insane with
her questions. Can't you find a location on her
planet I can deposit her?"

The voice of the AI sounded pensive. "The
human raised valid points. The Oracle did say to
keep her safe. If putting the female back on her
planet causes her harm, then you will have failed in
your mission. I see no option but for her to accompany you. We'll be back at Xaanda in approxi-
mately twenty full moon cycles. Since she is
destined to be a warrior's mate eventually, we'll
have just saved them a trip. Surely you can tolerate
her for that long. If you wish, I will answer her

questions. According to the files I dug up on an Earth network, she is a scientist and researcher. It is natural she would have many questions, and being the most knowledgeable entity on this ship, I will undertake her education."

Relief flooded him when Ralph offered to answer her seemingly infinite questions. "You speak sense, Ralph." The only problem with the plan, though, was Reg himself. Not only did he find himself unmistakably attracted to the female, even given her skinny state, an unfamiliar anger enveloped him at the thought of passing her on to another male. Surely, he did not wish to keep her? He barely knew the female and, besides, not that long ago, he'd made it quite clear to the Oracle and her staff that he had no interest in a mate.

Reg froze. *Why am I thinking in terms of mate?* Attraction to the woman was simply hormones. Easily cured with naked, sweaty sex. No need to bond.

He lay Penny on the floor and spread her limbs quickly before stepping away as if she carried the plague. Proximity to her seemed to affect his brain function. Perhaps she carried an alien Earth virus, in which case he'd better decontaminate her while she was docile and quiet. By the moons, he'd never heard one small woman speak so much, and without seeming to take a breath.

Reg felt the familiar tingle of the decontamination waves moving up his body, cleansing him of dangerous microbes he might have picked up. They stopped, though, before they'd reached mid-thigh.

"Ralph, is there a problem with the ship cleanser?"

"Sort of. The female's clothing is made of an odd material that the decontaminating rays can't penetrate. You'll need to strip her and throw her outfit into the incinerator."

Strip her? Reg's mouth went dry as all the moisture in his body collected in his cock. She remained unconscious, unable to disrobe herself, which left him with the task. With shaking hands, Reg found an odd metallic tab, which, when pulled down, split open her silvery ensemble, revealing creamy white flesh. Reg tried averting his eyes from the perky breasts topped with red berries and from the curly red thatch covering her mound. But he couldn't help feeling how silky her skin was when he peeled her jumpsuit down off her body. By the time she was nude, he was covered in a sheen of sweat and trembling. Never before had he wanted a woman so badly. *I think it's been too long since I visited my last brothel.* Something he'd definitely have to rectify, for, even slim as her figure was, he found himself aroused to an insane pitch at the sight of Penny's naked form.

Ancestors, help me find control for my lust.

The decontamination procedure recommenced, the tingling of the waves titillating his already throbbing shaft. He was thankful that she slept and could not see the state she'd placed him in. One he'd rectify before she awoke.

He knew when the sightless lasers touched her, for she sighed in her repose, her lips curving into a sensual smile and her nipples hardening into erect points. Dressed, the cleansing process was pleasant; naked, the tickling sensation could be quite arousing.

Cursing, Reg impatiently waited for the cleansing to be done and fled the chamber as if the hordes of Talkutta chased him. Out in the corridor, he leaned against the wall, unable to erase the image of her body—her beautiful and exotic body.

"Ralph, how long until she wakes?"

"At least two moon cycles?"

"Excellent. If her status changes, let me know. I need to take care of something."

"Yes, Commander."

Reg ignored the laughter in the computer's reply. He had more urgent things to take care of. Reaching his sleeping chamber, he stripped quickly out of his jumpsuit, breathing a sigh of relief as his turgid cock sprang from its confines.

He flopped on his back onto the bed, his hand

immediately gripping his shaft. It pulsed in his hand, thicker than he ever remembered it being and all because of one noisy, scrawny human.

Reg groaned. The image of her perfect, puckered nipples appeared clear in his mind, and his mouth watered with the urge to taste them. He could imagine so easily sucking on them, her breasts a perfect mouthful.

He slid his hand up and down his rod. The tip glistened with fluid, and he rubbed a thumb over that pearly drop, smearing it over his bulbous head, the perfect lube for him to penetrate her with.

He still couldn't believe she'd asked him if he would probe her. He now wished he'd said yes. How would she have taken him? She was so tiny compared to him. Would he lie her down and plunge between her creamy thighs? Perhaps on her hands and knees, her buttocks spread for him to watch as his cock rammed into her damp pussy? Or, perhaps, he'd perch her atop his prick and watch her sweet face as she rode his shaft, her small tits bouncing? He squeezed his cock tightly with his hand, imagining her cunt around it, velvety wet and welcoming. Faster he fisted himself, his balls tightening as he let his erotic fantasy push him closer and closer to orgasm. When he imagined her keening cry as her pelvic muscles crushed him in waves of bliss, he bellowed and shot his load.

Panting, he let go of his limp cock. Turgid problem solved, he now felt ready to face her again. He dressed in loose britches and no shirt, as he planned to go exercise for a bit after Penny woke and he settled her somewhere on the ship.

Scrounging through his clothes, looking for something of his for her to wear, for he definitely didn't want her wandering around naked—or did he?—Ralph suddenly spoke. "I've clothes for the female in the decontamination chamber."

Reg frowned. Why would his vessel be stocked with woman's clothing? His ship wasn't one of the ones designated for mate retrieval.

As if sensing his question, Ralph answered him. "All ships are stocked with female garments in case an emergency extraction of a future mate is required. The Oracle is always thinking ahead."

"Indeed she is." Discomfort tickled him, and paranoia reared its head. Coincidence that he happened to be in the right galaxy at the right time to save a female slated for mating and just happened to have clothing for her? And this right after he'd turned down the offer to mate? Reg wondered how far the Oracle would go to ensure her wishes were followed. Forewarned to the Oracle's possible tricks, Reg steeled his resolve to stay away from the human.

I'll not be shackled, intriguing female or not. Reg

strode back to the room where he'd left the unconscious Penny and walked straight in.

A piercing shriek met him, and he cringed at the sound, even as his cock immediately swelled at the sight that greeted him.

So much for taking care of my lust. By the three moons, I'm even hornier now than I was.

[5]

PENNY AWOKE ON A FLOOR AND BLINKED. SHE stared up at the curved ceiling, the very unfamiliar ceiling. It didn't take her long to remember her encounter with Reg, the big, blue alien who'd abducted her. She also remembered he'd injected her with some kind of sleeping agent, the jerk.

Sitting up, she gaped down at herself—her very naked self. Her first thought wasn't who'd undressed her and why but, *Don't tell me he probed me and I wasn't awake for it.* Just thinking he might have touched her made her blush, but there was no denying she was curious about her rescuer, scientifically, of course. As a woman possessed of a logical mind, she knew love and like and those other curious emotions people ascribed to were nothing more than a chemical reaction in the brain caused by a desire for the human race to band together for protection and procreation.

It did surprise her that an ET, even one who seemed to resemble a human male, would trigger the hormonal instinct in her to mate. It made her even more curious to explore the sexual attraction she felt. She wondered if his manly equipment was like a human male's, or if he was specially endowed. In the name of science—and to quench the fire in her sex—she'd have to find out. She wondered if he'd agree if she asked him to participate in a sexual romp as part of her study of him and his race. Penny bit back a giggle. How should she ask him? *Excuse me, but would you mind having sex with me so I can compare your body and technique to that of an Earth man?*

Speaking of whom, where had Reg disappeared to? And where were her clothes? She stood and checked her body to see if she'd been injected with anything while out. She didn't find any sign of punctures from needles nor did she feel any soreness in her pussy or bum. Oddly enough, this disappointed her somewhat. Apparently, her human shape hadn't incited extreme lust in her alien abductor.

A door slid open suddenly in the wall in front of her, and through it stepped Reg, whose eyes briefly met hers before traveling down the length of her unclothed body.

Regardless of her earlier thoughts, modesty prevailed, and she shrieked. "Don't look! I'm naked." Penny tried to cover herself, but with only two hands, she didn't get very far. The embarrassment in her cheeks burned bright, and she wondered if they matched her hair. To his credit, Reg looked for only a moment—a tummy-wrenching, arousal-pooling moment—and then turned away, but not before she saw his cheeks turning an interesting violet color, an alien version of a blush with his blue skin.

Reg shuffled sideways into the room toward a compartment that popped open in the wall. Penny knew she should say something, but her tongue was stuck in her dry mouth, and truthfully, she found it hard to concentrate. The reason? Her blue abductor was shirtless, and while she'd assumed him muscled, the reality of it was jarring to say the least —not to mention crotch wetting.

Penny squished her thighs together as tight as she could so the moisture seeping between her nether lips wouldn't be apparent. Her brief glimpse of his front was burnt into her retinas— rippled abs, flat, dark blue nipples, and a light dusting of hair that led down his chest to his tapered waist. His back, also muscled, was just as attractive when he turned. She found herself riveted by the sight of a black, swirling tattoo on his back.

"What's the tattoo on your back stand for?" she asked.

"Space, which is infinitely winding."

"Oh." She didn't know what else to say so kept quiet as he rummaged through drawers. Fluttering cloth came flying through the air and landed at her feet.

"Please put the garments on."

Penny picked up the silken mass and shook it out. *He's got to be kidding.* The outfit was made of some sheer material and looked as if it belonged in a sex shop window. She was a scientist. She couldn't wear that. "Where's my spacesuit?"

"The decontamination unit could not cleanse it of alien microbes, so I disposed of it. The outfit is the one the females of my world wear."

Lovely, I've been kidnapped by an alien culture that dresses their women like sex kittens. On second thought, this might advance my plan to explore further physical intimacies between our two races. Certain she would look foolish in such an erotic getup, Penny, nevertheless, draped herself in it. The material hung somewhat loosely around the waist, obviously made for a larger-sized woman and, as suspected, made her look like some kind of harem girl instead of a serious researcher.

"May I turn around now?" he asked politely.

"Yes, I'm dressed."

Reg turned around, and Penny waited for his mirth, sure she looked like an idiot dressed in such provocative gear. He seemed at a loss for words as he took a few steps toward her, his hand outstretched. He snatched his hand back before he could touch her and cleared his throat before saying, "We must go to the infirmary and complete your inoculation."

Penny's shoulders drooped. Foolishly enough, she'd hoped for a compliment. Silly really. She wasn't the type to inspire lust. But at least he hadn't laughed at her. "Inoculations for what? And why did you put me out in the first place? You said something about decontamination."

He held up a hand, stalling her questions. "How about I speak for a bit and explain what is going on, and if, after I'm done, you still have questions, then you may ask them."

Penny bit her lip to stall her tongue and nodded.

"My people have been galactic travelers for some time. One thing we've discovered in our years of exploration is that, while we might often come across beings who resemble us physically, physiologically we can be quite different. Common diseases or illnesses for one race that are easily vanquished can be deadly to another. This being the case, the first thing we do after encountering another race is go through a decontamination process. Using invisible particle lasers, our bodies and clothing are cleansed of strange microbes and other debris."

Penny couldn't help herself. "You mean this is how you bathe, as well?"

Reg gave her a stern look at her interruption. "Yes. Unlike many planets, the use of water for cleansing is prohibited by mine due to its scarcity. Your planet has not yet realized the preciousness of this resource and uses it in an appalling manner. When your world reaches a crisis, your people will more than likely follow suit and devise methods of cleansing not involving the use of water. Now, if I may continue?" He arched a brow at her, which made her blush and drop her chin. "The decontamination procedure is not the only process needed by visitors new to space and encounters with others. In order to protect you, we must also inoculate you against disease. There are a series of vaccines that you will have to submit to in order to prepare your body to fight the illnesses you will encounter since you are bound and determined to come with me. Now, do you have any questions?"

"Will it hurt?" she blurted out.

"Nothing more than a pinch and I will not administer them all at once, as we must watch you for adverse reactions."

She peered at him suspiciously. "What kind of adverse reactions are we talking about?"

He averted his eyes and shrugged. "It differs from race to race. Never fear, our medtech unit is first rate, so you won't die or suffer permanent damage."

And with those encouraging words, he signaled for her to follow him. Penny did so slowly, wishing now he'd kept his mouth shut and not answered any of her questions, or at least less thoroughly. *I need to buck up. Surely it can't be any worse than the shots I got back home in preparation for this mission.*

The medic room was smaller than the decontamination one and rather barer than she would have expected. It consisted of only one bed, which resembled a masseuse table on Earth. Where was the high-tech equipment? The real, live doctor?

Reg riffled through a tray, which slid out from the wall. Finding what he wanted, he turned and addressed her. "Hold still. I need to insert this in your ear."

Penny's eyes widened as he came at her with tweezers holding something small and buggy-looking. "Just a second. What are you trying to shove in my ear?"

"A translator."

"For what? I can understand you just fine."

"As part of my galactic training, I was taught your language. However, all sentient beings who've mastered space travel have these installed in their auditory sensors. Not all languages can be learned, due to physical differences that make it impossible for our bodies to recreate certain sounds and pitches. If you are to accompany me, it is standard procedure that you be implanted with one. When you sleep, the device will also teach you languages that you are capable of comprehending and speaking as an additional backup should the device fail."

Penny's head swirled, and not just in fear. The technology he so casually spoke of seemed almost magical, its very existence light-years ahead of the strides she knew others had made in the field back home. Biting her lip, she turned her head to give him access to her ear. She squeezed her eyes shut and tried to blank her mind from the crazy thoughts racing through it, such as, *please don't be some kind of brain-eating parasite.* To her surprise, other than a brief cold touch of the tweezers as he poked her ear canal, she felt nothing else.

He turned away and busied himself in another one of those odd drawers that slid out of what looked like a seamless wall. She stood on tiptoe and tried in vain to peer over his shoulder, but broad and tall, he blocked her view better than a wall.

"Please lie on your stomach."

Penny eyed the table and, for a fleeting moment, wondered—hoped—he would give her a massage. Such a flight of fancy and for a man, er alien, she'd just met shocked her. Disturbed at the direction her mind and body kept turning in, she did as told and lay on the flat bed. She stuck her face through the hole in the headrest and stared at the floor. At the feel of his hands on the fabric covering her butt, she protested faintly. "Hey, what are you doing?" *Mmm, is this where the probing begins?*

"I'm giving you the first vaccine. Please stay still."

Penny bit her lip and scrunched up her eyes. She was a real baby when it came to pain. *Please don't let me scream if it hurts. I don't want him to think I'm a wuss.*

REG LOOKED at the smooth skin of her backside, his cock, already semi-hard from seeing her nude, hardening even more. He shook his head, trying to regain control of his libido. He needed to do his job, and right now that meant poking her ass with the first shot. She'd clenched her cheek tightly, though, and if he gave her the shot now, it would hurt more than necessary. Taking a deep breath— and telling his cock to stop trying to escape his pants—he placed his hand on her ass and massaged her soft flesh. His erection grew at the innocent touch and strained mightily at the fabric restraining it. *Oh, by the three moons, since when does the touch of a female's flesh affect me so?*

"That doesn't feel like a shot," she said, her voice sounding soft and breathy.

"You need to relax," he said, his voice gruffer than usual. The more he stroked her butt to relax her, the more the urge to probe her like she'd suggested grew. With a sigh, he poked her loose cheek with the injector and pushed the plunger to give her the meds. What he really wanted to do was poke her with his rod and give her a different kind of injection—a cream-filled one.

Reaching behind in the tray, he grabbed the second set of meds and frowned when he saw it. The computer had mistakenly given him the fertility shot for the treatment of alien mates to make them more receptive to their seed.

"Ralph, I think you gave me the wrong set." He tried to whisper, but he should have known Penny's sharp ears would hear him.

"What? Have you poisoned me? Am I going to die? And who's Ralph? I thought you said we were alone." She tried to struggle upright, but he placed a heavy hand in the middle of her back and held her down.

"We are alone," Reg said through gritted teeth. "Ralph is the computer. Now would you hold still? Ralph, answer me."

"No mistake, Commander. Oracle's orders. She is to be given the full treatment."

Reg's brow drew together. He knew what that meant. The Oracle had plans to mate Penny with someone. Not that he cared. She was a noisy female, and he couldn't wait to get rid of her. What he was more interested in was, had the Oracle relayed these orders to the AI before or after he'd rescued Penny? His paranoia tried to escape, but Reg squashed it. The Oracle simply wanted Penny ready to bond. This didn't mean they expected him to be the one.

Annoyed and unsure of the reason why, he jabbed her with the inoculator, not bothering to massage her rigid backside first, and she cried out.

"Ouch. That hurt. You said it wouldn't hurt." Her accusing tone ate at him, and he immediately felt contrite.

He rubbed her abused cheek to ease the pain, and when she relaxed, he gave her the last set of shots for that cycle. He reluctantly tugged the material of her outfit over the ass his body begged to get better acquainted with and helped her to get up off the table.

Penny glared at him while she clutched at her sore ass. "Okay, buster. Care to explain again, starting with who Ralph is?"

"I told you. Ralph is the ship computer."

"Allow me to introduce myself," interrupted the AI. "I am the Alpha 400, artificially intelligent super computer, but you may call me Ralph. I will be in charge of making sure your voyage on the ship is a pleasant experience, well, if you can ignore the commander, that is."

Penny giggled while Reg glowered. He'd never understood why the computer needed a personality, never mind that, previous to this, he'd enjoyed talking to him—er it.

"Nice to meet you, Ralph. I would love to talk to you about, well, you. On Earth, there've been forays into AI units, but they've yet to fully come to life, so to speak."

"Yes, I am pretty magnificent, if I say so myself. It is nice to meet someone who can finally appreciate my abilities."

Penny continued to babble to Ralph, who flirted shamelessly, as Reg led her to the lounge area. While he didn't follow a regimented schedule for meals, it had been a few cycles since he'd last eaten. As he keyed in two meals to the food replicator, he scowled as Penny continued to laugh and talk animatedly to the computer. He didn't understand his ill humor. Surely he didn't care if she enjoyed conversing with a computer more than him. But much as it galled him to admit it, he was jealous of the AI. Which made no sense. Her questions were endless. He should be happy that he no longer needed to make an attempt to answer them.

The illogic caused his irritation and he slapped their food trays down on the small table flanked by two seats, disrupting Penny's avid attention to Ralph's comparison of Earth computers to himself.

Big green eyes focused on him and then down

on the tray he'd placed in front of her. Her nose scrunched up. "Eew. What is this?"

Reg looked down at their meals and saw nothing wrong with them. "It is a Xamian meal favorite."

"What's in it?" she asked, poking at it with a utensil.

"Heronian tentacles in a Jelaxian mount heart sauce with sautéed snails."

Penny's face turned an odd greenish shade, and she clapped a hand over her mouth.

Reg frowned at her. "Are you ill? Perhaps experiencing side effects from the shots? Have a bite to eat and see if it settles your stomach."

Penny shook her head. "It's the food. I can't eat this. Don't you have any human food?"

"Probably." Reg grabbed her tray and dumped it in the ship recycler and, using the food replicator menu, pulled up a menu for Earth dishes. "Name a food dish."

"Lasagna."

The food processor slid out a new steaming plate with a gross concoction of red sauce, lumps, and some kind of white slime over top of it.

Penny smiled when she saw it, though, so Reg withheld his misgivings. She took a bite and sighed. "Oh that's yummy. I missed food so much when I was on the pod. Stupid freeze-dried rations. I swear it's not the loneliness of space that will kill people. It's the food."

"What were you doing in that small habitat?"

"I was researching the effects of space on the body and mind. The government has been planning space missions to other planets, but there is, of course, concern over the effects of long space voyages on astronauts. I volunteered to go up in the pod to document how the lack of human companionship and lack of gravity affects a person's wellbeing. I'd just finished eight months with only four more to go before extraction when you kidnapped me."

"I can say with assurance that, physically, you need artificial gravity if you are to ensure the continuing health of your body. Our medtech unit will luckily be able to repair some of the stress to your internal organs and musculature caused by your sojourn."

Penny blushed. "Thanks. Like I said, they needed to study what would happen. Our scientists haven't quite found a way to recreate gravity in space yet."

"Then they shouldn't have been experimenting." Reg found himself angry that they would treat Penny no better than some animal, running tests on her that were detrimental to her health. Even worse, they'd left her to die.

"Why are you scowling?"

Her innocent question startled him, and he looked at her, startled anew at her beauty. How exotic she seemed with her fresh skin, bright green eyes, and even brighter red hair.

He could no more stop himself than he could stop a meteor shower. He stood and pulled her with him. She tilted her head to look up at him, her lips parted and, for once, silent.

He lifted her to meet his lowering head and kissed her.

PENNY MELTED AT THE FIRST TOUCH OF HIS LIPS. Firm and tasting sweet, they caressed hers intimately and sent a jolt of liquid desire roaring through her body. Her hands crept up and clutched at his shoulders. He felt so good, his solidness and strength increasing her arousal.

He slid his hands from her waist to her bottom, and his thigh nudged her legs apart to push itself insistently against her mound. She moaned against his mouth as she rubbed herself on his firm thigh, the friction creating pleasurable shocks. At the insistent press of his tongue, her lips parted, and he swirled it inside, slipping along the length of hers and drawing her tongue into his mouth to suck.

Penny's head swirled with sensation. Never had a man's touch set her on fire like this. Made her feel so desirable and wanton. With one arm curled around her waist and his thigh supporting most of her weight, he slid his free hand up her rib cage to cup her breast. Penny gasped when his thumb brushed the erect peak through the thin material of her harem outfit. A simple touch that drove her desire up even higher. If he were to place his mouth on her, she'd probably come. *Oh please.*

"Sorry to interrupt dessert, but we've arrived at Soturia. Docking permission has been granted and commenced."

Reg pulled himself away from her clinging mouth, breathing harshly. For a moment, she thought he would ignore Ralph's interruption and continue with his plunder of her mouth, but instead, he set her from him and took a deep, shuddering breath.

"I apologize for my sexual advances of a moment ago. I have long been without a female and did not mean to maul you."

Penny wanted to protest she didn't mind, but his words stung. *And here I thought he was overcome with lust for me. He's just horny from being in space too long.* Taking a shaking breath of her own, she waited a moment to rein in her hormones before she followed him out of the lounge.

With Ralph guiding her, she entered a room that finally corresponded with her *Star Trek*-induced image of what a spaceship bridge should look like.

Reg, looking the part of a commander—if shirtless and sexy—sat in a chair in front of a large window. She approached the screen, staring at the swirling, smoky mass.

"What is that?"

Ralph answered. "We are entering the outer edge of the gaseous planet your people call Jupiter. We are scheduled to rendezvous with the space station harvesting the hydrogen."

"Why?" The question popped out much like it had since she'd learned it at the age of two. Penny's curiosity needed to be sated.

"We are delivering some computer upgrades, which our planet produces, to the miners here. Keep an eye on the screen and you'll see the station docking arm in a moment."

Sure enough, out of the murky fog, something appeared, a boring metallic structure similar to an offshore oilrig. The spaceship glided along a projecting arm and, with a small shudder, docked.

Mundane or not, this was an alien construction. Penny whirled to face Reg. "Are we going to meet some more extraterrestrials? Do they look like you? Do I need to wear a space suit?"

"*We* aren't leaving this ship. The computer has already loaded the cargo into the transfer chute, and it's being transferred as we speak."

"Oh." Penny's bubble burst. She'd hoped for a

moment that she'd get to expand her suddenly new and widening horizons.

As if sensing her disappointment, Reg said, "There will be other planets on our route that will be safe for you to visit, and I promise you'll get to meet lots of species. Also, keep in mind," he said with a smile, "that who you call an alien is a matter of perspective. To most you will meet, you will be the alien one, for your race, having not yet achieved interplanetary travel, is not often seen unless they're visiting our planet."

Penny's eyes widened. Her, an alien? The thought seemed ludicrous, but thinking it over, she could understand it. Perspective was everything. But something he said caught her attention.

"Are you saying there are humans on your planet? Why? How?"

"Would you like me to explain?" Ralph interjected.

Reg looked at Penny and sighed. He scrubbed a hand through his hair. "No, I'll do it Ralph. You take care of the shipment."

Rising from his chair, he beckoned her to follow and led her back to the lounge. Seating herself, she watched him pace, his face thoughtful.

"I'm not sure where to start," he finally said.

"How about the beginning?"

"Very well, bear with me, as I need to give you a bit of a history lesson. As I mentioned, my people have long been space farers and explorers, but we are first and foremost a warrior caste. In order to expend some of this aggressive energy, we've, over the millennia, become involved in many planetary skirmishes for other races who were being subjugated by violent outsiders."

"So you're like space knights?" The blank look on his face told her he didn't understand. "Someone who defends the weak."

He smiled, but it was a chilly look that made her shiver. "Sometimes we fight for honor, sometimes we are hired as mercenaries, and other times we fight because we like it."

"Oh." Great, kidnapped by bloodthirsty barbarians with technology. The idea should have frightened her, but instead, it made heat pool in her cleft.

Reg continued with his history lesson. "We intervened in a certain war generations ago and, of course, won. The losers did not appreciate our meddling and retaliated in the form of a deadly virus. This virus was unleashed on our home world and had only one purpose—to kill all our females."

Penny gasped. Biological warfare was a word often heard on Earth, but to know such a horrible weapon also existed in space with advanced extraterrestrials was just downright scary. "Did it kill them all?" she whispered, appalled.

"Almost. Over ninety percent of our females

died, and of the ones left, most were barren. It devastated us."

"No kidding. What did you do?"

"Our ancestors killed the race that struck down our women. Every now and then we come across a stray one we missed and rectify the situation."

Penny swallowed at his dark smile. Vengeful. Another fact to note about his people. "How long ago did this happen?" she asked.

"Three generations. We are still rebuilding our female population, which is where humans come in. Well, female ones, that is. When the males finished their war, they came back to a world with almost no women. A lot of infighting ensued as battles were fought over the right to mate. In order to protect our dwindling numbers, the Oracle issued a decree."

She couldn't help asking. "Who's the Oracle?"

Reg sighed. "You truly are the lady of a million questions. The Oracle is the spiritual leader of our people. She can divine things with the help of our spiritual ancestors and guide my people."

"So, she's like a fortune teller?"

Reg's brows drew together in an annoyed frown. "Nothing so crass as that. She is a powerful being who has always been. Some of her power comes from the knowledge and aide that those who've passed on give her."

"Hold on a second. Are you telling me she

supposedly talks to ghosts? I so need a notebook to write this all down," she mumbled. She couldn't believe an advanced society like his still held archaic views about spirits and whatnot. Apparently, religion and intangible beliefs weren't a human-only domain.

"All that I am telling you is documented if you should wish to educate yourself instead of making insulting remarks." His brusque tone made her finally shut her mouth. *Oops. I think I offended him. But seriously? Ghosts and a woman who talks to them?*

"Sorry. This is all very different from what I'm used to. I'll be quiet so you can finish your story."

"I highly doubt that," he grumbled. "In order to rebuild our population, we needed women. The spirits of our ancestors went questing throughout the galaxy looking for beings seeded from the same master race as us."

Penny's hand whipped up, and she bounced in her seat, biting her lip so as to not blurt out her next question.

Reg rolled his eyes. "What now?"

"What master race?" Could this be the elusive answer to God humans searched for?

"Our progenitors were superior sentient beings who were humanoid in appearance. No one has ever encountered them, but it is well known they seeded many planets in the galaxies. Each race has, of course, adopted different characteristics depending on their environment, but biologically, we share many traits. Due to this shared genetic heritage, it is possible for our people to mate with yours."

"Back up a second. I want to know more about these guys who supposedly created life. Surely there is more known about them? I mean, did they all, like, disappear? Didn't they leave instructions?"

"I am not a historian. These are questions you will have to ask Ralph. I am just giving you the basics. Now, if I might finish before we both expire of old age?" He arched a brow at her, and Penny smiled at him sheepishly. "The females of your world are capable of bearing our children. Thus, when a warrior acquits himself well, he is accorded the honor of bonding with a mate and settling down to raise a family. It used to be the male filled out a questionnaire to aide in the selection of his female, but many of the Earthlings banded together on my home planet and protested this practice, claiming it was demeaning. So now, while the ancestors might guide a warrior in the selection of his female, they no longer just give him a name so that he might properly abduct and—"

"Probe her!" Penny blurted out and then felt the heat rise in her cheeks.

"What is it with you and probing?" Reg moved across the room until he loomed over her.

Penny ducked her head. "Slip of the tongue?" she said hopefully.

Abruptly, she found herself yanked upright. Startled, she opened her eyes and saw his peering back at her, and, yes, this time she was sure—they were glowing.

[7]

REG FOUGHT WITH HIS DESIRE TO KISS HER AGAIN. To feel her sweet, responsive mouth opening against his that he might taste her. "I'll give you a slippery tongue," he murmured, losing the battle with reason—and his body. He kissed her. The result was even more electric than the first time he'd embraced her.

She instantly melted in his arms, her pliant body molding to his. He rubbed his hands up and down her back, the thin fabric of her outfit frustrating him, for he wished to touch her skin. Her mouth parted eagerly under his, and her tongue boldly ventured to find his. He groaned, her caresses enflaming him. His cock throbbed painfully, begging for relief. He walked her backwards until she came up against the wall. Using it as a brace, he lifted her high enough for him to press his turgid shaft against her hidden core. Her legs wrapped around his waist, holding him even closer. He ground himself against her, enjoying the soft mewling sounds she made as she clutched tightly at his shoulders. Since he was shirtless, the simple skin-to-skin contact of her hands set him aflame. *If this is how an innocent touch affects me, how will it feel to have her naked body pressed to me, skin to skin?* He longed to find out.

He tore his lips from hers and trailed hot kisses down the edge of her jaw to the pink shell of her ear. He bit her lobe lightly, and she responded with a shudder. He sucked the spot he'd nibbled before moving his lips down the graceful column of her neck. Silken smooth, her skin tasted so sweet and encouraged him to seek even more delights. The material of her top impeded his progress, but when he pulled back slightly, her desire was evident in the sharp, excited points of her nipples protruding through the cloth.

He leaned forward and caught the hard buds in his mouth, one by one, sucking them through the fabric. She keened and shuddered in his arms. Reg was close to losing control, something he'd never had happen before with his usual iron control.

He needed to plunge his cock inside her. Claim her and make her his, body and soul.

Reg froze. *By all the moons, have I lost my mind?* He needed to put some space between them and think about what was happening. Examine—and squash —these strange feelings he found himself feeling in regards to Penny. He forced himself to release her delectable puckered berry, so clearly visible through the damp cloth of her top. His mouth watered, aching for another taste, and he clenched his jaw against the temptation.

He might have won the fight had Penny not whispered, "Oh please, don't stop. It feels so good."

With a groan of surrender, he found her lips again and claimed them in a torrid kiss. To the moons with it, he knew he was fighting a losing battle. Penny's allure was much more dangerous than he'd anticipated, but at least his loss would be pleasurable. But not here. No, he had a comfortable bed to cushion their soon-to-be pumping bodies.

He'd taken only one step with her clasped around him when the sound of Ralph clearing his throat loudly stopped him.

"Once again, sorry to interrupt, but, Reg, you have an incoming communication from the Oracle."

Those words took care of his erection and arousal, effectively dousing them. He let Penny slide down his body until her feet touched the ground. She swayed when he stepped away from her, her eyes heavy lidded and her lips swollen with passion.

Reg tightened his jaw as he resisted the urge to sweep her back up and continue with his plan of seduction. *Although I have to wonder if perhaps she is the one seducing me, for never before have I so completely lost myself.*

"Umm, the Oracle is waiting, Commander."

Duty called him, rescuing him from the madness that seemed determined to claim him. "If you'll excuse me, I must take this call. Ralph, could you please guide Penny to the stateroom that she might find some rest?"

For once, Penny was silent, although he could see troubled questions in her eyes, ones he had no answers for. This was uncharted territory for him, and he didn't like it one bit.

Reg grabbed a shirt on his way to the command center, still able to feel Penny's tentative touches. He growled at himself. *Why can't I stop thinking of her? Why must she plague my every thought? Here less than a full day cycle and, already, I am mad.*

As he entered the control room, the view screen lit up with the image of the veiled Oracle. He quickly dropped his head in deference. "Greetings, Oracle."

"Greetings, my child. I thought I would check on your mission status in person. According to the report we received, you rescued the female without incident, and she is now currently traveling with you."

"That is correct. The female claimed she would suffer hardship should I return her to her kind."

"This is actually perfect. We have plans for her."

"If I might ask, have you found a mate for her?" Reg held his breath, awaiting the answer. It wasn't as if he cared. Just because he wanted her body with a furious passion didn't mean he actually liked Penny and her talkative ways. Nope, he was eager to get her off his ship. The only odd thing he couldn't understand, though, was why the thought of her leaving made his stomach sink.

"A few possibilities have popped up, so the spirits are looking into it further. Of course, the final choice will be up to her. I'm sure things will have resolved themselves by the time you return. In the meantime, continue on with your missions."

Reg fought the urge to punch something at the words that several possible mates had cropped up. It was what he wanted. Now, if only he could convince his body—and his emotions—that this was the right decision.

The Oracle cut the communication, and Reg sat in his command chair, his face buried in his hands. Without the Oracle to distract him, he found himself aroused again and fighting an insane urge to find Penny and finish what he'd started.

But therein lay the path to madness. She was just about promised to someone else. It was just a matter of time before the Oracle and the ancestral spirits settled on a soul mate, one whom Penny would be unable to resist. It wouldn't be fair to her for him to seduce her, pleasurable as it would feel.

Or I could always claim her for myself. The Oracle did say I could have a mate.

The treacherous thought, so contrary to what he wanted, glued him to his seat better than any order. No matter what, he wouldn't be trapped— delectable Earthling or not.

THE BED RALPH guided her too was comfortable, but Penny found it hard to fall asleep. Confusion and arousal swirled in her mind and body. She couldn't understand her strong attraction to Reg, and not just that, but she was pretty sure she was developing feelings for him. She'd known him only a day, but he fascinated her. And it wasn't because he was an alien. *Am I falling in love?*

She scoffed at the idea. Love was just a chemical reaction of the brain. Reason or not, though, she wished he'd join her in this bed and finish what he'd twice started now. For science, of course. After all, hadn't she originally decided that having sex with him would make an interesting research subject? Of course, her justification would probably be more believable if she'd actually taken some notes on what had occurred so far. Maybe putting down her thoughts would explain what was happening to her, why she felt so drawn to him.

Perhaps it was her isolation that had her feeling this way. After all, she hadn't had any contact with other people in a long time and even longer since she'd had any sexual pleasure. Although NASA assured her the pod had no internal cameras to spy on her, she didn't quite trust them, and so, even though the urge occasionally arose to pleasure herself, she'd held back.

She was tired of being frustrated, though. Ralph had turned off the light so it was dark in the room, and she was under the covers, hidden. There was no one to see her, unless Reg was secretly spying on her using a camera that could see in the dark. The idea titillated her enough that she slid her hand under the silky covers and under the fabric of her top. Just thinking about Reg possibly watching had her nipples tightening into hard points. She pinched the erect peaks, remembering how good his mouth had felt sucking them. Heck, they were still damp, the fabric having not yet dried.

She tweaked and rolled her nipples, but the true heat that begged for relief lay lower. She left off toying with her breasts to slide her hands over her stomach down to her thatch of curls. *I wonder if alien females shave like we do on Earth?* She'd never actually shaved hers bald, being too afraid of looking stupid, but she knew from the media that a lot of women did. Would Reg mind her red thatch? Should she inquire of Ralph about his people's customs? Was it brazen of her to think of being with him in such an intimate way?

She had known him for only a day or so, but given the obvious sexual attraction, she thought it just a matter of time before they made love. She wondered if he'd mind her taking notes so she wouldn't forget what was sure to be the most erotic experience of her life, one she doubted he'd repeat. She had a funny feeling, once he sated his curiosity with her, the attraction on his part would be satisfied.

Knowing she was just some sort of exotic alien treat for him didn't diminish her desire for him. He was still the sexiest male she'd ever seen. As she touched herself, her sex's cream moistening her fingers for slick penetration, she wondered if he'd take a woman in the popular missionary style. Or would his kind have more exotic positions or preferences?

Just thinking of his hard body smothering her with his masculine weight while his hard shaft ploughed her channel made her quiver and pant. She plunged her fingers into herself while the fingers on her other hand rubbed slickly over her clit.

But her orgasm remained out of reach, frustratingly so.

"COMMANDER, the Earthling is showing an elevated heart rate, signaling possible distress."

"Is she hurt?" Reg sat up straight in his chair where he'd slumped looking for slumber, not daring to even attempt sharing his stateroom with Penny.

"I cannot tell definitely, but my auditory sensors did pick up a whimper."

"I'd better check on her then. I'll be back in a moment." Reg subconsciously knew there was nothing wrong with Penny, but Ralph had provided him with the perfect excuse to see her. And despite his vow not to touch her or think about her any further, like an addiction, he found himself unable to stay away.

He entered the dark stateroom without announcing himself, but a brief flash of light from the outer corridor momentarily lit the room. In that glimpse, he saw Penny, her eyes shut tight, her cheeks flushed, and her white pearly teeth biting down on her lower lip. He also caught the movement under the blanket, and guessing what she did, he almost dove on her to taste what she played with.

Swallowing and still pretending to himself that his check on her was benign, he asked, "Are you all right?"

"No," she answered honestly. "I'm horny."

Her claim shocked him but, even worse, made

him rock hard. "Penny, tell me to go," he growled at her, hoping she would have the sense to stop him.

"Why?"

"You are not meant for me."

He heard more than saw her sit up in the bed, the rustle of fabric giving it away. "I'm not asking for commitment. It's crazy, we barely know each other, but I can't seem to help wanting you. Maybe it's because I've been alone for a while. Honestly, I don't really care, for once, why I feel this way. I just know I want you to touch me, and I want to touch you."

Her soft plea ripped through his armor of good intentions. The right thing to do right now would be to walk away. Instead, Reg bit back several curses and gave in to the inevitable. Truly, whom was he trying to fool? There was no way he was going to make it through the remaining missions and the trip back home without touching her.

Screw fighting it. Maybe if they both indulged in a little pleasure, they'd be able to think more clearly.

He slid under the covers already warm from her body. Somehow, he found her lips in the darkness, and they kissed, mouths open and breath mingling. Somehow, even with their bodies pressed tight, he divested her of her clothing. The darkness hid her beauty from his eyes, but he could feel it with his touch, deliciously so. He let his hands travel the smooth skin of her body, enjoying her cries of pleasure and the way her whole body vibrated under his touch. She clung to him, her nude body pressed against his, and it was only the fabric of his breeches that stopped his aching cock from plunging into her sex.

He traced his way down her body with his mouth and hands, tasting first the soft skin of her neck then the indented valley between her breasts. Her cry when he took her erect nipple in his mouth was sweet music, but her scream when he bit her soft flesh and then sucked it hard almost made him come. His hands kneaded her breasts, pushing them together while his mouth tortured the erect tips. Her body was unbelievably responsive to his touch. He rolled his body so that he lay between her legs and sucked in a breath when the bulge in his pants pressed up against her molten core.

Oh, by the three moons, she was so hot and ready for him. He thrust against her mound and groaned when she pushed back. He was so close to losing control and taking her like a brutish animal. He rolled onto his back, trying to regain a measure of composure.

She followed, though, straddling his waist, her wet sex burning against him. She touched him tentatively, her hands stroking over his chest.

Reg groaned. "Stop, you're going to kill me."

She instantly froze. "I'm sorry. Am I hurting you?"

If she only knew how his cock and balls ached. Actually, on second thought, he decided to show her. He plucked one of her hands from his chest and moved it down to place it on his cock straining in his pants. "I'm sore with wanting you."

"Oh."

She removed her hand, and her delicious weight disappeared from his lower stomach. He thought for a moment he'd frightened her with his boldness, but she sat right back down on him farther up on his body. Her hand skimmed his hidden erection lightly at first then more boldly. His seeking hands found her body, and he realized she'd turned around on him so that her backside faced him, which put her face above…

Reg bucked before he finished that thought for she scooted suddenly, her slick sex sliding up his chest so that she could lower her face and nuzzle the fabric at his crotch.

He held on to his orgasm by a thin thread. *Please don't let me shame myself by coming before her.* He needed to regain control of the situation and fast. He found and gripped her thighs with his hands and pulled her back even farther until her mound bumped his chin.

Penny stilled, her hot breath steaming through the fabric of his breeches and making him go almost cross-eyed with arousal. He lifted and positioned her over his mouth, and then he tasted her.

Oh sweet moons, she was the most decadent dessert he'd ever had the pleasure of tasting. Her slick folds parted beneath his questing tongue, and he probed her with his tongue, her cream a heady aphrodisiac. She moaned as he explored her in the dark, using only his tongue and lips. He discovered her sensitive clit and flicked it, enjoying the way she shuddered against him.

But she paid him back. Her hands fumbled with the closure of his pants, but when she finally managed to open it, his cock sprang out, right into her waiting grasp.

It was his turn to buck and gasp as she stroked him with two hands, sliding them up and down his length. He worked her sweet nub faster, sucking and nipping it. She replied by taking his swollen cockhead in her mouth.

Reg cried hoarsely, the molten feel of her mouth sucking him wetly the most intense thing he'd ever experienced. Never mind he'd done all this before. For some reason, doing it with Penny was different, more intense, more pleasurable.

He could feel his body tightening, reading to blow. Not before she came, though. He brought one hand up and inserted two fingers into her tight, wet sex. Her pelvic muscles quivered at his penetration, and she sucked him faster. He slid a third finger in and pumped her while his tongue flicked quickly against her nub.

With a scream that vibrated against his cock still in her mouth, she came hard, her channel spasming in decadent waves around his still pumping digits. Her sweet surrender pushed him over the edge, and his body went taut as he finally found his own release, his rod shooting his cream into her mouth. To his shock—and intense pleasure—she swallowed his juices, even as she trembled from the aftershocks of her orgasm.

She rolled off of him, and he heard a rustle as she righted herself in the bed. Her slight frame snuggled up against him, and Reg curled an arm around her, more content than he could ever remember being.

He'd had sex before—many, many times—but what he'd just experienced went way beyond. Her breathing evened out, and he realized she slept, snuggled against him. Her trust in him brought out strange feelings of protectiveness, and he hugged her closer. He wouldn't allow any harm to come to her. She was his. And he couldn't wait to mate with her again and claim her, this time with his cock. To claim her forever.

Reg's eyes widened in the dark. *I've lost my mind.* He needed to escape now before the afterglow of good sex made him do something stupid. He snuck out of her bed, ignoring the voice that screamed at him to go back.

He wouldn't be caught in the mating trap like so many other good warriors before him. No matter how good she tasted, no matter how right she felt in his arms, no matter how much he longed to probe her with his cock, he wouldn't give up his freedom for sex, no matter how mind blowing it promised to be.

Penny woke and stretched, alone in the big bed. She frowned, wondering when Reg had slipped out. She'd kind of hoped for a morning wake-up probe. While their oral pleasuring had made her explode, she still desired him.

"Lights." Better than a clapper, the illumination for the room came on, not too bright, so her eyes adjusted quickly. More clear-headed than the previous night, she peered around with curiosity. The size of the room surprised her. She would have thought guest quarters would be modest. However, this room seemed quite opulent from the overly large bed to the silken sheets and soft, cushiony floor.

"Good morning, Penny," said Ralph from hidden speakers, startling her. "I trust you slept well."

"Yes, thank you."

Ralph snickered. "That makes one of you then."

Penny scrunched up her nose. "What do you mean? Didn't Reg sleep?" She assumed he'd gone to find his own bed. Apparently, he wasn't a snuggler. Penny knew she should be excited to be discovering so much about her alien, but instead, she found herself disappointed. She had so many questions still, like what kind of recuperative powers did he have? She knew his cock was thicker and longer than any she'd ever experienced, so how would it feel sheathed inside her? She really needed to change her train of thought, for her body was becoming flushed with arousal and she hadn't even brushed her teeth yet.

"Oh, the commander slept, of a sort," answered the AI evasively. "I don't think he found his chair as comfortable as his bed though."

"Why was he sleeping in a chair?" Penny still didn't get it.

Ralph chuckled again. "There's only one bed on board."

Penny almost slapped herself for being so dense. This was his room and it seemed kind of dumb of him to choose to sleep in a chair instead of sharing the mattress. The bed was big enough, after all, for the two of them—especially if she climbed on top of him. Penny blushed at the direction of her thoughts. And then an even worse one hit her.

Maybe he'd left for a reason other than the fact that he didn't like to snuggle. *Maybe he snuck out of bed because he didn't want to have sex with me.* He'd gotten off and assuaged his curiosity about making out with an Earthling. And apparently, it hadn't inspired him to have a repeat performance.

Penny sighed. *What did I expect? He's hot, and I'm just boring old me. If only I didn't want him now more than ever.*

"Are you hungry? I can have the food replicator prepare you a meal in the room if you'd like," Ralph offered.

"I'm not hungry. Just confused."

"About the commander I would assume?"

Penny bit her lip. She felt kind of stupid talking to a computer, but who else did she have to talk to? She didn't even have a journal anymore. "Am I that obvious?"

"To one with my superior intellect and observation skills—yes. If it's any consolation, the commander seems to find himself just as befuddled."

"I doubt that," she grumbled.

"Take it from one who has known him many cycles, I've never seen the commander so uncertain and out of control with his emotions."

"Well, he could have fooled me. I mean we are

talking about the man who snuck out of bed to sleep in a chair so he wouldn't have to wake up beside me, right?"

"Proving my point," said the AI. "A man who didn't care would have taken advantage of what you offered without remorse."

"So, because he left me and didn't try to probe me, he likes me?" Penny tried to follow the AI's logic, but as usual, convoluted emotions escaped her. She'd always had a hard time following human behavior. Throw in an alien element and she was completely lost.

"Correct."

"I'm not sure I believe you, but let's say I do. Then what do I do next? I know I've only known him a short time, but he makes me feel things, Ralph. And I know it's just a chemical reaction in my brain, but I have to say it's even better than chocolate. So how do I get him to admit he feels things for me too? " Penny found talking to the AI remarkably easy. Perhaps the fact that he didn't have an actual face helped. He was like a diary that talked back.

"I think perhaps you need to understand more about his people and their ways to find the solution to your dilemma. Reg is a warrior descended from a long line of warriors. They don't speak of feelings and, believe it or not, until they met humans, had never heard of the emotion you

Earthlings call love. Now this isn't to say they never felt it. I'm sure many have. With them, mating with a female is a ritual that results in a mental harmony that transcends the need for words."

"But the females of his world died. I guess mating with other species like humans isn't the same." In other words, her geeky self might have been a letdown, regardless of what the AI thought.

"Yes and no. While human females might require special fertility drugs to procreate, when it comes to mental harmony, they are more than compatible if matched with the right male. The spirit ancestors of his people are quite adept at finding the perfect female. And in the past, once a warrior was given permission to mate, he would abduct his Earthling and perform the mating ritual."

"So they get married?"

The computer paused. "It's more than marriage. From the written studies on it, apparently during the bonding, the souls of the two join and become one."

A society that believed in soul mates. That surprised Penny, given their technological advances. "This is all really interesting, but what's it got to do with Reg and me? I'm not looking for commitment." *Just hot sex, regardless of what the organ known as my heart thinks.*

"Reg was given permission to mate by the Oracle."

"Oh, so he's already got some girl lined up to marry then." Penny's heart plummeted. It would explain why he tried for aloofness. *I guess I was just a fling before he settles down.* Which was perfectly fine because she wasn't looking to get married. She just wished the thought of him mating with someone else didn't give her an urge to have a hissy fit.

"No, the commander refused the honor."

Penny's head shot up. "Why?"

"When a pair bond, they return to the home planet, where they are given a home and the male is given a job planetside while the female tends to the babies she is expected to have. The commander thinks this is a fate worse than death, as he prefers to roam the galaxies."

"Can't say as I blame him. I wouldn't want to be stuck barefoot and pregnant. I'd much rather be out in space, too."

"Exactly his opinion."

"But I still don't understand what that has to do with me."

"The Oracle has informed him that the spirits have chosen several males suitable as your mate."

"Whoa. Back up. I don't want to get married. Not to him or anyone else. I'm a scientist. Now that I've discovered there is life out here, I want to see it, and not just on some video screen, but in person. I'll just have to tell your Oracle I'm not interested."

Ralph chuckled. "Now that I would like to hear."

"I'm glad you think it's funny. I don't think it's amusing at all that some ET who talks to ghosts thinks she can arrange my future for me. But that's getting away from the point. If I understand you correctly, Reg doesn't want to get married, and because he thinks I'm supposed to get married, he wants nothing to do with me."

"Exactly." Ralph sounded pleased she'd summarized the situation, but understanding did nothing to help.

"Well, that's just dumb." And she intended to tell Reg just how stupid the entire situation was. That was if Ralph was correct in his assessment and Reg had pulled his disappearing act out of fear they'd end up shackled together or that he'd be cheating on one of his kind.

Penny still wasn't 100 percent sure that Reg's disappearance wasn't because he'd had a taste of her charms and found himself not impressed.

REG WORKED the kinks out of his body shadow fighting with a computer simulator. The thrusting and running at his fake opponent helped clear the fogginess from his mind as well as ease his aching muscles.

I should have stayed in the bed. It was stupid of me to sleep in the chair. But he knew if he'd stayed in bed with Penny, he'd have crawled between her legs and pounded into her sweet flesh until she clawed his back and screamed his name. And then he had a feeling he would have started all over again for, like a drug, he didn't think Penny was a craving he could vanquish with just one probe. *By the moons, I can still taste her on my tongue, and I am so hungry for more.*

Growling, he threw a flurry of punches.

"Feeling a little frustrated, are we?" said Ralph with chuckle.

"Shut up."

"I just thought I'd let you know Penny is awake."

"Why would I care?" Reg's fist flew in a flurry of blows at his shadow opponent.

"She was wondering where you were. She was hurt you left her alone. For some reason, she likes you."

"What?" Distracted, Reg forgot to pay attention. The animated boxer struck a blow and snapped Reg's head back. "Simulator off." Rubbing his face, Reg tried to tell himself it didn't matter if Penny liked him. He didn't want a wife. He wanted his freedom. And besides, she was just as good as promised to someone else.

"She's just as opposed to marriage as you are. Says she'd rather travel the galaxies than stay on the home world to birth babies."

Reg found himself listening and eager to know more, even if he'd decided during his sleepless sojourn that he would do his best to avoid her until he could deposit her planetside. "She said that? What else did she say?"

"You know maybe the two of you should try talking to each other directly. I think you both have more in common that you think."

For a moment, Reg allowed himself to dream of roaming the universe, Penny at his side, sharing adventure—and his bed.

The Oracle would never allow it. Females were safer at home. Besides, the Oracle already had some warriors in mind for Penny.

Suddenly enraged, he needed to hit something. "Simulator on," he barked. The ship might be small, but he knew it well. Avoidance was his best option, no matter how his cock and balls ached— and, even stranger, his heart.

[9]

"You will stay on board while I conduct my business here."

"Why?" This was the third such stop he'd given her specific instructions to stay out of sight. It was getting annoying, especially considering it was one of the only times he talked to her voluntarily. In the close confines of the ship, it was hard for him to avoid her completely, and when she did manage to corner him, she'd attempted to engage him in conversation, to baffling effect. She'd discovered smiling at him or laughing made his face tighten, almost as if he suffered pain, and then he'd make an abrupt U-turn and just about run to get away from her. On other occasions, he pretended to not see her at all, avoiding her as if she had the plague. Ralph tried to reassure her that it was because Reg was afraid of his feelings for her. Penny disagreed. *If he liked me, he wouldn't be so aloof.*

"You will stay on board out of sight because the place we're docking at is too dangerous."

Penny bit back the words "Yes, Daddy" at his condescending attitude. However, having glimpsed their docking location on an honest-to-goodness asteroid, riddled with buildings and covered tunnels, she couldn't resist trying again. "I promise I'll do whatever you say. I just want to observe. And besides, you'd be there to protect me."

He ignored her, to her annoyance, and finished suiting up. She didn't cringe when he wrapped a belt around his waist and holstered a gun. She did, however, swallow hard when he also added two long, gleaming knives. *Okay, so maybe he's telling me the truth and this place really is dangerous.*

"Our next stop will be more suitable. Now be a good girl and go study or something."

His dismissive words made her flush. *What else am I supposed to do with my time when he practically ignores me?* She wondered what he'd think if she divulged that her current notes were all about him—and the diagrams she kept tearing up were amateur scribblings of his nude body. She'd tried to lie to herself that she was simply researching him as a new species. The truth was she found comfort—and titillation—in remembering what they'd done together. Not that it helped the pain in her psyche since he'd so callously avoided her after their one and only intimate encounter. She had tried to view what had happened dispassionately. After all, emotions were chemical reactions in the brain and thus unreliable, but it was cold comfort when she slept alone, her thoughts centered around him. Even worse, she existed in a constant state of arousal.

Penny fell back on what she knew best to fight the hormonal imbalance that caused her to feel irrationally—research. Ralph proved to be an invaluable fount of information about Reg. She knew all about his accomplishments as a space warrior, both in battle and during planetary off-world business. She knew he was an only child, his father a full-blood Xamian and his mother a human/Xamian born mix. She'd browsed images of him kept on file, which Ralph pulled up for her, and she studied them intently. Her interest in him, almost obsessive, made no sense, and neither did her emotional turmoil. Given his treatment of her, logic said she should hate him. Instead, she wondered what she could do or say to get him to skip the banal conversation and visit the stars he'd shown her before in bed.

Oblivious to her thoughts, without a backward glance, Reg left, his big black boots thudding as he headed toward the decontamination chamber and the door that led off the comfortable ship that she'd mentally renamed her prison.

Penny ran to the command center and hit a series of buttons to pull up the cameras outside the ship. Bored, she'd learned a lot from Ralph about the ship and Reg's world and his people and...

Simply put, she now knew a heck of a lot of facts, none of which helped her or chased the boredom away. She watched Reg as he strode tall and confident down the tube connecting them to the docking port. She fidgeted as she waited, the empty corridor on the view screen mocking her. Seconds ticked by while she drummed her fingers. Surely it wouldn't hurt if she took a little peek. She wouldn't go any farther than the end of the connecting tunnel. How was she to learn anything if Reg kept her sequestered everywhere they went?

I'll just poke my head out for a minute and be right back. He'll never even know.

Of course, she hadn't counted on Ralph.

"And just where do you think you're going?" the AI asked as she placed her hand on the door control to slide it open.

Penny jumped as if she'd been caught sneaking out by her mother. But there was a big difference. Not only was she a grown woman Ralph was also a machine. Tilting her head regally she replied, "I'm just going to look. I'll be right back."

"The commander told you to stay on the ship."

"Oh please, I'm not going far or long. Come on,

Ralph, I promise, one tiny look and I'll be back before you know it."

"The commander wouldn't like it."

"Please, Ralph."

Machine or not, apparently he couldn't resist her plea, and the door slid open. "Make it quick. I'd rather not become intimately acquainted with a scrap heap."

"You're the best, Ralph." Penny scurried down the narrow hall. At the end was a closed door. Slapping her hand on the control panel slid the door open and she stuck her head out to look.

From space, she'd seen buildings embedded into the asteroid surface, appearing tiny and far between, but looking around wide eyed, she now realized what she'd seen was just the tip of the asteroid, so to speak. The reality of the place was a lot bigger than she'd given it credit it for. They'd dug into the mini world rotating around the gaseous purple planet it orbited and, if the hangar was any indication, built quite the city underground.

All around there was movement from machinery moving pallets and machine parts to beings—real ET's!—striding about purposefully. Penny's excitement made her forget her words to only look quickly and return. How could she with so much to study? She stepped out of the tunnel to look around better. *Pinch me because I can't believe I'm standing in the presence of honest-to-goodness aliens.*

Just a few feet away an eight-foot lizard waved stubby arms while his long tail thrashed on the metal grate floor. In front of her, on fluttery gem-colored wings, a pair of chubby creatures flitted past, so cute to look at if you ignored the sharp teeth and claws. Tall and short, fat and skinny, beings of every color went about their business. Her inner researcher, always on the lookout for interesting things, noted how the aliens mostly followed humanoid lines and where bipedal. *I wonder if they were also seeded by that master race Reg told me about?* The scientist in her was positively giddy with wanting, make that needing, to know.

"And what have we here?"

The words sounded harsh and guttural, but the translator allowed her to understand clearly. How marvelous. Penny whirled in excitement, eager to meet another ET. She recoiled slightly when she saw a creature that surely had porcine ancestors leering at her. Not as tall as Reg, the warty speaker was thick with an olive green skin tone that glistened either with sweat or slime—it was gross either way. Beady eyes squinted at her above a nose that could easily be termed a snout. A pair of small tusks flanked his mouth, and when he smiled grotesquely at her, she noticed his teeth all ended in points. She sucked in a frightened breath and almost gagged, for he also really stank.

"Um, hi. I was just leaving." Suddenly realizing

she might have overstayed her peek, Penny took a step back toward the tunnel to the ship. She was brought up short, though, by a rancid-smelling body at her back. *Oh, this can't be good.*

"But we were just getting acquainted," said the boarish-looking ET, showing his sharp teeth in what might have been a smile.

In the off chance she was wrong about his intentions, Penny smiled weakly. "Gee, I really wish I could stay and chat, but my very big boyfriend is waiting for me so I'd better get going."

The ugly beast chuckled, a wet sound that made her gorge rise. "I think you lie, for no male would let his female wander this place, especially unguarded."

Okay, screw playing nice. Time to run. Penny tried to dart away quickly, hoping to catch Phlegm Voice and his smelly friend off guard.

A pinch at her nape, though, gave her a nanosecond to realize how stupid she'd been.

Curiosity killed the cat, but I think my fate is going to be a lot worse.

10

Penny came to on a cold metal table, naked. With a squeal, she rolled off and peered around frantically. A wet chuckle from behind had her whirling to see her porcine abductor, still just as ugly, holding out scraps of material to her.

"There is no escape, female. Now dress."

"Or else what?" she asked in a squeaky voice with a bravery she didn't feel.

"Or else instead of auctioning you off as a concubine, I'll eat you for dinner."

Given the options, she snatched the clothing and began to dress. Once she was done, though, she had to wonder if her naked body might have been less alluring. Dressed like Princess Leia visiting Jabba the Hut—in other words in a very skimpy outfit that left not much to the imagination—Penny was led through a series of corridors until she and the pig who dragged her by one wrist emerged onto a small raised dais.

She blinked in the bright lights but almost wished she'd remained blind when she saw what was around her. She seemed to be in some kind of bar—a very crowded bar. Surrounding the dais on three sides were tables packed with aliens of all types, most of them leering at her. Odors of all kinds assailed her—rancid, unwashed, totally gross—and made her slightly nauseous. She really wished she'd listened to Reg. Once again, her curiosity had landed her in a royal mess. *Maybe I'm overreacting.* Her captor's words did nothing to quell her fear, but she did almost pee herself.

"Lookee here, varmints and mates. I've got a lovely unclaimed human here with enough holes to satisfy even those of you with multiple appendages." Penny swayed, trying not to swoon in terror.

"I thought they was illegal," shouted someone in the crowd.

"Illegal to any but Xamians to poach from their home planet, but if found off-world, there ain't no laws against them offering themselves up."

Loud guffaws echoed in the room.

"Now, she ain't a virgin, but she's healthy. Her red hair is real and matches her woman's hair. Now who's gonna start the bidding for this choice morsel?"

Penny bit her lip to keep it from trembling as

shouts of credits rang around the room. Bidding was steady and rapid, dashing her hope that nobody would want her.

"Come on, ye cheap bastards," said her kidnapper, coughing something gooey onto the floor. "With skin like this, imagine how well the whip marks will show up."

Penny almost fainted as numbers were thrown out with a speed that would have been flattering under less life-threatening circumstances.

"She is not for sale."

His voice rang clear and loud, and the clamor died down. Penny lifted her head to see Reg standing tall and furious amidst the scum who would buy her.

Hope bloomed in her. Despite her logic telling her it was impossible, she knew Reg would save her.

REG HEARD the clamor as he headed back from his successful transaction to his ship. He meant to bypass it, not interested in the type of entertainment found in a place like this, but when he heard the words "red hair," he stopped dead, forcing those following behind to divert around him.

"Ralph," he said aloud, knowing his embedded communicator would put him in contact with his ship. "Please tell me Penny is still on board."

"Yes, well, she—that is—" the AI stuttered, and a cold finger of fear traced its way up Reg's spine.

"Stubborn Earthling. I am going to beat her ass right after I save it." Reg did an about-turn and strode back to the galactic bar that served not only the vilest drinks in all the galaxy but also had the worst patrons, too.

Trepidation and anger battled for supremacy in his body, especially when he caught sight of Penny cringing on the platform at the back of the smoke-filled and putrid-smelling bar.

"Damned foolish woman," he muttered under his breath as he pushed his way through the leering crowd that impeded his path to her.

The amount of credits being shouted out for the purchase of Penny staggered him. Apparently, he wasn't the only one who found her to be a rare beauty. Of course, they hadn't heard her talk yet.

When he got close enough to be heard, he spoke. "She is not for sale." His voice came out louder than expected, obviously amplified by Ralph, and while the crowd surrounding the dais quieted, the announcer continued on as if he was deaf to his claim. Penny, however, heard him and fixed him with hopeful eyes. In the face of her despair, something in him groaned. Odds against him or not, he wouldn't leave here without her. What was that Earth expression that Ralph had told him using some kind of odd accent? Ah yes, *it's a good day to die.*

"I said she's not for sale."

At his booming words, bidding came to a stuttering halt, and the pirate running the auction finally squinted at him. He spat on the floor before saying, "And who are you to say she isn't?"

Reg spoke without thinking. "She's my mate." Oddly enough, the words didn't make him cringe or want to run for the stars. Instead, they felt...right. But he'd have to analyze that—as well as have a panic attack over it—later.

The filthy slaver snorted. "She bears not the mark. You lie."

Reg shrugged. "My mate wished to become accustomed to me and my world's ways before saying the words. She is mine, though, and as such, you have no right to her."

"Prove it. Speak the words."

"What?"

"If she is truly your mate, then conduct the ritual. If you speak true, then her mating band will mark her. If you speak false, well, you die, and she will go to the highest bidder."

Reg was surprised that the slave auctioneer's requirement to bond with her didn't anger him. Surely he didn't want to be mated? What had happened to being free and roaming the stars? *Ah, by the moons, her life isn't worth the price of my freedom.*

He leapt up onto the dais, and Penny threw herself at him, hugging him and whispering in a choked voice, "I'm so sorry. I should have listened to you. What are you going to do?"

"Marry you, apparently, and pray the spirits are watching. You're not hurt?"

"No. Just feeling stupid and cold in this outfit. So, how are we escaping?"

The sharp prick of a knife made him turn his attention away from Penny.

The pirate sneered. "How touching. Now, say the words and let us see if you spoke true."

Reg turned back to Penny and held up his hands. "Usually, we'd do this naked, but I think your outfit has shown quite enough of your flesh off already to this bunch. Put your hands on mine."

Penny held his gaze and placed her smaller hands against his. A tingle jolted him where their skin touched, an electrical current he'd heard of but never thought to experience. Penny sucked in a breath, and her eyes widened, but for once, she kept quiet. Damn, it looked as if, regardless of his feelings on the matter, Penny was his soul mate, which meant the mating ritual would work. In the off chance he was mistaken, he did have a plan. Escape the hard—AKA bloody—way.

"Hurry it up," said the impatient slaver with another jab of his knife.

Reg debated for a moment fighting his way out,

but looking at Penny so frail and trusting, he knew he had to try to get her out without violence if possible. "I need you to repeat after me." Reg took a deep breath and prepared to change his life forever. "My life, my soul, I pledge to thee."

Penny swallowed, her eyes flicking between him and the knife. Her hands against his trembled, but finally, she spoke. "My life, my soul, I pledge to thee."

"Forever joined for eternity."

Penny repeated after him, and as soon as she said eternity, it hit them. With a loud crack, energy thrummed into him and then out into Penny. Back and forth, mystical power spun between them, joining them irrevocably, melding their souls forever more as one. Reg had only a moment to sense her emotions—fear, hope, and something warm, something sweet he could put no name to. He'd figure it out later. First, to find out if the pirate would keep his word for, as per the bargain, Reg was now mated to Penny and she bore the mark.

Reg twined his fingers through her left hand and pulled her arm up for all to see the smoky mating band that now moved in sinuous patterns around her wrist.

"What is that?" she asked, staring at it in fascination.

Instead of answering her directly, he spoke to the slaver. "As I told you, the woman is my mate and bears my mating band. Now, if you don't mind, my wife and I would like to retire to our ship for some privacy."

Reg had known it wouldn't be this easy, and as soon as the pirate's face squinted into something even uglier than his usual mien, Reg tucked Penny behind him and drew his knives.

"Get th—" The ugly slaver's word were cut off as Reg sliced across his throat, almost decapitating the brute with the sharpness of his blade. One down, a horde to go.

11

THE DARK BLOOD THAT SPURTED FROM THE SLAVER'S neck made Penny blanch. She'd never seen or experienced violence firsthand. And apparently, she wouldn't have the time to come to terms with it, for Reg pushed her toward the door at the back of the dais. She stumbled along, hearing numbly the roar at her back as the bidders expressed their displeasure at the turn of events.

She still couldn't believe Reg had arrived to save her, and in the nick of time, too. And he'd married her! An event she'd love to analyze when he stopped dragging her through the maze of corridors.

"Ralph," he barked aloud. "Prepare the ship for immediate departure."

Penny didn't hear a reply and assumed Reg wore some kind of transmitter. "Are we close?" she whispered loudly.

"More or less, but I expect we'll have to fight our way on board."

"Why not teleport?" she asked as he tucked her behind him to peer around a corner.

"The whole asteroid is shielded against it," he replied, tugging her along again.

Once again, at an intersection, he stopped, but instead of scouting around the corner, he turned to face her with serious eyes.

"Here, take this. The safety is off so just point and shoot."

Penny looked at the gun he shoved in her hand and offered it back. *He wants me to kill people, um beings?* "I can't use this."

"You will if you want to live. Or would you rather end up a prostitute in a galactic brothel?"

Put that way… Penny grasped the gun tightly.

"Stay close to me. When you see an opening, you run for the ship and don't look back."

"But what about you?" she asked.

"Don't worry about me. I have no intention of missing our wedding night, *wife*." He followed up his words with a fierce but brief kiss that made her tingle from head to toe. "Don't hesitate if you see someone coming at you. Shoot."

And with those final words of comfort, he dragged her out into the wide hangar area. To Penny's relief, there wasn't a bloodthirsty crowd waiting for them. Actually, the place was surprisingly bare except for a handful of porky-looking miscreants standing in front of a docking door. Of course, it happened to be the one door they needed to escape, and while there were only about five thugs, they were big and nasty-looking—not to mention smelly, even from where she stood.

They grinned in welcome, their pointed teeth making her shudder. Reg didn't even pause. With a battle cry that both chilled and thrilled her, he ran toward the pirates. Penny could only watch, stunned, as he danced among the beasts, his silver blades flashing. The flying blood was kind of gross and distracting, but to her amazement, against all odds, Reg was winning.

And I would never have thought it, but it's kind of arousing to watch. Reg moved with a fluid grace that astonished her, his body twisting and bending to thrust, dodge and slash, not a movement wasted in his deadly dance.

One down, two down, three. He prepared to dispatch a third when she caught movement to her left, and she turned to see another dirty pig approaching stealthily with a pistol rising to shoot. Without even thinking about it, Penny swung her gun up in his direction, vaguely aiming it. She squeezed her eyes, shut even as she pressed on the trigger. There was no recoil, just a sizzling sound followed by a faint cry. She opened her eyes to see the sneaky pirate lying on the ground.

Oh sweet niblets, I killed him. But there was no time to freak out about her new murderous capabilities, for Reg, having dispatched the last of the slavers, called her.

"Move it, Penny. Now!"

Penny ran for him and the door to their ship and, hopefully, freedom. Reg watched warily as she ran past him into the tunnel. She'd just reached the safety of the ship when she heard him pounding up the connecting tube behind her.

He slipped into the decontamination chamber, and the door swished shut.

"Get decontaminated," he barked at her and ran out of the room.

Penny frowned at his back, tempted to ignore his order and follow him. But the fact that he'd thought it important and, admittedly, the idea of being covered in possibly dangerous alien germs made her decide to delay for the few minutes it would take to cleanse herself.

Besides, she wanted to be clean, for he'd promised to give her a wedding night. The thought was enough to make her wet. *It's about time he probed me.*

"GET US OUT OF HERE, RALPH," Reg said, breathing hard. He threw himself into the command chair and, with lightning-quick taps, pulled up the defense systems for the ship.

The sound of the docking clamps releasing sounded faintly, and with a slight shudder, the ship lifted.

Reg drummed his fingers, waiting for signs of pursuit. Only after they'd reached the edge of that particular solar system with no alarms or signs of other crafts did his tension leave him. Another tightness took its place, though, as he thought of what had almost happened to Penny, his wife.

"Ralph, I'm off to see to my mate. Notify me immediately if there's trouble."

Reg stalked to the decontamination chamber, his body taut with anger. He wasn't furious at having been tricked into getting mated—which surprised him—but he was livid that Penny had disobeyed him and put herself in so much danger. *She could have died.*

When he didn't find her in the cleansing room, he went to the bedroom next and found her quite calmly reading a vid screen. For a moment, he just looked at her, still wearing the slaver's provocative outfit. The top, two triangular scraps, revealed a decadent amount of creamy flesh while the slitted skirt hung low on her hips and gaped over her thighs. It stunned him to realize, *She's mine now to touch whenever I want. And by the moons, I want to touch her, kiss her, fuck her...*

She raised excited eyes to him and shook her wrist with the mating band. "I was curious about the smoke bracelet that appeared after your marriage ritual. It's quite fascinating. Did you know scholars on your world believe it's created from the actual spirits of your ancestors?" As he stood there glowering at her, her smile faded, and uncertainty pooled in her eyes. "Is something wrong? Didn't we escape?"

"Oh we got away all right, no thanks to you."

Penny put aside the tablet and sat up straight in the bed. "I said I was sorry. I just wanted a peek."

"After I told you to stay in the ship." Reg needed her to understand the danger she'd put herself in. A danger they'd escaped by some miracle.

She stood in front of him, bristling. "I am not a child. You can't tell me what to do. And, besides, we got out all right."

"Barely, and that's not the point. You're my wife now, and as such, you will do as you're told."

Her jaw dropped then her green eyes flashed with ire. "Ha! Not for long. I want a divorce."

"A what?" The word divorce wasn't one he could translate.

"Divorce. It means I want the marriage annulled."

His brows shot up. "Impossible. Once a Xamian mates, it's for life."

"Well, I don't want to be married to you," she

said, stubbornly crossing her arms under her bosom, which only drew attention to them.

Reg's cock twitched. However, much as he wanted to claim her body, first he needed to punish her.

"If you didn't want to be married, then you should have listened to me. It's too late now. But don't worry. You won't have to suffer me for long. I'm making a straight course for my home planet to drop you off."

"What do you mean drop me off? Where are you going?"

"I still have missions to complete and, apparently, since I can't trust you to listen to my orders, I need to put you somewhere where you can't get hurt." She looked at him with a wounded expression, one that caused a sharp pain in his chest. *I really need to see the medtech unit about that.* "You brought this on yourself. Which brings me to the next thing. Your punishment."

She laughed. "What are you gonna do? Ground me to the ship? Dump me on a planet alone with nobody I know? Wait, that's already your plan. Do your worst," she said, tossing her head imperiously.

"I intend to." He grabbed her by the wrist and yanked her along with him as he crossed the short distance to the armless chair in the room and sat in it. He dragged her down and pushed her over his lap.

She struggled against him, but he held her over his thighs with a firm hand.

"What do you think you're doing?"

"I'm punishing you for disobeying." He ripped away the fabric covering her buttocks, exposing her pale skin. For a moment, lust almost overtook him, making his thoughts of punishment fade. But then, he remembered the fear he'd felt when he saw her standing in front of all those scum.

Crack!

[12]

PENNY SQUEALED AT THE FIRST SPANK ON HER bottom. Fiery pain shot through her, and she struggled in earnest on Reg's lap. But his muscles were more than just hot to look at. They also contained strength. He held her bent over his lap effortlessly and proceeded to paddle her bottom, turning deaf ears to her pleas and tears.

"You meanie," she railed. "Stop it right now!"

When threats didn't work, including a rather inventive one about what she'd do to him and his manparts with a beaker of acid, she resorted to bribes.

"I'll be a good girl. I promise. Let me prove myself." She proceeded to recount in embarrassing detail what she would do to his cock, and while said rod poked her ribs solidly, he didn't falter.

"I'm doing this for your own good."

Penny wanted to retort, but deep down—really deep where she would never admit it—she knew she deserved it. Funny how getting spanked forced her to reconsider her decision to flout his command. *In the end, he was right. It was dangerous, and I guess, much as it galls me to admit, I should have listened and never left the ship.*

She stayed quiet after that realization, of a sorts. She still yelped and whimpered as he punished her. She wasn't sure when the slaps stopped hurting so much and, instead, ignited desire. All she knew was, suddenly, instead of cringing away from his hand, she arched into it and her cries of pain turned into moans of pleasure. A change came over him as well, for his smacks became lighter, and he stroked her burning skin between slaps. When his hand slipped between her buttocks and stroked down her damp cleft, she whispered his name.

The spanks to her bottom stopped, and instead, he delved between her nether lips, probing her aching sex with his fingers. Penny panted, aroused and wanting more. She squirmed against his touch, unable to stop the gush of fluid as her desire lubed her channel.

"Stand," he ordered gruffly.

Penny stood, the torn remains to the bottom of her outfit puddling on the floor at her feet. She looked down at him, for he'd remained seated, and found him gazing at her, his eyes glowing violet. It made her even wetter. His hands reached out and grabbed her thighs, spreading them. He pulled her forward until she straddled him, but his goal remained out of reach. He pressed and held a concealed button on the underside of the chair's armrest until his seat sank down, bringing her mound level with his face. With a groan, he buried his face against her pubes. He nuzzled her curls before moving lower and found her clit with his mouth. At the hot wetness of his mouth on her swollen nub, Penny hissed in pleasure. She grabbed at his hair to steady herself, her knees wobbly. She needn't have worried. His hands held her steady as he licked and sucked between her thighs. His tongue probed her sex hotly. Penny gasped and swayed, hot pleasure building in her.

He finally stopped his oral torture after driving her to the brink and stopping several times. He let her sink down to sit on his lap, but when her sore bottom came in contact with his thighs, she winced. In a nanosecond, he had her on her knees on the floor with her hands braced on the chair he'd vacated.

His mouth brushed hotly against her abused backside, the pleasure/pain of it making her twitch. "Please, Reg."

His mouth disappeared, and she felt the hard head of his cock sliding between her thighs to rub against her moistness. Slick with her juices, he probed between her plump lips, taking it slow. It was exquisite torture.

Finally, he sheathed himself inside her, his long, hard length driving deep and striking a sweet spot inside that had her body tightening. With his hands on her hips, he pumped her, his hot mouth seeking and then sucking the hot skin of her nape.

Penny gripped the chair for dear life, welcoming the thrusts of his cock and only hissing once when his body came into slapping contact with her burning backside.

Pleasure swirled inside her, a rapture that coiled tight as a spring. Her tension burst into a screaming orgasm when his hands slid from her waist to cup her breasts and his thumbs brushed her nipples.

She quivered and shook, the intensity of her orgasm making her mindless. Eventually, her body finally calmed, and she found herself cradled in his arms, somehow in bed. He brushed her temple with his lips, and Penny smiled, but it wasn't in her nature to be quiet, even after great sex. Her anger over his treatment of her had faded, especially since the spanking had turned into something so decadent. But she needed to make him understand that, while she appreciated he'd been frightened for her, she refused to be treated like a child. If they were, in truth, married, then she wanted equal status in their relationship. About to give him a lecture on the rights of women in society, she changed her mind when he rolled her on top of him and she felt something hard nudging at her soft belly. *Maybe later…*

"Ready so soon, husband?" she asked, almost giggling at the word husband.

"Warriors are always ready to please their women," he teased back then grabbed her ass cheeks.

Penny reared up as the heat in her posterior flared up.

"Ow!"

———————

AT PENNY'S cry of pain, Reg found himself submerged in remorse. While he'd meant to punish her, he'd not intended to cause her lasting harm. It would seem, though, that his Earthling wife was of a more delicate constitution than he'd realized. He dumped her onto the bed on her stomach and, naked, jogged to the infirmary to retrieve a jar of lotion to ease her abused buttocks.

He returned to the bedroom and found her watching him when he strode in. She gave him a half-smile that made his heart stutter oddly. He'd have to run himself through a medical later on and see what was the matter with him, for he'd suffered these heart palpitations since he'd met Penny. While he'd balked at marriage, now, suddenly wed to his exotic human, he realized he wanted a long life with her. But forget his funny heart problems, he could now see the brightness of her ass, and his chagrin grew.

"I'm so sorry," he apologized, sitting beside her on the bed and opening the jar. "I didn't mean to punish you so harshly."

"I'm sure it looks worse than it is. With my skin, it doesn't take much to get some color. Just don't do it again."

Scooping the lotion on his fingers, he replied, "I will devise a better punishment for next time."

Penny choked as he rubbed the healing cream on her fiery skin, and he hated he caused her more pain.

"Next time?" she finally screeched. She reared up on the bed and twisted her body to look back at him. "There will be no more punishing, buster. We're married now, as in partners for life. That means you can't treat me like a slave."

Reg returned her gaze calmly. "You are fragile and must be protected. As such, if I give you an order that pertains to your safety, I expect you to obey it or face the consequences. But don't worry, soon I'll have you at my home planet where the only danger will be if you trip on your own feet."

Penny gaped at him, and Reg smiled, well pleased he'd finally managed to render her speechless.

"No."

Reg's smile faded at the anger he could see flashing in her narrowed eyes. "No what?"

"No, I will not become some meek little house-wife while you go off and have adventures. There's no reason I can't come with you."

"A women's place is on the home planet." Where he'd probably be grounded in short order, too, as a mated male. The idea of no longer roaming the stars stuck in his craw, but Penny was sure to liven things up. Maybe it wouldn't be so bad.

"I think I'm going to have to teach you about women's lib," she said, moving to sit on her bent legs. "But before I do, what the heck did you put on my bottom? I can't feel the pain at all anymore."

"See, there are many things for you to learn about on my planet. It won't be as dreadful as you fear."

Penny cocked her head at him and smiled. "Or I could prove to you what an asset I'd be with you in space. Starting with this." She placed her hands on his chest and leaned up to kiss him.

Her boldness enflamed him, and his cock swelled to press up against her lower belly. She pushed at him, and he complied, lying on his back. She remained kneeling beside him, and her gaze devoured him hungrily.

"What are you thinking?" he asked when she bit her lip, her eyes locked onto his cock.

"I wish I had a notepad right now."

Reg's brow creased. "I'm probably going to regret asking, but why?"

She tore her gaze from his shaft and smiled at him seductively. "I would love to do a sketch of your penis and take a few notes on the oral techniques that most arouse you."

Reg almost choked. He wasn't sure if he should laugh at her strange urge or beg her to find a notepad and do what she said. Sanity prevailed at the thought that some of his warrior friends would find out his new wife liked to draw pictures of his cock. "No notepads, but feel free to experiment with my body all you want. I'd be really interested in the effect of your mouth sucking me while your hands massage my balls."

Penny smiled, but instead of diving on him with her mouth, she grabbed his rod in her hands and squeezed him tightly. His cock, already throbbing hard, pearled at the tip. His naughty mate pounced on him, her lithe tongue lapping at the clear drop, making him hiss in pleasure. He closed his eyes and enjoyed the sensation of her laving the head of his cock. He expected to feel her mouth at any moment, taking his prick deep into her throat, but once again, she surprised him. She kept her hands on his rod, but her wet tongue flicked across his balls.

Reg shouted. "Sweet moons!"

Penny didn't reply. She couldn't, for she'd taken his sac into her mouth and sucked him. Reg clutched at the sheets, his body trembling with effort as he forced himself not to buck. She explored him intimately, sucking his testes one at a time then taking both into her mouth. She played with them, and Reg almost came, so pleasurable was her foreplay.

When she finally stopped teasing him, he panted as if he'd run a mighty distance on a thin-atmosphere planet. She gave him no reprieve though. She straddled him, and her hot sex sheathed his cock. Reg couldn't stop himself from thrusting up into her, his poor, overly teased cock seeking her sweet spot.

He felt her hands brace on his chest, and he opened his eyes to see her staring down at him, her face flushed with passion. She looked so beautiful to him, and even more arousing. *She is mine.*

He gripped her waist with his hands and helped her rock on his shaft. She gasped in pleasure as her clit rubbed against him and her channel muscles quivered around him. Faster, he slid her back and forth, increasing the friction between their bodies.

When she would have closed her eyes, Reg growled. "Open them."

She opened them, her eyes glazed and heavy lidded with passion. Reg found himself hurtling toward the edge of pleasure, and he pumped faster, bringing her with him. He thrust up into her, his cock finding her sensitive place and spearing it. Her body tightened, her muscles squeezing him tightly, and Reg let go, joining her in rapture.

"I love you," she cried out, throwing her head back, her orgasm sweeping her.

Reg didn't reply, for he didn't know how. Instead, he let his body speak for him, holding her tenderly as she quaked with pleasure in his arms. He might not know what this Earthling emotion love was, but as a warrior, and now her husband, he would never let anything happen to Penny. *I will cherish and protect you, my sweet human wife.*

13

PENNY AWOKE WITH A SMILE, HER BODY SENSITIZED from the all-night lovemaking. She'd orgasmed more times than she would have ever thought humanly possible. She hoped she'd also managed to change Reg's outdated ideas on women's roles. She'd lectured him at length on the advance of women's rights back on Earth in between bouts, and he'd listened to her, even if his gaze tended to stray to her naked body parts. She was pretty sure she'd managed to make him understand logically the reasons why they should stay together in space, and then to add sugar to sweeten the deal, she'd shown him physically.

I can't believe he expected me to become some kind of Suzie Homemaker popping out babies. My research on the effects of space travel on pregnancy and children, rare as those cases seem to be, doesn't lead me to believe there's any reason why we can't continue on to travel the galaxy, which is where I know Reg wants to be.

Speaking of whom, where was her sexy blue husband? She dressed and went to find him. Not seeing him in the lounge area, she headed next to the command center. She paused just outside when she heard Reg speaking. She knew she should announce herself and go in, but instead, she surrendered to her curiosity and eavesdropped.

"Greetings, Oracle," she heard Reg say. "I regret to inform you that the human Penny is no longer eligible for mating," he said in a serious voice.

A female voice replied, "Explain yourself, first class space warrior. Your mission was to bring the Earthling back here safely."

"The female is safe, but due to unforeseen circumstances, I was forced to bond with her to keep her unharmed."

Penny bit her lip as disappointment flooded her. She'd known he wasn't keen on marriage, but he'd shown himself more than eager to bed her. His words, though, seemed to say otherwise.

"Mated, you say? That is not such a calamity. What are your plans now?"

"We should be arriving home within three full cycles. I will drop off the human as per custom, and then, with your permission, I will return to space to complete my remaining missions."

Penny clapped a hand over her mouth as tears brimmed in her eyes. She'd heard enough. She ran back to the bedroom.

How could he want to abandon me like that? I thought after last night that surely he'd change his mind. Apparently, she'd guessed wrong.

Penny scrubbed at her tear-stained face, and her mind raced furiously, analyzing the situation and coming up with a solution. *Fine, he doesn't want me, then I'll make sure he doesn't have to see me anymore. I refuse to give up my dreams and to live alone just because he thinks women don't belong in space.*

Penny didn't take long to plan, even as her heart ached. She couldn't believe she'd allowed herself to succumb to the hormonal imbalance known as love, especially since she knew better. Heartbroken, she knew what she needed to do. *Leave my husband.*

"WE SHOULD BE ARRIVING HOME within three full cycles. I will drop off the human as per custom and then, with your permission, I will return to space to complete my remaining missions." Reg said the words to the Oracle with a heavy heart. After last night's long talk with Penny, where, for once, her loquaciousness hadn't driven him nuts, it occurred to him to take Penny along with him as she wanted. But policy with alien females was very clear. They needed to be brought planetside for their own safety, something he could understand after the terror he'd felt when he'd seen her in danger and knowing now just how delicate she was. The thought of her coming to harm made his blood run cold with dread.

"I realize that usually it's protocol for females to reside her at home. However, we have great need of you in space. I also have a confession to make. Penny was chosen long ago to be your mate."

Reg stared at the screen and the veiled Oracle. "What do you mean? I told you I had no interest in mating."

"You only believed that. We knew you would change your mind once you met the right female."

"We? What do you mean we?"

"Myself and your spirit ancestors, of course. They've been looking for a long time for the right female and then had to manipulate certain situations to put the female in a place where you would have to rescue her."

"You've manipulated me this entire time just so I would mate with Penny?" Reg waited for the anger over the Oracle's actions to hit, but when it didn't, he realized something. He didn't regret meeting or even marrying Penny. She might have given him a heart condition, but she also made him feel alive. *And gives me more pleasure than I ever imagined.*

"Manipulate is such an ugly word, my child.

Think of it more as nudging you in the right direction to ensure your future well being and happiness."

Reg wasn't about to let the Oracle off that easy, even if he wouldn't give Penny up for anything. "And how is grounding me planetside by mating me supposed to make me happy?"

"Who said anything about forcing you to live planetside?"

Reg dared not breathe, certain he'd misheard the Oracle. "But that is custom when a warrior mates."

"For other couples, perhaps. We need your experience in space, but at the same time, it would be unfair to deprive Penny of her mate by forcing her stay at home. Then there's the fact that she's an intelligent scientist whose fresh outlook might provide our own researchers with unique insight. Your ancestors didn't just choose any female for you. They chose your soul mate, one who will you join you as a partner on space missions."

Reg wanted to whoop with joy. *I can stay in space and have Penny too!* But then a sobering idea hit him. "But what about if she becomes pregnant?"

"Unless there are grave health issues, there is no medical reason why you shouldn't have healthy children. Of course, we would like to see you planetside when the time for the birth approaches just in case complications arise, but the medtech units on board are well equipped to deal with most situations. Now, shall I assume then that you and your new mate will continue your work in space together?"

He remained stunned for only a moment before beaming. "It would be our great pleasure to continue on as galactic travelers for the empire. However, if I might make one small request. I believe that perhaps it might be more prudent to assign us less risky missions, especially given Penny's curious nature." Let some other unattached warrior visit the dangerous outposts. It was a compromise he could live with to keep Penny safe and both of them happy. He couldn't wait to tell her.

Reg signed off with the Oracle and drummed his fingers, wondering how to tell Penny without making it sound as if he'd caved completely to her demands. *Maybe I should make her convince me a little more. Make it seem like I'm giving in reluctantly and, at the same time, wring some promises from her to keep her safe.* The thought of a repeat of last night's attempt to change his mind made him hard and eager to seek out his wife.

"Ralph, where's Penny?" The AI didn't reply, which made Reg frown, and he went to call for him again when the object of his thoughts spoke.

"I'm right behind you," she said.

He turned to see her looking fresh and beautiful, her hands clasped behind her back. His body reacted as if it hadn't just spent several intimate moments with her just a short cycle ago. With a smile, he bent to brush his lips across hers.

Her arms came around him, and she pressed herself against him, her lips hot and eager against his.

Amidst his building arousal, he felt a prick in his shoulder. He pulled his head back and looked down at her with incomprehension.

"I'm sorry," she said, her green eyes swimming in tears. "But I refuse to be some baby-making machine stuck on an alien planet by myself." As Reg felt his consciousness slipping and his knees sagging, he heard her whisper, "I love you."

14

REG REGAINED CONSCIOUSNESS ON THE COMMAND room floor, his head pillowed and his body covered in a blanket. With a curse, he jumped up.

"Ralph, where's Penny?" The AI still wasn't replying, and Reg took off jogging to check the ship. It didn't take him long to determine Penny was gone.

He returned to the ship's command center and paced the area in front of the view screen.

She left me! He'd known she was upset, but to do something this drastic... Why couldn't she have waited? He now wished he'd told her immediately about the Oracle's permission for them to travel together. Not that Penny had even given him a chance.

No matter, he'd find her. "Ralph? By the moons,

computer, I know you must have helped her. Speak to me, dammit."

Silence reigned, but across the view screen, words appeared.

Penny disabled my auditory function so that I couldn't warn you of what she planned. That human is much too smart for her own good. She managed to override my controls and teleport herself off ship.

Reg laughed. He couldn't help himself. Both he and a super computer outwitted by a wisp of a female. *And to think I thought she lacked the strength to survive in space.* Immediately on the heels of that thought, though, was the realization that she wasn't on this ship, but somewhere on a strange planet— alone. Unacceptable. For all he knew, she could be in danger at this very moment.

"Ralph, do you know where she is?"

Not exactly. She wiped the records of planetary halts and transports, but she was unaware of my separate backup system. You'll have to manually connect me to it that I might upload the information missing from my databanks. While I do that, I don't suppose you would restore my vocal abilities?

"I'll get right on it." He needed something to distract him while Ralph pinpointed his mate's location. He just hoped he arrived before danger found her.

PENNY AWOKE to a hand clasped over her mouth. The inside of the survival tent was dark, but she'd recognize those glowing violet eyes anywhere. Her husband had found her.

I should have known I wouldn't get away that easily. Well, if he thinks I'm going to let him drag me back to his ship just so he can dump me, he's got another thing coming.

She bit him. With a curse, he pulled his hand away.

"Go away."

"No," he said calmly, pulling her from the tent.

She breathed in the fresh air of the sentient pink planet she'd chosen as a perfect place to hide and research while waiting for another alien vessel to pass by and hitch a ride on. When she'd first arrive, she'd sighed in relief when she hadn't convulsed at the first inhalation of the strange atmosphere. Her research had claimed the air wasn't harmful, but she'd had her doubts. With nothing more dangerous than four-eared bunnies, and with tantalizing reports that the planet itself was alive, she'd thought the strange world would act as a salve to her bruised emotions, but now, seeing him again, even annoyed as she was, she couldn't deny she was glad to see him. But that didn't mean she'd willingly go back to a life of genteel slavery. She prepared to tell him so, but before she could speak, he'd scooped her up—caveman style. He flung her over his shoulder so that her head and arms dangled down his back.

"What do you think you're doing?" she said in a disgruntled tone—an attempt to hide her mounting elation.

He smacked her lightly on her bottom. "Silence, woman. I am abducting you that I might probe you as all aliens do to their captives."

Penny gaped at his back, stunned speechless, then she giggled. "Don't you mean rescue me?"

"I tried rescuing last time, and all it got me was a lot of headaches and questions. This time, I'm doing it my ancestors' way. I'm kidnapping you for my mate, so now be quiet that I might get us safely to my ship to have my way with you. Well, right after we get the punishment out of the way."

Penny remembered her last punishment and her cheeks—facial ones this time—burned with heat. She squirmed half-heartedly, moisture pooling in her sex as he slapped her ass again then caressed it.

"I didn't do anything wrong," she stated stubbornly. "I told you I wasn't interested in being some stay-at-home wife."

"And I should have listened to you." His reply stunned her into silence. "I'm the one who should be punished for trying to force you to be someone you aren't. I'd come to that realization after our talk, even if I didn't know what to do about it. Even better, the Oracle realized it, too."

"What are you saying?" She was afraid she'd misunderstood. She still couldn't believe he'd come back to find her. *He wouldn't have done that if he didn't care.*

"Congratulations, my wife, you and I are now both officially in the service of the Oracle and Xaanda."

"You mean we're both going to travel the stars and see…everything?" Penny grinned.

"Yes, now be quiet that I might properly abduct you. It has been a whole cycle since I probed you, and I find myself in great need."

And he isn't the only one, she thought, her cleft already damp with arousal.

Moments later, they found themselves in the dimly lit decontamination chamber. Reg let her slide to the floor but held her loosely in his arms.

"I am sorry," he said seriously. "Please don't ever run from me again. It made my heart condition even worse."

"What heart condition?" she asked with concern.

"Since I have met you, my heart has this strange tendency of racing or stopping, and when you disappeared, I thought it had shriveled up and died."

Penny grinned at him. "Gee, it sounds just like what my heart has done since the day you rescued me."

"Abducted," he corrected. "I wish for our children to think we met in a time-honored fashion."

"Speaking of babies, I think you're going to have to show me, naked of course, just how a big alien like yourself impregnates a woman. I think it might take several tries."

"Really?" His smile beamed brightly, and before she could laugh at his eager look, he'd torn her clothes from her body and stripped himself. Then, he did something surprising. He knelt on the floor in front of her, head bowed.

"What are you doing?" she asked. "Is this another type of ritual?"

"I am awaiting my punishment, wife. Do as you will."

Penny bit her lip to hold in a giggle. "Get up. Why don't we call ourselves even and forget about this punishing stuff? Well, maybe not the spanking bit. That part is kind of fun."

She'd no sooner spoken than she found herself lifted in the air. Reg held her up effortlessly, his swollen cock probing at her damp sex. With a thrust, he sheathed himself, and his fingers clutched at her buttocks to balance her. Penny wrapped her legs tightly around her husband's blue waist.

"I love you," she said before kissing him.

"You are mine," he replied against her mouth. His claim, while not a declaration of love, warmed her. She hugged him tight as he pumped her.

As the decontamination chamber cleansed them and heightened her pleasure with its tickling touch, she visited the stars with Reg, twice.

EPILOGUE

REG WATCHED HIS MATE ON HER HANDS AND KNEES examining the silken pink grass of the sentient planet they'd come back to visit. He never tired of watching her, and he'd even become used to her endless questions. He especially enjoyed her inquisitiveness in the bedroom, where she delighted in exploring his body over and over, as well as experimenting with techniques. Although he did draw the line at her taking notes during the act. He, instead, allowed her to videotape them, although he wasn't sure what value the videos had from a scholastic point of view, for, whenever she watched them, the result was the same. They both ended up naked and fucking wildly. Not that he was complaining. He didn't mind sacrificing himself for science.

Ralph's voice crackled in his earpiece. "So,

when are we upgrading to a bigger ship? I've got my eye on that new luxury model with the improved warp drive."

"Bigger ship? What for?" Reg replied absently, smiling when Penny, with a giggle, threw herself on the tickling grass and rolled.

"Why, for the baby, of course. It's going to need its own room and a nanny bot. Did I mention I met an AI one last time we were planetside?"

"A baby? What baby?" Reg grinned when Penny began flinging clothes in his direction.

Ralph interrupted the visual striptease. "Surely the two of you didn't think with all the sex you were having that she wouldn't get pregnant?"

Reg's smile froze on his face, and he fought the panic that tightened his throat. "But…"

"And just so you know, the baby is perfectly healthy. I can't believe I'm going to be the first AI uncle. Wait until I brag to my predecessor, Alphie."

Reg tuned out the computer and worked on controlling his breathing so he wouldn't hyperventilate. Penny, pregnant? By the moons, it would explain several oddities, like her sudden liking of his native food and the fullness of her breasts and waist. Dear moons, a baby with blue skin and red hair and…

Suddenly, Reg grinned. He and Penny were going to be parents.

"Wife," he shouted, striding toward where she lay in the grass now fully naked, a blissful look on her face.

She opened one eye and peered at him. "Shh. I'm researching," she said, ruining her serious mien with a giggle as the grass tickled her again.

"I've just received news that you're about to embark on a huge research project."

"I am?" She sat up, eyes wide with anticipation. "Are we going to go native with some indigenes? Discover a new solar system? Examine some ancient ruins?"

"Even more exciting," he said, grinning. "And you even get a title."

"I do. Stop teasing me. Tell me."

"Your new title is…" Reg drew out the moment. "Mother." Her jaw dropped, and she said not a word, just stared at him bug-eyed. "I think you should title this project 'The Effects of Alien Probing.'"

Instead of replying, her eyes rolled up in her head and she fainted. It was quite illogical, given she had to know this would happen, but vastly entertaining. Reg sat beside her and pillowed her head in his lap, brushing her red hair from her face.

It still amazed him that a simple rescue mission had changed his life, all for the better. To his wife's amusement, he'd finally discovered his heart problems were nothing more than a case of human love. And having had a taste of that addictive emotion, he'd give up even the stars to be with his Earthling soul mate, forever.

THE END

For more Sci-Fi and Alien Abduction books visit EveLanglais.com

CPSIA information can be obtained
at www.ICGtesting.com
Printed in the USA
LVHW011652291021
701929LV00009B/961